'[Jones is] one of the most interesting and talented novelists at work in Australia today...daring enough to express a complex, original and passionate vision; she writes with a belief in the power of fiction to express meanings unavailable to other forms of art or inquiry.' *Sydney Morning Herald*

DREAMS OF SPEAKING

'A captivating, analytical inventory of consciousness-altering technical developments of modernity, from the telephone to the atomic bomb.' *Australian*

'Jones is an extraordinary writer no matter what genre she is working in.' *Australian Book Review*

'Shards of poetry stud Jones's writing like diamonds.' *Independent*

SIXTY LIGHTS

'There is no doubting Jones's flair for luminous and accurate prose...In her hands, words feel chosen and juxtaposed in new ways.' *Guardian*

'Jones writes scenes of such simple love, fear and beauty that they will break your heart...[She] consolidates her place in the category of our truly great writers with *Sixty Lights*.' *Telegraph*

BLACK MIRROR

'*Black Mirror* shows the beauty of things in dislocation, the wonder of the ordinary.' *Bookseller + Publisher*

Gail Jones is one of Australia's most critically acclaimed writers, the author of two short story collections and seven novels. She is the recipient of numerous national literary awards, including the *Age* Book of the Year, the SA Premier's Award, the ALS Gold Medal and the Kibble Award, and has been shortlisted for international awards including the Dublin IMPAC and the Prix Femina Étranger. Her work has been translated into twelve languages. Originally from Western Australia, she now lives in Sydney.

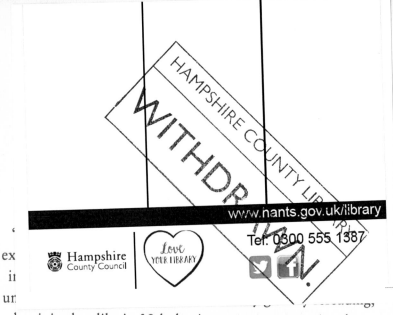

but it is also, like its Nabokovian parent, a narrative that pulses with feeling. Its pages finally summon not one ghost but millions of them.' *Australian*

'A remarkable investigation of reading and speaking, and of the interaction between high literature and immediate human experience...The novel is a demonstration of both the power of storytelling and its limitations...a full and moving exploration of the experience of knowing others through literature and life.' *Monthly*

'*A Guide to Berlin*, like memory itself—how it forms, what we remember, and in particular how childhood memories can shape the person we become—is complex and layered with meaning. An extraordinarily rich and enriching reading experience.' *Newtown Review of Books*

FIVE BELLS

'Gail Jones's magnificent new novel propels her to the forefront of Australian literature...Her prose is poetic and infinitely pleasurable, imbued with a rare capacity to

awaken. She reconciles what is richly human with mundane and alienating aspects of our sophisticated world...The novel is a profound meditation on memory and emotion, as well as a rhapsodic evocation of place. Neither Jones nor Sydney need putting on the map, but the combination is a winner...a brilliant work, both explicitly Australian and insistently cosmopolitan.' *Australian*

'Thoughtful, intelligent and intensely lyrical... Jones's skilful negotiations with the past—with individual and collective memory, as well as with the literary canon— have provided her with a framework for a novel of unmistakable contemporary relevance.' *Guardian*

'*Five Bells* is many things: a love letter to Sydney and its physical beauty; a deeply moving exploration of the effects of grief and loss; and, perhaps most importantly, a luminous and shimmering reflection on time, memory and mortality. Yet like all of Jones' novels, *Five Bells* is also a remarkably intricate creation: a highly sophisticated, thrillingly allusive web of implication in which a wide range of literary and cultural references are woven together, reinforcing and counterpointing each other in fascinating and often surprising ways.' *Griffith Review*

SORRY

'The great beauty and depth of Jones' writing, in this novel as elsewhere, has simultaneous appeal for lovers of intricate, elegant thought, and lovers of verbal style. There's also a great deal of her signature literary "sampling", with quotations, allusions and echoes from fiction and poetry vying for space inside her own sentences: Emerson, Dickinson, George Eliot and of course Shakespeare, who haunts these pages like a colossal, chanting ghost.' *Age*

GAIL JONES

THE DEATH OF NOAH GLASS

TEXT PUBLISHING MELBOURNE AUSTRALIA

textpublishing.com.au

The Text Publishing Company
Swann House
22 William Street
Melbourne Victoria 3000
Australia

Published by The Text Publishing Company, 2018

Cover art by W. H. Chong; figures derived from Piero della Francesca's *The Dream of Constantine*
Page design by Jessica Horrocks
Typeset by J&M Typesetting

Printed in Australia by Griffin Press, an Accredited ISO AS/NZS 14001:2004 Environmental Management System printer.

ISBN: 9781925603408 (paperback)
ISBN: 9781925626445 (ebook)

A catalogue record for this book is available from the National Library of Australia

 This book is printed on paper certified against the Forest Stewardship Council® Standards. Griffin Press holds FSC chain-of-custody certification SGS-COC-005088. FSC promotes environmentally responsible, socially beneficial and economically viable management of the world's forests.

Schwerer werden. Leichter sein.
(Grow more heavy. Be more light.)

PAUL CELAN

PART ONE

IN THE CORAL light of a summer dawn, Martin Glass recalled a tale. Two brothers in their late seventies attended the funeral of their father, aged forty-two. The father had disappeared as a young man skiing across country, and in an unseasonable thaw, years later, his frozen body had been exposed. The bright sun shone upon him, ice melted and slid away, and he became a gruesome, implausible and shiny surprise. The trekker who discovered him felt both lucky and appalled. The body might have been a slow-motion swimmer lifting through the surface of the water: first his nose met the air, then his leathery cheeks, and then his damp face, with eyes closed, was revealed to the sky of Chamonix.

Martin imagined the two brothers identifying their father, looking baffled at a version of themselves when young. The corpse was part figurine, with the skin hardened and made inhuman by its preservation, like those bog-men, he supposed, who have the appearance of wood. The father's clothes would have been old-fashioned and possibly familiar. Perhaps his sons saw again a particular scarf, red and cosy, or recognised a belt, or a woollen hat, or gloves they remembered, stretched long ago over the flexing star of his fingers. Perhaps they stared at these details in order not to dwell on the face. Perhaps one of them thought *mummy* in a fleeting irreverent second, struck with the impertinence that might come with accident or death. They would have been silent, observed by strangers, formally bereft, looking down at their dead, impossible father. Both must have felt the collapse of time. One brother, the younger, died three weeks after the funeral. The older followed a few months later.

Though he'd not thought of it for years, Martin was awoken by this story. Three faces alike, sorry timing, mortal coil. The vex of an accident, its meaninglessness. It afforded the interest of a chance occurrence seeming supernatural. Each man anticipates looking at the face of his old father, possibly standing by the deathbed, possibly assessing his own mortality in the presence of the patriarch: this inversion in sequence compelled and fascinated him. As he lay half-dozing on his back, Martin saw himself as the iceman, confronting the white wall of an untimely death.

Wednesday. This was the day of the funeral. Today he must retrieve the suit he was married in and prepare himself. He must be cautious of his own precarious feelings, he must be manly, and upright, and not lose control, or weep. Martin kicked his legs free of the sheets. He turned from the window and struggled hungover from his bed. His body, always slim, felt abnormally heavy. He rubbed his face with both hands, then his stiff neck, then ruffled his receding and thin grey hair. He felt his skull and wondered with idle alarm about diminishment of memory. Only forty-three, he suspected that his brain was already fretted with holes. Almost every day he found evidence of incipient dementia or a biochemical dysfunction that had no name. Objects receded from definition. People became generalised. Book titles were often difficult to recall. It seemed a dopey belittlement. He was growing smaller in the world, and now, with his father gone, there was a dread, or humiliation, entering the texture of things, like the feeling of walking into a dark room, fumbling for a switch and finding the electricity gone.

In the bathroom, shaving, he barely recognised himself. He was tempted to say his own name aloud. Outside, in the world, he was oddly more credible, an artist who appeared in the news-papers, feted by collectors with a shrewd eye on the markets, linked to the burnished figures of the mysteriously rich. He tilted the mask of his face towards the mirror at a cubist angle. This, apparently, was what it meant to be parentless. One changed appearance, something was peeled away. Shaving cream spattered as he flicked his razor. Martin wiped it to a bleary swirl with the back of his forearm, turned on the tap, and watched the foam of his shaving mess circle and disappear. It would be a day sullied, he knew it, a day full of objects and substances turning into emotions and symbols.

When he heard the phone he started, as if it sounded his nervousness. He considered refusing the command, but realised it was Evie, checking up on him.

'So how's it going?' he asked.

'Did I wake you? Have you remembered?'

'No. Yes. Of course I remembered.'

'You found the suit?'

'Not yet, but I know it's here somewhere. Fuck, Evie…'

Martin paused. He must not swear at his sister or sound exasperated. She'd seen him drunk the night before, wallowing in self-pity. She'd seen him stumble on the pavement and whine like a bullied boy, as though the death of their father, Noah, was a personal affront. He felt the grip of a juvenile shame.

'Still ten-thirty?'

'Yes, that should give us time.'

Martin waited for Evie to resume the conversation. There was a pause that he could not decipher.

'You okay, Martin?'

She'd seen him red-eyed and pathetic. He'd gazed not at a father-artefact, preserved to outlast him, but at an outstretched stranger, already tomb grey. It was not true what they said, that the dead appear to be sleeping. Their father was stony and gone. His mouth hung slightly open. Martin would never tell Evie about the official identification, how he'd been disgusted by the force of his own revulsion, that there was a foul odour in the air and a mortal sting. Someone professionally impassive, standing by, had known not to speak or touch his shoulder. Someone else, a stiff clerk, asked him to sign a form. And now Evie was phoning, to check if he'd found his suit. He hated the way his younger sister called him to account, made him feel that his misery was undisciplined and trite.

'No worries. See you soon.'

He hung up. She would guess, no doubt, that he was ashamed of his behaviour, of having made a scene at the restaurant. She was the practical one. She had taken his face in her hands and kissed his moist forehead and said, 'We'll get through this, Martin, we will, we will.' She'd hailed the taxi and held his hand and dragged him snivelling into the house, and propped him against the wall with her own body as she reached to flick on the lights. She'd guided him with difficulty to his unmade bed, lowered him to rucked sheets, arranged him, chided softly—*Jesus, Martin*—pulled off his stinking shoes and foetid socks. He'd made a weak

6

joke about cowboys dying with their boots on and wanted her gone. Their roles should have been reversed. He should have been the strong one.

In the kitchen Martin half-tripped on his daughter's Barbie dollhouse, left behind after her weekend access visit. It was three levels of tiny kitsch, in which everything was coloured fuchsia and open to view—wee tables and chairs, a four-poster bed ringed by a shred of looped gauze, a stove with a minuscule chicken roasting in the oven. He'd won the argument with Angela, who was offended by what she considered its domestic malevolence. Like a pedant Martin lectured her on mass-cultural knowledge, on how charming things in miniature really were, on how children in play are instinctively radical. When she said no, he bought it anyway, wishing to secure Nina's love with a plastic token. He liked to watch her small hands exploring the rooms, pushing furniture here and there, redecorating with her index finger alone. She had the scowl children achieve when they are concentrating with pleasure.

Just as he'd never known Angela, he would never truly know Nina. Women were alien, communicating in arcane languages, exulting in something delectable he couldn't see the point of, or outwitting him with an observation he didn't quite understand. Mars and Venus—wasn't that it? A formula that possessed the crude vigour of a cliché and made everything intractable comic. Once, enraged and casting about for a novel insult, Angela had called him Martian. It was meant to hurt. But by then both were too docile in their marriage to revert to wit, and they had walked off in opposite directions, defeated, frowning.

Martin bent his face to the level of the tiny house, and then lowered his whole body. He stayed like that, curled on the floor, looking into the Barbie rooms as one might seek a saint's face in the galleried spaces of a quattrocento painting. There was a chessboard floor, and he thought of those early works that situated figures in geometry—Piero's *Flagellation*—those visions beyond walls in which the eye calculates significance by lines of conjunction and perspective. Martin could have slept again there, acquiescing in his own unhappiness, as children fall asleep in the company of toys. But at length he rose. He needed an aspirin and strong coffee and to greet his sister with resolution.

In his grief he was thinking: I've had my vision for the morning and it was a crap toy doll's house. He was missing his daughter. He was missing his father. Self-deprecation was his default against difficult emotions.

The crematorium chapel resembled a bunker, with the anomalous addition of stained-glass windows. It was a dull building, unsuited for any function but disposal. Already, before the service, the community of mourners was dispirited and the summer heat added sweaty discomfort to an ill-timed event. For Martin and Evie, exposed by their status as his children, weak with fatigue, ravaged by memories, each convinced of the incapacity of the other to cope, the service was a trial.

At the funeral they sat so close they might have been lovers, just met. Evie rested her whole body to his, and he to hers, as if their two bodies would make up for the one suddenly gone. Bereavement was like exhaustion; they could barely stay vertical.

There were twenty or so people there, Angela among them, though she kept her distance, hiding behind sunglasses. Most of the others were friends of their father's, those who also moved in the comfortable world of art-historical scholarship—snobs, Martin thought. His insecurity prevailed. There were one or two younger scholars, and an attractive young woman in those heavy-framed glasses that were now all the rage; and two men about his age beside her, competing for her attention. She had black hair and dark eyes and might have been Italian. Martin wondered who she was, and if they might meet here and whisper tenderly before the wreathed coffin of his father. The air of grief would make him appear mournfully seductive.

He was in control in this way, even sexually and artistically speculating, until the minister began the eulogy. Hearing the name of his father made him anxious again. Martin felt a wasteland spread open inside him; every word seemed to bring him to the verge of tears. Evie was distant and silently weeping. Her shoulders sloped away, arousing his pity. What he feared above all was his own lack of dignity. He might blubber or call out. He might make a spectacle of himself, as he had in the restaurant. He sat clenched, imagining a series of desperate blunders: falling in the chapel aisle, uncontrollable sobbing, opening his mouth to speak and finding the bubble of nothing to say.

Two wreaths of mauve roses, with sprays of baby's breath and leaves that might have been plastic, sat high on the coffin. *Death-buoys*, he thought grimly, pleased with his own morbid wit. But he held it together; he sat fixed as a corpse.

For old times' sake Evie had chosen a Scottish hymn:

Abide with me; fast falls the eventide.
The darkness deepens; Lord with me abide.

The faint consolation was only of memory. Martin recalled standing in church between his parents as a seven-year-old; it would have been the year their mother died. She was wearing a white cotton dress, or possibly linen, something with a dry, papery rustle. She was holding a hymnbook down to his height, so they could share the words. Her thumb keeping the book open. The musty scent of the pages. The twin pillars of his parents aligned beside him. All around, droning voices created an aura of contentment.

Martin couldn't remember Evie there, but she would have been almost four and old enough to join them. She must have been present, surely, standing at his side, singing 'Abide with Me' in an infant mumble.

From the tedium of so many Sunday services, he had recovered the solace of this one, small moment. He would have brushed at the fabric of his mother's dress. There would have been a mother's or father's hand come to rest on his head, or a low formal whisper to make him lean closer.

For the dreadful interlude during which the coffin slid behind the gold curtains, Evie had chosen Albinoni's *Adagio in G Minor*. How their father had loved it. His taste had been mostly conservative and predictable, yet the music seemed to swell in the hot hall as if in a cathedral, the organ continuo rising up, the strings vibrating with their pulse-like effect. Something—was it the tempo?—encompassed and held them all, like a rhythm inside the body. Albinoni had never before sounded so sensual. Others heard it too; Martin saw it in their faces, this throbbing appeal of an easy sadness, this pressurised emotion.

Together Evie and Martin watched their father slide away. The mauve roses wobbled, the hall light might have flickered, or dimmed, as the melody repeated, and repeated, in an accumulating sob. And since this was the logic now, and since he'd remained bravely calm to the end of the service, Martin embraced his sister and avoided looking at her wet, distressed face.

They stood in the windy chute near the door and shook the hands of departing mourners. They heard their father praised. They saw the courteous manners of genuine sadness. Some mourners introduced themselves, most simply filed past. Martin was gratified to see that the attractive woman had been crying. She shook hands weakly, and didn't make eye contact. A former university colleague of his father's was there, murmuring platitudes, his turtle throat quivering. Martin had to suppress an impulse to yawn. An old student announced himself. Strangers passed by. A distant relative, a woman in her nineties and more rumour than real, blew her nose and called their father 'a lovely boy'.

Martin's attention wandered.

'Lovely,' he repeated. 'Yes, my father was a lovely boy.'

What a ridiculous thing to say. Someone in a smelly suit escorted the old lady away, down the steps and over the crunchy gravel.

There would be no wake at the house, no small talk, warm brandy or soggy ham sandwiches. There would be no laborious reminiscence or false sociability. When the group dispersed, when the minister had climbed into his prehistoric Datsun and cheerfully waved goodbye, Martin and Evie phoned a taxi, went speedily to the pub, and together commenced the business of serious drinking. Now, they were companionable. Now the task was done and they felt like truants.

Searching for topics of conversation, Martin considered, at one stage, mentioning the Barbie house, and how it had reminded him of the Italian painting. But this would have sounded pretentious. In a private scandal of inattention, he'd been thinking of it all morning, even during the funeral service. There was a possibility there, perhaps a video installation, or a painting that used fuchsia and chequerboard and acute angles of perspective. Instead he rambled on, itemising the trivial offences of the service, displaying his control, ordering another round of drinks.

Evie was mostly silent. Another alien woman. Since she'd moved to Melbourne, they had become strangers to each other. He knew that she worked in a bookshop. Lived in a flat somewhere.

11

It pained Martin how little he knew of his sister's life, and in a pledge to himself he resolved to find out what she was planning, if she had a partner, if she needed any help, or money. He'd noticed with a pang her cheap and unflattering clothes and the first threads of grey in her dark wavy hair.

And it was Evie, this time, who was the alcoholic wreck. She was gulping and stumbling. Wine trickled down her chin. Her averted face showed the miserable struggle of the day. When they returned to his house, Martin laid her down on the couch, arranged her legs, and shuffled to the kitchen to make coffee. Noah had once announced, 'This family drinks too much,' his tone a mixture of severity, charm and rebuke. They'd felt helpless and irresponsible, celebrating a shared weakness.

They'd missed lunch, but Martin realised he was not hungry. It was late afternoon, too early for dinner or sleeping. Outside, the sun was the acrylic gold of crematorium curtains, and the city hummed with irrepressible life. He forgave cement and high-rise and the deadening rivers of traffic, for barking dogs, shimmering trees, and the roar and heave of busy streets. He loved it all, the jumble and jubilation of inner-west Sydney. Everyone said it: *life goes on.*

Now he stood at his sister's side, holding the coffee. She'd fallen asleep and commenced a meek, female version of a snore. How depleted she appeared. Her eyelids were cyan blue, her blotched skin was pasty, and she seemed thinner, a heap of bones, even since yesterday. In a slight distortion, her face was creased against the cushion. The two French brothers must have looked at their father in this way. They must have seen this combination of the meagre and indestructible. He would tell Evie about them—as children they told each other everything—but not yet, not until this time had passed, with its heavy silences and evaded questions. Instead, he sat at his desk with paper and pencil and sketched a few ideas, pleased to discover that he was still alert and intact, and content to be artfully moving his hand.

When Martin looked up, it was dark beyond the radius of his lamp. This was the lip of the night, the black mouth he might fall into. Leaving his art-absorption, becoming aware of his body at the desk, silent and alone, he recalled his father drinking sherry in semi-dark at the kitchen table, the night after the funeral service for his mother. It must have been an illicit childhood glimpse. The brown bottle, his head bent, the woeful stare. The way lamplight made an ellipse that contained only him. It had been like a sentimental painting, theatrical and touching: *The Widower Alone*, or *Portrait of Grief.* But there was something ample in this memory that seized and undermined him. It was a wrench to childhood, elsewhere, and a sliding away. The past that held his father was like that now, threatening to intercept him. Martin must be equal to Noah's self-composure.

About eight he pushed back his chair, rose and padded through the unlit house, careful not to disturb his sister. He used his mobile phone as a weak torch. The rooms seemed immensely still and vague. The hum of the day had gone, and the golden light. All around were ordinary things, his possessions, his furniture, translated to block shapes and shadowy presences. The night spoke to him in the language of child sensations retrieved: a clock that might have been a face, the taste of warm milk at bedtime, the secret lives of keys and cupboards and windows and paintings, a head resting on a pillow, the strange menace of hanging clothes. To this property of abstraction he added the faint sounds of the outside, a scrape, a trace of voice, the sigh of a slow rising wind. The house in darkness remade him; here, where nothing was happening, where he was listening to his sister's snore.

Martin didn't switch on the light in the kitchen but opened the refrigerator door. Something in its small wing of lemon glow sinking into the darkness gave him pause. He saw half-empty shelves of inedible leftovers, he saw incompetent living, waste, indulgence. He stood like an idiot staring down at the wedge of light across his shoes.

Yes, he thought, *my father was a lovely boy.*

The fridge emitted a frail animal rumble. Beyond this lit space, the night was fearsome and huge. He felt a wave—was it a wave?—pull him down and under. Martin buckled to the floor. He let out a moan, a heartsick release, and then he wept.

2

EVIE WOKE TO discover she'd been asleep for almost thirteen hours.

She had fallen into the skull-space of her own drunk mourning, and found an annihilation there that soothed and calmed her. Six a.m. To be nothing for thirteen hours: what sweet relief it had been.

Martin must still be asleep. Evie sat on the edge of his couch for a minute or two, stalled by the unfamiliar household. She lifted herself stiffly and tiptoed on bare feet to the toilet, and then to the kitchen. The refrigerator door was open and a pool of water glistened on the floor. There was the fecund scent of spoiled food, or of something organic unfreezing. She bent and wiped up the mess, relieved to perform a domestic chore. Then she made herself coffee, using the pot their father had given each of them as teenagers, insisting it was essential to the civilised life. Evie filled the water chamber, spooned the grounds into the filter, screwed on the top and set it upon the low gas flame: the small ritual of making coffee was part of her inheritance. After death, one summarises. Noah's concluded life was now a story running backwards. He had already become inherent in objects, and in words, and in the wide-scattered emblems of her father-memory. Like God, she thought cynically, the dead are everywhere and nowhere. Here was her father, eternal, in these small movements of her hands, in the way she lifted the lid to check, in the careful pouring.

The funeral: he would have approved her choice of music, how Angela had spoken to her and not to Martin, how Martin had not wept, or made a scene, as he did in the restaurant. He had seemed, in fact, rather like Noah; he had seemed self-contained, even preoccupied, in the ceremony of loss, as if his training to see the world converted to art was a handy displacement on public occasions. When the mourners filed away, Martin looked older; she saw him in the future, slightly greyer, slightly bent, and with a caution in his movements that betrayed arthritic knees and stuck joints. He was vain and would hate to be imagined like this by his sister.

As if she had summoned him, Martin appeared. He stood aslant at the kitchen door. Her sense was correct: future age hung over him. He looked ragged and infirm. Two days of solid drinking and little food had taken its toll.

'Me too,' he said. 'One sugar, no milk.'

And then he sloped away, crashing onto the over-cushioned couch. He was not quite ready to join the world of the fully awake. No 'good morning, how did you sleep?' They might have been students in a share house, comfortably sloppy and accustomed to acting on the barest instructions.

Evie looked at her bony wrist turning off the gas flame. She would not allow herself to be irritated, but would take her time. She would practise forbearance in dealing with her brother. She poured the coffee carefully into two small cups and found a tray, tucked behind plates, and a few dry biscuits. She watched her own hands fluttering, making her spirit behave as if busy.

Martin was huddled on the couch, staring between his feet. Like her, he was wearing yesterday's clothes. No jacket, but he still wore the black tie, loose and askew, and it seemed pitiably inappropriate so early in the morning. How like Martin—and how forgetful to have slept in a tie. She saw that he hadn't yet shaved, and then remembered her own unkemptness.

'Who's de Saussure?' he asked her abruptly.

'Linguist or Neptunist?' She always enjoyed these tests he set for her. It was their mode of exchange; she was the brainy one dealing with his curiosity, his histrionics, his bouts of depression.

'Fuck, is there anything you don't know? Some connection to the Alps.'

'That would be the Neptunist. Eighteenth-century scientist. Climbed Mont Blanc. Believed the Alps had been formed by the oceans, hence Neptunist.'

Evie handed her brother his coffee and placed two biscuits in his lap. They drank in silence. Martin devoured the biscuits. Evie wondered where the de Saussure question had come from, but knew not to inquire. She hoped he'd ask about the linguist.

'The police want to talk to us,' Martin said. 'There was a phone message, the day before the funeral.'

'And you didn't tell me?' Evie was filled with dismay by his casual withholding. 'What about? Didn't the coroner say heart attack, "natural causes"? Isn't that why he released the body?'

She felt a chill overtake her, as when she heard of her father's death for the first time. Noah had just returned from a holiday in Italy; he had new theories, he said, and new ideas. He had rung her to say: *visit me. I miss you. Come up to Sydney and see me. Let's speak more of these things.* Only a week ago she had heard his voice on the telephone.

Martin looked up at her. 'They didn't say. They just asked that we come in after the funeral. Detective somebody or other. We could go today.'

Evie searched his face for more information, but found none. He was as ignorant as she. As worn out by grief. Both still existed in the below-zero world of the newly numb, those for whom everyday tasks were necessary, but scarcely real.

From beyond the wall came the muffled sound of a neighbourly bump. They glanced at each other, as if both had childishly thought *ghost*.

Martin attempted a smile. 'I'm sure it's nothing. A formality. There are probably more papers to sign.'

He opened his arms. Evie accepted the implicit invitation for a hug. *Abbracci*, she thought. Martin enclosed her in his stale funereal clothes, holding her firm.

'A formality,' he repeated.

And they stayed like that, listening to the sounds of the morning. Evie noted this time the state of the house: Nina's toys all over the floor, a pile of sketches on the table, dirty plates and cups, old newspapers, empty bottles. Beneath the windowsill stood a dead pot plant, still holding aloft its parched leaves. On the walls were paintings by fellow artists, mostly gifts in exchange, she guessed, and in one corner of the room his guitar, leaning upright. The paintings were wildly mixed in subject and style: a neo-surrealist figurative next to a few minimalist smears of red, a landscape—central Australia—that must have been done in the fifties, a portrait of Martin—how could she not have noticed this before?—large and grotesque enough to be entered for a prize. The Archibald, surely. Evie wondered how Martin could live with this outsized image of himself, staring back with orange eyes and the drippy brushstrokes of a face. Narcissist, she told herself. Martin is a narcissist.

'We should eat,' she said.

Martin roused, loosened his embrace. 'Yes, take care of me, Mama.' He included a moan.

Evie made a fist and gave him a sharp punch to the arm, as they did when they were children. He had no idea how much this joking upset her.

We have just endured, she thought, the funeral of our father and my brother is still as he was, negligent, self-centred, without a clue. He is still the cocksure adolescent bound for fame and glory, still contesting his father's authority. They were so alike, father and son, that they had loved each other in self-confirmation. The equation of what they were was a tangled knot. They had mirrored each other's expressions, taste in women, in food, an admiration for all things Italian and for stories of miracles and saints. How they talked about human frailty (superciliously); how they ate (omnivorously); how they walked (comically), leaning forward like mime artists, as if battling a high wind.

Evie looked up at her brother. She would need to stop thinking in this way, seeing her father undead in the person of her brother. If she was to lay Noah to rest, she had to break them apart. If she was to go on, and to be strong, she had to love Martin separately. She understood what it was she was feeling, a kind of resentment that Martin had been more loved. It surprised her to name it for the first time. *Martin had been more loved.* She trembled her hands over her frowsy hair, and patted it pet-like, to reassemble herself. She rose with the tray, playing Mama, and returned to the kitchen.

'There's eggs,' he called to her.

And so there were. Evie fried four eggs in butter in a small pan and they sat eating them together. There was salt, nothing more. How could he live like this? She looked into her brother's face. With rapt inattention he was staring down at his greasy plate.

'If we're going to see your detective, we should get ready,' Evie said. It would be her role to defeat the torpor that threatened them both. 'I'll return to the guesthouse to shower and change. Take your time, I'll come back, and we can walk into town from here.'

The love of walking: this was one thing they shared. In this confusing time she was looking for reliable connections.

She thought back to the funeral. The moment of greatest difficulty had been the solemn singing of the hymn. Her heart was in the coffin with her father; she had to pause until it returned to her. She would not even pretend to join in, but the words unwound themselves inside her atheist mind, following the furrowed track Noah had made for her, years ago. She was an ungrateful daughter, refusing his beliefs, but she could not resist the beauty of the word 'abide', or the congregation of others, conscientiously in tune, each engaged in a private elevation. Some no doubt believed. Some were strengthened against the golden curtains and the slide into flames. Some offered up their voices in a piercing purity. She could hear both their commitment and their self-satisfaction. And it had amazed her, disconcerted her, that Martin was among those singing.

As she closed the door behind her, Evie felt the reviving

beauty of the Sydney morning. She'd been in Melbourne five years, loving her relocation, but had forgotten this electric sky and buzzy soundtrack, the slight savage edge. Traffic at a distance, joggers on the street, a terrace door slamming; these notations seemed the hoot of a more confident life.

Walking quickly, she skirted an oval-shaped park. So much energy here, Evie thought, so much extroversion. Not her city at all. Dogs in friendly clusters were tossing themselves upwards. Birdsong rang out. The massive canopies of fig trees gave a dense looming shade. A watery aspect to the sky foretold imminent rain. There was vivacity everywhere, people starting the new day, streaming to work in cars and trains. Somewhere, further away, the harbour glittered.

Perhaps this too was grief, she thought, this omnipresent liveliness, marking one's own exclusion.

3

IT WAS MID-MORNING before Martin recalled what it was about de Saussure: he invented the cyanometer, a little pie chart to estimate the shade of blue of the sky. In a circle he had painted graded slices of blue, all derived from carefully diluted tinctures of Prussian, so that the sky itself submitted to the calculations of science. How blue is the sky? Today it is *this* blue. Today it is blue number twenty-seven, a fraction darker than twenty-six, a fraction lighter than twenty-eight. He must have come across the name when he read of the brothers of Chamonix. Or perhaps, reading of the cyanometer, he discovered the story of the two brothers. Perhaps there was no connection at all; there just happened to be a colourist in the same location as the dead father and this sudden recollection had been entirely coincidental. Martin glanced out the window. How false was European knowledge. No Prussian tint out there: the sky was *cerulean*. A different pigment entirely, its blue verging not to grey or darkness, grizzled and leaden, but to elements of gold.

Martin and Evie set off under the southern sky and walked all the way to the Central Police Station. It was strenuous exercise in the humid air, and with the queasy after-effects of a hangover and eggs. But each felt the release of movement, the way the body wishes to walk. To be still is death, Martin told Angela, when she revealed she had taken up meditation.

He'd been a fuckwit; he was arrogant. She'd been right to leave him, he reflected.

It had always been a mystery to her why he strode around his studio, why he danced by himself, with the radio tuned to eighties hits, why he went for long walks, hours long, with no purpose or explanation. He felt warm now, even hot, as if he'd dispelled the chill of the father-corpse; and the reeking fumes from the buses in City Road made him aware of his own lungs and tight breathing. There was a moment he took Evie's hand—they were crossing the busy intersection at George Street and a car had swerved towards them—and Evie clenched his grip, startled, or in sudden gratitude. He liked having her by his side. He liked holding her hand. They should talk more, or travel together, or work on some project or other.

Cerulean was leaving the sky and rain clouds were massing to the east. There was the faint green tint that often preceded rain. Martin looked skywards and hoped that the cloudburst would catch them.

By the time they made the shortcut through Chinatown, striding up Dixon Street between the red façades and gilt lettering of competing restaurants, the concrete lions, the menu handbills, the oriental bunting aflutter above temple shapes and archways, both were bright with sweat. Their clothes were clinging to their bodies. Evie bought bottles of water from a squinting old lady who held the dollars up to her face, as if to check they were real. They drank under a canvas sign that advertised Aussie-Chinese New Year.

Chinese Sydney. He enjoyed its collision of images—characters, pinyin, a dragon banner, murky aquariums in the glaze of mirrored restaurants, faceted silk lanterns alongside blatant fluorescence. This was a zone of riddled mingling, and a dream of artistic connection.

As they arrived at the police station, rain began to fall in emphatic drops. Dark coins appeared on the shoulders and bodice of Evie's dress. Martin had always adored these sudden transformations. He might incorporate this vision into his Piero-Barbie artwork; he might depict his father as a saint, spotted with lustrous drops and made mystical by rainfall. Or he might simply admire his sister, who still resembled him.

Chinese bunting, saintly rain. He was having trouble staying focused. Wrecked by the last few days, he needed to pull the world in, to make it resourceful. He must remember that his artwork gave him purpose. Noah had known this. It was Noah who had taught him how attention could be arrested and pattern made. Noah understood the everyday tussle of images, that we select what we see and are made into selves by our selection. 'Perseverance is all': Martin remembered that much. He'd been a junkie when Noah first taught him this slogan, sitting beside him in a cane chair, speaking in kindly tones, touching the back of his hand. This was the true accomplishment of his father, that he had helped his son stay alive.

~

The young constable at the front desk called the detective, Frank Malone, whom Martin and Evie agreed later was a gloomy fellow. He had a long, ghoulish face in permanent shadow, and his deep voice seemed to portend dark disclosures. They stared at him, disturbed by so distinctive a face. The news, Martin decided, could only be bad. They all shook hands. With barely a greeting the detective turned and led them to a regulation grey office, devoid of ornamentation but for a large clock in the centre of the wall. It featured Roman numerals and the legend *Glasgow 1910*. It was encircled by oak. The detective's face, together with the touching legend, made Martin confused. He glanced at Evie and knew she too had seen these ill-fitting omens, this overlap of arbitrary signs.

'Sorry for your loss,' Detective Malone began. It might have been a lost watch or kitten, judging by his muted tone. 'This is not about the coroner's investigation. There is another matter.'

Here Malone paused, as if on television. He leaned forward, elbows on his desk, commanding their attention. Martin looked away from his compelling face.

'Before your father's death, only three days before, a report came from Italy alleging a certain object had been stolen. This object was of Italian origin.' Here, defeated by police-talk, he slowed to consult a sheet of paper. 'From Sicily, in fact. The report names your father, Noah Glass, as a suspect in a gallery theft and the handling of a stolen national treasure.'

Detective Malone looked up, expecting a response, a denial, some acknowledgement, at least, of his extravagant and enticingly foreign information. His grey, foreboding face again loomed before them. Evie was staring into space, Martin at the clock.

'Can you confirm your father spent ten weeks in Sicily and returned about four weeks ago?'

'You clearly know this already.'

'The Carabinieri Cultural Heritage Protection Agency have

asked for our help in investigating the case of Noah Glass. We need to know what you know. We expect you to be frank.'

The case of Noah Glass. Was there a case?

It was Evie who spoke up. 'We were told nothing about this. Doesn't it throw suspicion on the death?'

'Coincidence,' said Malone. 'The death was initially thought suspicious because of the Italian report, but, as you now know, the coroner ruled natural causes.'

He spoke in a matter-of-fact way that Martin found infuriating.

'But it seems he's some kind of suspect? What,' added Martin, 'is Noah *alleged* to have stolen?'

He liked the way his own voice sounded; this was the right question and he'd remembered to say *alleged*.

'A sculpture, a bust, late nineteenth century, by an artist named Vincenzo Ragusa.' The detective extracted a printout from a file and placed it before them on the desk. Under a satin sheen the face of a Japanese woman stared out at them. Japanese? Surely a bungle. They noticed her beauty.

Martin snorted. 'There's obviously some mistake. My father's field was quattrocento painting, mostly Florentine. He had no interest at all in nineteenth-century art, certainly not sculpture. He visited Italy a great deal and wrote art-historical articles. That's it, that's all. They're looking for someone to blame.'

Detective Malone said, 'Nevertheless.'

Martin and Evie waited.

'Nevertheless, the blokes upstairs love an international request. Makes them feel important. Some desk-bound bugger is hoping for a trip to Palermo. Take the missus, have a holiday. Drink some vino. It's not your usual break and enter, with some loser from the suburbs ripping off a phone or a telly.'

They noticed wry scepticism, almost disloyal, in the detective's attempt to charm them.

'So what was your father doing in Palermo?'

Martin could have said 'research' but was suddenly unsure. Why, he was thinking, would the Italians care about a local piece from the nineteenth century, when there were so many important thefts to chase? It sounded phoney, some speculative pretext or other. And his father was a model of bourgeois rectitude. No criminal, no way.

'It's a mistake,' Evie said softly. 'Why do we even have to deal with this? The funeral was only yesterday.'

Martin heard an implicit plea in her voice. She was right, it was monstrously insensitive, someone's balls-up or Walter bloody Mitty fantasy; a minor official in Sicily needing a name to pin to a mislaid artwork. There was a world out there of dodgy art deals and the sneaky smuggling of treasures. But no one here knew of Noah's righteousness. The hard light of the office was beginning to annoy him. They were all bluish beneath it, vein-coloured and strange. Martin examined his own wrists and considered the ugliness of skin.

When Detective Frank Malone dismissed them ten minutes later, he handed over his card. 'Anything you think of. Call.' Fed up with their failure to be impressed, he lifted his long, dark face and pointed with his chin towards the exit.

It had been the swiftest of meetings, for so grave an accusation. Was this how the law worked, all implication, no nonsense, and the hint of urgent procedure? Language like strategy. Rigid adherence to codes. Even the word 'detective' was flagrant when linked to his father.

Without umbrellas they were beginning to soak. Martin's hair was flattened, his round face glowed. Evie looked bedraggled and overwrought. Already a mess, Martin thought; she shouldn't have bothered. They ducked into a café and ordered macchiatos.

The scent of arabica coffee was reassuring. Then, realising they were both hungry, Martin ordered again, two gigantic 'all-day breakfasts': baked beans, fried eggs, cooked tomatoes, avocado, bacon, mushrooms, with a toppling ziggurat of toast on the side. This inelegant assemblage intimidated Evie. Martin watched as she lifted the eggs with her fork and placed them atop his serve. Four eggs, six this morning. He studied her face.

'I thought policemen didn't believe in coincidence.'

'It's crazy, it's like a *giallo*,' Martin responded.

Evie remained silent.

'*Giallo*, you remember? Italian detective stories. Yellow covers. Hard-boiled, nuggety crims, dodgy perps, that kind of thing. Something grisly and revolting in the backstreets of Naples.'

'Jesus, Martin. It's our father we're talking of.'

'That woman who sold them from a stall outside the place we used to stay in—where was it, now? The woman with the evil eye and the mole on her chin.'

Evie sighed, shuffled her food.

'Nevertheless,' he added. He saw that she was hurt, and that he'd failed to judge her mood. She'd missed the *nevertheless*. Though she'd wiped her face, there were still tiny moisture beads clinging to her hair and a liquid pathos to her flushed dishevelment. Rainfall amplified the traffic sounds and there was the whoosh-whoosh of passing cars, all heading down the hill, then up again, towards Anzac Bridge.

'Eat up,' he urged, finding nothing better to say. Then he added, 'Detective Malone?'

And she smiled and nodded with a mouthful of toast, and they were collusive again, brother and sister again, seeing the world with one pair of eyes.

'Glasgow, 1910?'

And she let out an involuntary laugh, lifting her hand to her mouth too late to prevent a small spray of crumbs. Neither could have said why the clock amused them.

This was what Martin relied on. In his own disintegrating state, he wanted her to be funny. He wanted his sister to confirm the illogic of things, to notice what he noticed, and to corroborate his mental agitation. The loss of their father was more ruinous than he could yet express. It was a void for which he had no clarifying words or images. He would ask Evie more about the sky man, de Saussure. He would tell her of his artistic project, inspired by Barbie and Piero. And he would speak to his sister of private matters that he could reveal to no other person alive.

4

AT THE GUESTHOUSE Evie changed her clothes once again, spreading her damp cotton dress across the back of a chair. Why had she not decided to stay with Martin? It would be wise to save money, to talk more, to share the same space in a companionable grief. But she knew that they would both need time to retreat, and this pastel room, budget-furnished, suited her well. It had a grumbling air conditioner and a mouldy smell, but it overlooked the street, so she could lean on the windowsill and envision her nowhere an anywhere. This contraction of existence felt appropriate to her mourning. Here she might feel what she must—here, in a small anonymous room, where she could fling her bag in a corner and hang her scarf over the mirror, covering it as they did in traditional rituals. Evie liked the idea that she prohibited her own reflection. Corpses and mirrors. No corpse here, but had there been a clock, she would have stopped it; had there been a black armband, she would have worn it. Nothing had added nobility to his passing: a crematorium service, not a burial as he would have wished, a brother and sister, mostly estranged, still prickly in conversation, and now cops and robbers and an almost overwhelming sense of absurdity. The dead did not rise. Christianity was a lie. She imagined the scorn of believers, even as she enacted minor ceremonies of appeasement.

Unlike his atheist children, Noah had retained his religious beliefs and might have expected a crystalline hereafter. He had enjoyed provoking them with God-talk, mostly of transcendence and the persisting soul, with pious Christmas cards—always a classical nativity—and intolerance of the casual blasphemies of swearing and wealth. He'd been a Methodist before he became an Anglican, and something misfortunate and austere remained, an insecurity he attributed to unspecified events in his childhood.

They'd loved their affectionate banter, she and Noah. Neither owed the other an explanation, but to preserve their dignity and connection, they fought and teased. To express feeling, they'd practised indignation, each unyielding and a little fierce. What to others might have appeared as discord was their expression of love.

The warm rain continued, slowing to a drizzle. From her window Evie could see a large fig tree, dome-shaped, its black leaves sagging low under the afternoon showers. The road was silver. The traffic was light, seeming behind the glass to float noiselessly past. Martin had agreed they would meet later for dinner, and that they would not drink alcohol.

Evie sat on the double bed of her rented room and allowed herself to contemplate the accusation that her father was a criminal. That he had stolen an artwork was inconceivable. He

31

deplored the art market and was appalled at the prices Martin's work commanded. He had always insisted on the immaterial aspects of art, so that when she had objected to religious symbols and institutional power, he had sighed and told her that she was missing the point. The point was the magpie on the roof of the stable, he said. It was the fallible body displayed. It was the unearthly made visible. It was the way one was obliged to stand still and peer into the stopped world of a single image, to consider first things and last things and the threshold of a frame. She had joked: how mystical he was becoming, how like the figures he studied.

Noah's apartment in Elizabeth Bay overlooked the harbour. It was full of souvenirs of his travels, unusual objects, curios, but nothing particularly valuable. Evie now wanted to visit his rooms, to see evidence of his work, his papers, his library, his notes, to encounter again the small items he had daily cherished. Though she was at home in the guesthouse, it occurred to her only now that she might stay at her father's apartment. She would rest her head on his cool pillow and dream him back into life. His rooms would comfort her, or perhaps not; his traces would at least slow or moderate her reckoning of his passing. The more she thought of it, the more solid the idea became. Martin had the keys; she would ask for them at their dinner.

Evie had locked up her flat in East St Kilda, and told her boss at the bookshop that she was taking a few weeks' break. She sent farewell messages to her friends, and a vague note to her sometime lover, a man inconveniently, or perhaps conveniently, married to someone else. It had been easy to leave. She'd been untypically decisive with the shockwave of the news, but in truth wasn't sure what she would do in Sydney. Already she was feeling inert and superficial. Three years ago, she'd abandoned university work as a philosopher, and she didn't want to resume her academic contacts; she knew few people in Sydney beyond her old field. There was no defining purpose now that the funeral was over. In any case, she imagined herself unrecognisable.

Evie kicked off her sandals, climbed onto the bed and opened the book she'd brought with her, a history of the Russian Revolution. In her peculiar habit of mind, she was committing the names of revolutionaries to memory in alphabetical order. She already knew she would start with Abramovitch and end with Zhukovsky and Zof. Good to have some Zs. How rare it was to have Zs to play with. It must be a failure of the English-speaking world, she thought, to have neglected the suave authority of a name or thing beginning with Z. With no chores and no wish to be a wandering tourist, she sank into the easy sublimation of reading, and forgot her despondency almost at once. The only interruption was when Angela sent a text message saying that Nina wanted to see her favourite aunt. Evie replied that she would come tomorrow. The afternoon was entirely hers.

She considered another series of sub-lists—Decembrists, perhaps, or Narodniks. She was aware of the archaism and oddity of her indulgence. Her alphabetical inclination and wish to order might be a named pathology. Someone somewhere must have studied it, and found a distant cause. A childhood germ, a trauma perhaps, a mean genetic malfunction. But in this practice Evie passed her time serenely, and relished the merit of learning in her idiosyncratic way. As if tuned to a devotion or spiritual exercises, she became still, centred and closed in on herself.

When it was time to prepare to meet Martin again, Evie was ready. She rose and brushed her hair by touch. Loaded with her new alphabetical lists, she felt almost replenished.

~

He'd made a serious effort. Martin had tidied his house, stowed the dead pot plant behind the couch and even bought flowers, lisianthus. He'd arranged them in a black plastic vase on the kitchen table. Evie stared at them, wondering how long ago he must last have bought decorative flowers. For Angela, perhaps. For an anniversary or celebration. She looked at the purple and white blossoms, blazoned in a loose composition against the lime green of a fresh tablecloth. He had placed three navel oranges, just so, at the base of the vase. She saw her brother's skill. He understood the transforming juxtaposition of things, he noticed hue and texture, he knew how a bloodshot vision could be revived by setting three colours together.

Martin stretched out an arm. 'Come,' he said. Pasta was bubbling in a pot on the stove; a salad—almost unnaturally multicoloured—awaited its dressing on the sideboard. A bottle of fizzing water was open alongside two tumblers. She watched him hover over the stovetop, checking and tasting. His shirt was speckled with oil, proclaiming the slapdash of his cooking. There was the flourish of a tea towel handling a saucepan. Her brother served the meal with an inexperienced rush; he hurried back and forth, could not find the parsley, and fretted with the service as he made her sit at the table. But his efforts were triumphant, and he beamed as he spooned penne arrabbiata into bowls and sprinkled it with parmesan. They both ate their entire portions and were pleased they'd resisted wine. After he had cleared the plates, Martin made coffee. They were enveloped in a unanimous and absent-minded calm. The best meals, Evie thought, are casual and fast.

'We need to talk,' he said.

'Later, we'll talk later. I can't now, Martin. I can't talk about Noah right now.'

'That crime, what do you think?'

'Not now.'

Why did he make her repeat? How could he not know her feelings?

'Later, then.'

'Later.'

They sipped at their coffee. She waited for him to resume; there was a boyishness in the way he seemed energised now, and returned to the world.

'I've been thinking,' Martin said, 'about a trip to Italy. Sicily. I'd like us to go together.'

So this was the purpose of the meal, this was the proposition. With dour satisfaction Evie thought 'no'. But instead she said, 'Why?'

'Obvious reasons. To get away. To honour the old man. To eat more pasta.'

Here he smiled, but was cautious. She could detect in his offhand manner a wish to persuade and please her, yet all the while she was thinking: what a disaster that would be, to travel with Martin, to have to deal with his moods, and his self-importance and his immature copying of their father.

'I have no money,' she said.

'No problem, I have plenty. Just think about it—you don't have to answer me now.' Martin was losing his composure. 'Don't you want to know too? What Noah was doing there?'

Evie stared at the vase of lisianthus. She could not respond. She choked at the idea of an investigation into her father. And though reluctant to concede it, she knew that Martin, inexplicably, had more intrinsic vitality to counter their loss. She was irritable, dull; he was already imagining new beginnings and the resumption of real life.

'I need to go to his apartment. Would you object if I stayed there? I need to sort some things out...'

Martin raised his tumbler of water, as if offering a toast. 'So sort,' he said.

When their evening concluded, she had agreed to nothing. They stood closely, silently, facing each other. The importance of what had not yet been said hung fog-like between them. But Martin had given her the keys to their father's apartment, and she was already anticipating the taxi drive in the morning and the relocation of her luggage.

The guesthouse room looked dreary when she returned. The daylight and sheltering fig had given the room its air of hospitality, but by night the furnishings were clammy and oppressive. The covered mirror looked pointless; *no corpse here*. A television hung from the ceiling like a black dead eye. Evie located the remote and watched the screen, unseeing. American crime drama. An improbably good-looking detective was going through her generic motions: confrontation, argument, rapid talk into a phone. A car pulled up in front of a brownstone, and detectives in long coats slammed its doors, turned in an arc and strode up the stoop. There was a female body, prone, and a fabricated tension. There was a babble of law language and a mishmash of cop threat.

At the ad break Evie switched off, showered, then fell onto the bed. The thin curtains admitted a chalky street light, traffic sounded in a continuous rainy shoosh, and in her troubled mind there was too much distraction to sleep. Somewhere in the dark was the gift of lisianthus, set forth for her benefit on her brother's kitchen table, the pot plant hidden away, the effort of a meal. These signs of his concern had unaccountably moved her.

When at last Evie slept, it was on the slide of a partial memory, the scary Italian woman with a mole on her chin. She possessed the *malocchio*, the evil eye. Framed in a booth like the illustration of a tourist attraction, she'd called out to the children from behind her wall of yellow-covered books. Yellow magazines were pinned with wooden pegs on a string above her head. She flapped a magazine and its pages fell open and gaped. They'd been frightened by the swatting motion and the loud appeal for their attention. They'd held hands, nervous, inventing the terror of her gaze. Naples. The *malocchio* of their childhood had lived in Naples.

Evie slid away, darkly certain, on the inner surf of her zzzs.

5

NOAH GLASS WAS born in Perth, Western Australia, in 1946.

He died in Sydney sixty-seven years later, fully clothed, face downwards, in the pristine turquoise swimming pool attached to his apartment block. A woman in a voluminous striped blouse, Irene Dunstan, long-time resident of number fourteen, came upon him as she sought her cat, Socksy, at about seven a.m. Socksy, she explained, always woke her early, but was nowhere to be seen. It was fishy, she declared, in the light of what happened.

Socksy turned up two days later; now residents were reluctant to use the pool and there was talk of having it drained or disinfected. Irene Dunstan had used a leaf scooper to poke at the body, as if it might be a joke in bad taste or a mistake of some kind, but the drowned man had wavered only a little on the still water, revolving slowly like a synchronised swimmer. She rang the police, more excited than upset by the delicious horror of having a death to describe. The discovery gave her special authority, and the more she spoke of it the more she embellished her story. She fingered the cloth of her blouse as she offered the details; she was, if temporarily, the centre of attention. It had been a lifelong ambition.

Of her neighbour, she knew little. Not even his name. Worked in an office, maybe. Kept mostly to himself. Quiet bloke, reserved. Not one to give a wave, or stop by in the evening for a chat.

From the age of eight, Noah lived for four years at a leprosarium in the north of Western Australia. He knew that this time and this place had shaped him more than any other, but he rarely spoke of it, or wished to recall.

His father, a doctor missionary, defied advice by taking his wife and two small sons with him, certain that faith and anti-biotic breakthroughs would keep them all beyond harm. It was the mid nineteen-fifties. The world was still rebuilding after the war, and Joshua Glass, returned soldier, working off some undisclosed debt or secret thanksgiving, was doing his bit. He was a man convinced both of the bitterness of the world and its possibility of redemption, and filled, though obscurely, with higher purpose. He was also blunt, remote, authoritarian in his vocation, and too reserved with others to be easily loved. His patients were all Aboriginal, and this community of blighted black people, perishing in slow stages, confirmed his belief in the durability of suffering. Though dedicated and hardworking, he was a man apart. Secretly, he thought himself a creature of spiritual corruption.

Noah would later reflect that he never knew his father, and what little he understood disturbed and confused him. There

39

were rare gestures of connection, shy with tenderness and gruff in expression. He would remember most clearly his father's hands, the wormy blue of raised veins, the long, rheumatic fingers, knobbly and mustard from the smoking habit he'd acquired in the army. How stiffly they splayed across the table or the cover of his Bible. How huge they had seemed, compared with his own. When he could not look at his father's face, he stared at his large, bony hands.

Only many years later, when his own children arrived, did Noah understand what was possible between parents and children, what unexpected feelings might open and release. He had missed his chance. Paternal power, he later reflected, meant that many of his generation had missed their chance. Joshua's stern command, his cloak of sadness, his secretive wartime, his embarrassed, evasive air, made him largely unsuited to social intercourse; all these aspects of character removed and silenced him. Noah knew he was not alone—his mother and younger brother, James, felt this distance too—but would seek to ingratiate himself with his father, sacrificing a more intimate connection with his mother. He was perhaps forty before he understood the implications of this choice. Belatedly, he knew his own emotional stringency. When his mother whispered words of comfort, he despised her weakness, as well as his own.

The community of lepers numbered one hundred and fifty or so. Some appeared comparatively healthy and were employed in baking and butchering, wood-carting and washing. A small garden of straggly vegetables was tended with particular pride. There was an 'orchestra' of violins, irregular cricket matches and a quarterly mass when a priest visited from afar. Two sisters of St John of God, smiling in their stifling habits, administered the community. Noah had assumed his whiteness and good health would secure a kind of status, but from the moment of his arrival he felt ignored. Just a kid, after all. His father was admired and respected for his labour; he was insignificant.

In the privacy of darkness Noah felt outraged. Nightly, tossing in the heat, he was aware of James's restful breathing, close by in the same room, and the syllables of unknown languages, drifting outside. Bird calls startled him, the nocturnal screech of something predated, and the click and ping of corrugated iron contracting. Dogs seemed to bark at all hours, apparently at nothing. There was no electricity. Obliged to reckon every day with evidence of disease, to learn new ways of being and behaving, he thought only of escape. In the future he would recall the stench of an extinguished kerosene lamp and those nights in which he turned to the wall, huddling and desperate, trying to seal himself away.

The older, more disfigured residents filled Noah with panic. The sight of eroded faces and missing ears, of clawed hands, flattened noses and crusty patches of skin, made him distressed and afraid. Some of the elders were blind, several had amputations. One man had no forearms and a stub for a leg. Noah was aware of looking away, of ignoring a hello from figures at the edge of his vision, sitting in the shadows. There was guile in his behaviour, in the way he spun a rope around himself, as if to say 'don't come near', in the way he bullied his little brother, pinching and punching, or spat after someone unknown called out to him. Desperation was a rough and inventive mood. Noah possessed the terrible energy of the miserable.

Nothing made any sense. The few children of the community kept to themselves, and he had no resources to fill his new-found emptiness. Once his father appeared at the doorway with a headless chicken tucked under his arm, its neck still dripping blood. His father, the doctor, was now brutish and inexplicable. Noah

41

had bolted outside, furious, to vomit into the dirt. Everything conspired to alarm and revolt him, and instinct told him this was a place to which he would never adapt. The earth was Mars orange, the baobab trees with their bloated bellies and spiky limbs signified nature deformed. Mangy dogs with yellow eyes hung about everywhere, claiming space and attention. There were two dormitories, one for men and one for women, a few corrugated-iron huts and water tanks, a weatherboard infirmary and a cluster of small sheds. Beyond the buildings lay the graveyard, a collection of neat timber crosses; and beyond that, terrifying distance and the dissolve of figures into space.

Joshua consulted on the verandah of the infirmary—dentistry, medications, the setting of broken limbs—and seemed busily content. Noah watched as his father, gallant as a lover or a bridegroom, took a young woman's palsied hand and gently, one by one, flexed her stiffened fingers. The woman looked away; she knew the intimacy of the act. Yet Noah remained gripped by flinch and recoil; he could not imagine touching anyone but his mother. Disease was everywhere implicit, in the rust-coloured drinking water, the sticky swarms of black flies that clumped on his back, the spiders in the sink, the snakes beneath the back steps. They'd been exiled not for a higher cause, but as a vile punishment.

It was the isolation that truly terrified him. His family could die out here and no one would ever know. They could disappear from the face of the orange earth and no one would even come searching.

In the first weeks Noah argued incessantly with his father, who seemed pleased by his son's torment, which he evidently regarded as a spiritual test. His mother, Enid, was weak and withdrawn, and only later did Noah realise she'd been depressed, that the days she didn't rise from her bed were her own kind of trial, undistinguished by biblical precedent and more lonely than his own. Within a few months she returned south to live with her mother; they were a ruined family and Noah missed her quiet caress of his head, the way she plastered down his hair along the part line with her spit. He missed her fumbling for a hug and her desultory attempts at cooking. Had she stayed, he might have enlisted her as an ally. Together, they might have defeated his father. James, three years younger, was simply useless and exasperating.

Later on, Noah was ashamed of his boyhood cowardice. He would have liked to tell his adult children of some outback adventure, but he kept his secrets close. In truth, he'd been a sullen, self-centred child, with no fellow feeling that might have helped him appreciate Joshua's work, or understand that the banishment was not his, after all, but belonged to the suffering people around him. Most of all, he would regret his selfish revulsion, but it could not be forgotten, or disavowed.

There was an exemplary moment; it would return clear as a wound. Once, when a man nearby began bleeding from the nose, his father impulsively jerked Noah and James away, telling them that sneezes and blood were all they had to fear. This attempt to reassure made him more afraid. Noah believed he'd breathed something in, and that germs had flown like tiny arrows to lodge in his throat. He loathed his father. Hysterical, he begged to be sent south, to live with his mother and grandmother. Joshua quaked, crossed the dirt, and struck his son across the face with an open hand. It was the only time in his life his father used violence against him. There was a pleasing second in which Noah saw that Joshua's anguish was greater than his own. It was amazing, this sudden, inverted signal of love. James had burst into tears. Their father looked aghast, his mouth rigid and empty. It was plain to each of them that Joshua had no comprehension of his action, could not apologise, could not explain.

Noah never forgave him. He ran into their shack, all obstinacy and pride, all jangled rebellion, and drank cup after cup of water to remove the leper germs. He wanted the fear gone. He wanted comfort. He wanted his father to express deep regret and beg for forgiveness. For the rest of his life, Noah's anxiety appeared as a rash at his throat. The rash resembled the livid plaque symptomatic of the early stages of leprosy. It was both the disclosure and the return of his own faulty humanity.

By degrees his father's convictions began to make sense. Not quite old enough to dissent fully, not quite in control of his need to ingratiate, Noah eventually complied. He adopted the saving mentality of the religious. He was twelve when he left the colony, to attend boarding school in Perth, never to return. During those four years Noah had grown pragmatically servile, calming himself in study and rationalisation, sometimes engaging his distant father, hoping to win favour with a shrewd query or a casual display of knowledge. But he'd hardened his heart. He was tough, egotistical and emotionally absent.

It was the strained peace of a truce. Some weeks after their mother left, Joshua permitted his sons to attend the school run by the nuns, Sister Agatha and Sister Perpetua, and despite his initial reluctance, Noah felt less alone. There was another life there: the books, the singsongs, the Bible stories, the saints. To be organised for half a day was a huge relief. To have somewhere to go. To have a desk to sit at. And in this barest of schools, every object was special. A blackboard, chalk, a pale-coloured map of the world. Sister Agatha gave music lessons with donated violins, some of which she'd repaired herself. Playing helped to exercise the fingers, she said. No musical knowledge needed, just following a tune. Years later Noah heard a fiddle and an accordion play in a backstreet in Lecce and tumbled as if in a dream to remembrance of Sister Agatha and her lessons, the way she nudged a violin under a chin and arranged fingers into a musical position.

In a dusty pile of books Noah found *Great Art Museums of the World*. It bore the fuzzy stamp of a library in suburban Melbourne, but ended up in his own hands and before his own astonished eyes, and lived under his pillow, a treasure, and a night window to elsewhere. This single book marked the arrival of exotic visions. Other worlds and times blazed as portents from the pages, drifting into focus, contained and set apart in a shiny strangeness. He stroked the glossy paper and studied the legends to the paintings as if his future life depended on it.

The younger of the nuns, and his teacher, was Sister Perpetua. Although Joshua had warned him about the fanatical Catholics, Noah found her unlike his father's description. She was clever and listened to him when he spoke. She used his grandmother's expressions—'My word! Goodness me! Heavens above!'—which made her seem timeless and almost family. Occasionally she mentioned the gospels, but not as often as his father, nor with his stern theological absolutism. She said she was living in the community simply to serve. She didn't think that Aboriginal people were sinful—no more, in any case, than anyone else. In fact, people in Adelaide, where she was from, were much more sinful, she said with a wink. Noah had no idea what this implied, but he was thrilled by what seemed a confidential remark. He was thrilled to have an adult pay him special attention.

It was Sister Perpetua who sat Noah next to the boy called Francis, and encouraged their friendship. Francis was originally from Halls Creek, and, but for a few scattered macules and lesions, he looked more or less healthy. He was almost a lifelong resident of the community, having arrived as a toddler with his mother, Maggie, who was now one of the truly defaced.

Noah was afraid of Maggie. He saw her often, sitting outside cross-legged, quietly observing. Her features were worn and scab-like, so that her eyes appeared prominent; she peered at him and smiled without lips, pleased that her son had another companion. Noah kept his distance. He was still a boy afraid. For all his compliance and acts of submission, religion had not dispelled his fear. In nightmares Maggie's mouth opened crimson and appalling, and a contagious sneeze exploded in droplets all over him. She inspired a horror against which he defined himself, not to be one of those, not to be touched by this godforsaken woman, whose rotten face appeared to have been slashed at with a knife.

When he recalled this time as an adult, he discovered his love for Francis. It was not affection, it was love. He'd longed for his presence. They'd grinned at each other, silently knowing. Yet his memories were mostly simplified, or gone. They must have passed time as boys do, mucking around. They must have shared unusual objects, and games and words. With James tagging along they often dawdled down to the creek, and made boats out of bark cut with pocketknives and assembled with string. He remembered that Francis taught them how to hunt for goannas and snakes, then how to use their thumbs to remove charcoal and taste the clean flesh of their killings. He remembered the shape of Francis's back as he bent over a cricket bat. He remembered that with his friend beside him he'd felt brave and undefiled. This was a version of love, surely, to receive what was best in oneself, acknowledged and sweetly returned. They exchanged stories, but he recalled few details, something elusive that devolved to a tone of voice. Noah, in return, spoke of the city in the south. There were buildings as big as mountains, he boasted, and there were rivers of cars.

This he remembered for sure—they had both loved cars.

At the leprosarium a single wartime jeep spluttered in the dust. Sometimes they sat in its high-up seats, or watched as the driver, Jeremiah, tinkered with its engine. In the city, Noah told Francis, there were lines of brand-new cars, different colours, different sizes, moving along hard roads. Together the boys developed an obsession. Both received a Dinky car from Joshua dressed as Santa. It was as if God himself had chosen a gift for each of them.

At some stage Noah realised he could tell Francis anything, since his world was bounded by the colony and he had little idea of what lay beyond. Like heaven, Noah said. Perth was like heaven. There was more food than anyone could eat and there was a river covered by swans. When they rose up, their wing-beats were like thunder in the air. Sometimes, in a mass, they blocked out the sun, casting the city into darkness. The houses were cool and full of furniture and plaster ornaments. There were trams, like long cars, and people stepped on and off to the sound of bells. A man in a gold-brocaded cap took money for the ride. There was a zoo, with an Indian elephant, and a street full of shops, where rich people stared at their reflections in sparkling windows. James sat hugging his knees, silent and credulous, and did not contradict him. Francis, Noah thought, ought to have been more impressed.

When Noah left for boarding school, James became Francis's best friend. Noah missed them terribly, but was also relieved. It was easier to think of those years behind a scrim of distaste: he imagined a man turned away, pissing hot against a wall; there was the stench and the acrid vapour of something you couldn't quite look at. James dutifully wrote, in a neat hand, of his continuing adventures with Francis. But it was a gone world now, fifteen hundred miles away, and Noah believed he had made a great escape. Though helpless in the face of nightmares, he was still released, far away, and most of the time unblemished.

He heard that Francis became a car mechanic and an electrical handyman, self-taught from books. The colony of lepers was disbanded in the 1980s, and the patients moved to the coast, to Derby. Francis joined them. After his schooling, James returned for a while to work in the north, and maintained his friendship with Francis for the rest of his life. Noah intended to stay in touch, but never did. He once thought of writing to Sister Perpetua, returned to Adelaide, but when he lifted his pen he had nothing to say. He recalled her occasionally, with confounded feelings, but it was hard enough writing with confounded feelings to his own estranged parents.

In his thirteenth year Noah discovered the meaning of his boyhood experience. He pushed his shame away. In the movie *Ben-Hur*, he saw the hero descend into a leper colony, tucked into caves, and retrieve from the darkness his mother and sister. Both were bundles of rags. Ben-Hur witnessed Christ carry his crucifix on the road to Calvary and the shadow of the cross passed over his family. In a magnificent rainstorm, the women were cured. Their complexions cleared, their rags fell away, they possessed the innocent glamour of the saved. Noah was captivated; his boy's heart was full. He could hardly believe it: the restored beauty of the ladies, the weepy hero, the crescendo of violins and the soft light illuminating their salvation. Charlton Heston's profile was aristocratic and his skin shone bright and holy, with an antiseptic glow. Noah was interested less in the famous chariot race, round and round, each cycle more terrible and shattering than the last, than by this sentimental story of descent and return, divine blood in rainwater, contagion overcome.

With this story Noah hauled himself into another country. Now that he was away from the leprosarium, he could consider

48

himself a kind of hero. He too had looked at rags that might be people, and his fear and revulsion could be reworked into a ripping yarn. Even as he knew this was false, still he asserted it. Noah reconstructed his shame as a story: 'Just like in *Ben-Hur.*' And he could see that the boys at Guildford Grammar, rapt, gullible, their eyes wide as cinemascope, imagined caves and bloody rain as Francis might have imagined a sky full of swans. In his story Francis became the one he rescued ('You actually *touched* him?' they asked), a boy like themselves, but pitiable and tragic. A black boy, waiting in a cave to be saved, squinting in a gritty wind, moping in shadows, solitary, sad. It was something, Noah told himself, to do with the tangible and the intangible. You started with what you could feel, and soon enough you could visualise a picture, or a story. It was just like religion, it was just like belief. As an adult he understood how assiduous he'd been, sealing his confused desolation in this way. The film logic reassured him, even if his version of the colony was the product of cynical lies.

In the neurotic and competitive community of his school, Noah was one of the elect. He was tall and smart, and he carried an inner conviction. His teachers assumed he would become an engineer or a doctor, perhaps even a surgeon or a famous scientist. He was brilliant at maths and physics, and could do sums in his head. Everyone was disappointed when Noah took Arts at university, and ended up in the poncy, embarrassing business of writing about paintings. The school hero shrank into a kind of joke. As his friends made money, bought large houses, and found their own models of perfection in mining shares and real estate, he continued his studies. He went to Cambridge—Pommy-land, they said—and thence to a small university in the south-east of England. When they heard he had married, they were also surprised, having decided that his art studies were conclusive proof he was a poof. Noah heard all of this through the devoted reportage of James, who dropped out of school, joined a local band and, as one loyally obedient, wrote weekly to his brother.

A scrap returned, one day, in the shape of a small religious card. Noah discovered it tucked in the dust jacket of his childhood copy of *Great Art Museums of the World*. Jeremiah, the jeep driver, had given Noah a palm card depicting St Lazarus. The leper saint was an old man, covered in sores, his thin body leaning on a wobbly stick. Two dogs, of some gentle but unidentifiable breed, licked with compassion at the sores on his legs. The card was one of those old lithographs in which the magenta and cyan are too bright, so that the saint appeared garish, propagandist, and unworthy of sombre regard. He was smeared with old grime. What possessed him, Noah wondered, to make a keepsake of this card? He clenched the found image into a hard, tight ball. There. Dealt with. From that moment, vicious in its pleasure, he considered his early life crushed and flung away.

'He was a nice gent,' Irene Dunstan announced to her newer neighbour. 'But kept to himself, mostly.'

She worried that the swimming pool was forever spoiled, and that, if word got out, her property would fall in value. Now a young woman had come, claiming to be his daughter, and she also worried that there'd be other young people traipsing here and there, parties and whatnot, wandering strangers scaring Socksy. Irene had never seen the woman before—not one to visit her old dad, clearly—and they'd barely spoken when she arrived in an unironed dress, tugging a battered case up the driveway, looking disgraceful, looking for all the world like the wreck of the *Hesperus*.

6

EARLY IN THE morning Martin returned to the police station. He wanted more details, but without Evie present. A week ago he'd seen the coroner's report, and the findings were straightforward. Their father had died of a heart attack, a myocardial infarction. The incident had been assumed suspicious because the official note from Italy had just arrived, and the proximity of death and a possible crime seemed unusual, to say the least. There was also a red patch of inflamed skin at Noah's throat, as if he had been grabbed there, or suffered an abrasion of some kind. His doctor's records confirmed it was a chronic problem and, though distinctive, not the consequence of mishap or attack. There were other questions, too: how he came to be fully clothed in the swimming pool; why he had left his front door open. His blood-alcohol reading was high, but not excessively. No drugs in his system. If he was a criminal himself, now exposed, this could have been a cause for suicide; but this too had now been conclusively ruled out. Noah had a heart attack during the night and somehow fell into the swimming pool.

Martin was seeking the reason Noah had been named as a suspect. Might his father be involved in some disgrace? The investigation was launched from Palermo, so there could be something internationally nefarious to consider. The business of the sculpture was also puzzling. Noah would have told him or enlisted his help if he had been in any trouble. Until their interview with the detective, Martin had never heard of the sculptor, Vincenzo Ragusa—a minor figure, surely.

Malone reiterated that he wanted to pursue the Italian connection—perhaps he was the one who hoped for a trip to Sicily with the missus. Something in his doleful look made anything possible. He was too sure of himself, too gravely in the baritone with which he declared, as if singing, 'Carabinieri Cultural Heritage Protection Agency.' Martin shook his hand, once again, and felt no fellowship at all. He had learnt nothing new. Malone gave laconic and almost surly responses to his questions. The detective seemed aware he might be the object of sly derision; he must have known that his looks inspired aversion. This made him act as if self-conscious and on guard, Martin thought, or perhaps it was simply a policeman's manner, to seem unyielding and professionally unhappy.

Martin returned to the café he'd visited the day before with Evie. The waitress recognised him and gave a flirty smile. He ordered a macchiato again, and the same all-day breakfast, though he consumed it this time with little satisfaction, feeling the absence of his sister and the need to talk to her of their father. Now the café seemed almost unbearably noisy. The air crackled and the sound of crockery smashed and clattered. Martin looked down at the remains of his meal and felt grief sweep over him—some larger, confused feeling of being alone in the world, some intimation of abandonment at the knowledge that his father had secrets. They had been close, Martin and Noah. Both were proud of the fact that they spent time together, liked each other, planned trips to galleries, and the cinema, and went walking along the beach. In all that had happened to Martin—the failure of his marriage, his time in the clinic, his wavering sense of worth—Noah had been a wise and dependable support.

What Martin feared was that his memories would throw him off balance. Somehow this did him in. Small recollections were overtaking him and seemed a kind of weakness, almost feminine. There was a moment he could have sworn he felt the sensation of his father cutting his hair. Gentle fingers hovering at his nape, the soft click-click of silver scissors, his hair lifted, lightly combed, then falling away. His father fluffed his hair up at the back, as he'd seen real barbers do, before he combed it again, lifted it again, found a small section, parting it both languidly and precisely, to begin again his neat clicking. How Martin had loved the feel of his father's fingers in his hair, and the moment when he blew on his neck, to clear away stray remainders, when he patted his head and proclaimed the haircut complete.

At about thirteen Martin insisted on going to the barber's. It was a matter of self-respect, he told himself, to sit in the uphol-stered chair tilted before the mirror and watch a true professional at work. Martin could not admit it had been a disappointment, that the real barber had pushed at his head and cut his hair too short. He had glowered, curt at the till, refusing even to say thank you as he paid. But it was important to join the world of other boys, and not have his sissy dad humming and chatting and playing mum as he wielded his scissors. Martin never allowed

Noah to cut his hair again, even though he longed for it, and wanted again the feeling of boyhood trust, and of his father's hands, those particular hands, fussing over the vulnerable surface of his scalp. The force of this memory made him giddy as if from a slap. How could he protect himself from phantom assaults that came from nowhere?

The waitress hovered at the table as if she wanted to ask a question. Martin ignored her. In the end, rather too sharply, she said, 'Finished?', annoyed at his lack of responsiveness. Martin heard the espresso machine behind him issue a cyclonic roar. He felt flustered and guilty, though he had no reason to be. He felt like announcing that his father's funeral was only two days ago, enlisting her pity, shaming her into kindness. Instead, he left a large tip and slipped away. He wished he wore a symbol of some kind—a black armband, say—that would warn the ordinary world to offer respect and allow him his intervals of stupefied grief.

He texted Evie to ask if he could see her at Noah's flat, and she responded that she was waiting for the ferry, heading to the North Shore to visit Angela and Nina. 'Come for dinner, 8,' she replied. Not even her name. His phone shone with her blank unfeeling message.

His last 'episode' had ended in pneumonia, naltrexone and disgrace. Now he craved that subdual of feeling again, and the soft hit of shadows. But there were Nina and Evie, and the promises he had made, not least to his father. *The promise to his father.* He began a swift walk, his thoughts disastrous and racing. Insecure, he imagined himself as a crash-test dummy, the mere shape of a man, hairless and featureless, hurtled forwards, filmed in slo-mo as he was yanked and damaged. As a boy he'd loved that kind of footage: the wallop of a body, the crumpling moment of impact, the almost joyful brutality of a human shape broken.

Now, he needed to be anchored by Evie. Martin had a vision of her on the harbour, sailing away into sunlight, her thin form receding into a silhouette. The leporello opera house, the restless ferries, the dazzle that made any foregrounded figure black. It was a vision of her leaving. It implied her impermanence. The force of her image passed over him like the shadow of a bird. Nothing touched, but he was darkened, momentarily, and visited by shapes unbidden.

Martin set off towards the harbour. It was the long way home, but he wanted to clear his head. Instead, driven by images, he found himself free-associating on his crash-test self. There were those life-sized figures used for CPR training, shop-store mannequins, inflatable sex-dolls. There were the small articulated wooden shapes that artists studied, there were robots in movies, with lit chests and eyes. And there was Marcel Duchamp's *Nude Descending a Staircase*, a dummy of paint-strokes and the impression of movement in time. This itemisation calmed and externalised Martin's feelings. There were any number of brainless man-shapes existing around him, a mock world of art-stuff and anthropomorphic intention. He would paint a sequence on fake humans. He would place his own portrait in there somewhere, specific and identifiable among the anonymous faces.

As Martin walked he realised that Noah's death had renewed his desire to paint. It was a resurrection—though he baulked at this word—of what for almost a year now had gone stale, producing only indecision and preparatory sketches. Martin watched the people walking ahead and towards him, their impulsive coordination, their rhythmical grace, the engine of so many diverse organisms pumping away, driving a mass of flesh forwards with tremendous confidence. Walking, that's all it was. Pushing into time. He thought of Marey, of Muybridge, of the fascist Futurists. No one since them had seen it better. He could feel a strong fresh wind blowing from the east. He ran his hand through the worry of his thinning hair. He would like a gaudy palette, as in fifties movies. And a disciplined style, like the nude descending. As he took a short cut up a set of steps, he thought, *Martin Glass, Ascending a Staircase.*

For almost an hour he'd barely thought of his father, floating face downwards, limbs outstretched, his childhood fear ablaze at his throat. Just yesterday it had seemed that he and Evie were caught up in a story, a *giallo* written as if to disturb their memories. There was dishonour and vulgarity in what the detective had told them. It was a grubby fiction about a blameless man, felled by ill health. His drifting form, suspended, was a challenge to the scheme of things that said one should die in an armchair or a bed, eyes closed in a decorous, private conclusion.

Martin caught the whiff of fresh-roasted coffee once again. As a child he loved to sniff at pencil shavings—there was piquancy there, and an obscure sense of ambition. Now he breathed in the scent that his father had truly given him, and more decisively set off for his home, and the apathetic ease of his studio. Against what Sydney displayed, against the summer city, he was thinking *Piero della Francesca, Prussian-blue Neptunist, crash-test dummies*; he was thinking of the almost erotic moment when paint squeezes out, depositing the sludge of its glossy impasto onto the palette. All he needed was the strength to keep walking, to keep painting, and to stay relatively sane. He would go to Sicily with or without Evie. He would solve his father's mystery there.

7

AS SHE STOOD on the deck of the ferry at Circular Quay, Evie was conscious of storing up things for future recollection. Here was the lustily gleaming harbour, the absurdly golden midday, and the bridge, swinging away like a door on brass hinges as the ferry executed a slow turn. Above was an infinity of blue-becoming-black reaching far into space, almost shocking after the grey security of Melbourne. The scale of things was all wrong, too lavish, too sunny, too geared to applause.

Nevertheless.

There was a solace in being upon water that might be the trace of ancient feelings. The idea of drift, perhaps, of not being entirely solid, as the essential state of any self. She had always thought of the mind as adrift in sensation: phenomena wash over us; we are less intention than ceaseless flow. It was anxiety, perhaps, that caused her to assemble a structure. In alphabetical order Evie compiled a list of oceans and seas of the world: *Adriatic, Aegean, Andaman, Antarctic, Arabian, Arctic, Atlantic, Azov, Baltic, Bering, Bismarck, Black, Caribbean, Caspian, China, Coral, Dead...*

Through the glass panels of the ferry she saw faces animated in chatter, addressing invisibles with mobile phones, holding up a screen to take a photo. A child, staring back at her, poked out his tongue. Evie did likewise and he mimed a peevish frown. Then he dived headlong into his mother's lap, and she saw how very young he was, not far beyond babyhood. Small children love exchanges of petulance, she thought. How open their feelings, with their arbitrary attractions and unfixed capabilities. How unfaithfully volatile. Now the boy had already forgotten her. He was pulling at his mother's jacket, and climbing her body.

As she turned back, Evie saw the opera house, its fins falling into the water, scattering in white reflections, and the cartoon-form of another ferry bobbing alongside, also leaving the quay, but faster. Others stood with her on the deck, their faces in the wind. The opera house exerted a peculiar pressure: it carried hypnotic command; it was a wrench to avert one's eyes. Whatever was embodied in this structure was innate art-sense. Lighthearted, in the present, she withheld an impulse to wave, to no one and everyone. Then she devised a witticism, droll and superior, for her friends in Melbourne. It was irresistible, possibly ethical, to denounce such splendour, to assert the claim of her own, more serious city.

Evie could see Angela and Nina floating towards her, on the small wooden dock of the ferry stop, the sun in their straw hair, mother and daughter alike. Angela still had her near-sighted, unfocused look, and she had dressed up for the occasion of Evie's visit. Always stylish in a boho manner—dangling scarves, silver jewellery, eastern fabrics—she wore an embroidered kurta tunic in saffron over baggy pants. Nina wore a sun-frock covered in a pattern of lemons. Together—had Angela contrived it?—they were a vision in storybook yellow. Others had a knack of suitable elegance she'd never quite accomplished. Evie was aware of how shabby she must appear in her creased shirt and jeans. Nina was holding her mother's hand, and Evie's affections flew in a swift gust to the child's sweet face. How good to be an auntie. How vividly this child was alive to her.

On the dock she bent and swept her niece upwards, laughing. Nina threw her arms around Evie's neck and made a mushy drama of kissing her. It was an intense and easy happiness, carrying a child, loading her weight, having her face so breathy and close. And the manifest pleasure of children was so admirable, Evie thought; it was a comfort to recover this grasp of blithe unconcern, generation to generation, as if the future had been made physical.

In Angela's apartment at Lavender Bay Evie played on the floor with her niece, who had glue and magazine images to paste in assorted combinations. The polished paper crinkled with the glue, so that Nina was constantly smoothing with the heel of her hand pictures that would not behave and lie flat. She was a tidy child, devoted, like her aunt, to system and order. She bent at her task with tight lips and studious concentration. After pasting, they scribbled affably with felt pens for half an hour, while Angela prepared a salad. The silence between them was an enveloping contentment. When it was time for her nap, Nina kissed Evie on the cheek, and with unnatural obedience headed to her room with her favourite soft toy, a ragged penguin. She was five years old. She was self-possessed, and complete.

'You've never seen her cranky,' Angela warned. 'Another child entirely.'

They sipped a dry white wine and fell into their old, easy exchanges.

'Because of the deafness people think that she doesn't cry or scream,' she added. 'Just hang around a while, you'll see.'

It was an invitation. They had been good friends, and confidantes. They had swapped tales and intimacies as sisters did. Implicitly, Angela was asking her to stay in Sydney. Evie's eyes filled with tears. 'I can't bear it, Ange. The thought of him dying alone.'

She was ineloquent in her grief and felt banal in her misery. Angela leaned across the table and took her hand.

'Some old biddy at the flats told me she found him. Fully dressed, face downwards. It creeped me out.'

Angela squeezed her fingers. There was a moment of silence. 'What about Martin?' she asked.

'What about him?'

'How's he taking it?'

'I don't know, really. At the restaurant a couple of nights back he was a terrible mess. Guzzled the booze, swore at me and collapsed in a heap, sobbing. I practically had to drag him home. Then at the funeral—you saw it—he seemed to cope fine. It hasn't sunk in, I guess.'

'Always one, our Martin, for delayed reactions,' Angela said.

Evie noticed the 'our' as though they had equal claim. Ange was the ex but she was his sister, who had known him forever. She felt a possessive sense of competition, but was wisely quiet, and realised she was edgy, now that Nina was not there to calm and distract them. Evie told Angela of the trip to the police station. The Italian connection. The detective. The Palermo accusation.

'It doesn't make sense,' Angela said.

'That's what I said.' Evie paused, took a sip. 'Martin wants us to go to Sicily together.'

Now it was Angela's turn to look taken aback. She might have been recalling a holiday together, a time when they were happy.

'No way,' said Evie, as if to reassure her, and Angela didn't ask why.

When her niece woke, they went for a walk together along the foreshore, Nina riding for a time on Evie's back. It was a good weight to bear. Evie felt the child's fingers clasp at her neck, and the way her skinny legs hooked loosely at her hips, the fitting bracket of another body. She clasped her hands behind her, under Nina's buttocks, and jiggled her lovingly, and just for the fun of it. And they were friends again, the three of them, though it had been months since her last visit, and she'd worried that Nina would not remember the ease of their affection.

A squall lifted from the water, changing the weather in seconds. The sky lowered and darkened. Fine spray whisked about them, and soon the force of the wind pushed them back inside. Nina looked grave, then began to laugh. Excited and flustered, she made soft drumming noises. Angela ushered them in. She paused to correct her hair in the mirror near the front door and to her reflection said crossly, 'Another day ruined.' Her many bangles jingled. Evie recalled she'd said this often when she and Martin were together, always expressed emphatically, as though irrefutable. Ruined and ruinous days; how little one knows of others' relationships. She'd silently taken Martin's side, though she couldn't imagine him blameless.

From their second-floor window they saw trees thrash about and the water surge. Waves had sprung from nowhere to break across the low harbour wall, pushing foamy scum across the grass and discolouring the paths. Evie was kneeling at Nina's height, watching the sky shift, when they saw below them a boy blown sideways from his bicycle. A man ran to him and set the bicycle upright. The boy wheeled it away, and affected a limp. Nina was transfixed by this mini-drama of accident and kindness, and by the windblown boy who should have been, like her, cautiously indoors.

The scene had a shivery, aquatic quality, and might have been, Evie thought, a kind of visitation. She was irrational in her grief, just as Martin's sadness seemed more unbearable than her own. She recalled falling from her bicycle when she was a child, and Martin rushing to aid her, his face blue-tinged and alarmed, his mouth agape with fear. She'd not thought of this incident for many years. Now, through the glass, she could see her brother inspecting her grazed knee, dabbing it with his shirt, pulling her hair back from her eyes. He helped her stand as if she were a soldier, dragging her arm over his shoulder, and she limped dramatically, to show how he'd rescued her. He'd offered a daft, reassuring smile.

'The ferry will be too rough,' Angela advised. 'Wait a little longer.'

By the time Evie returned to Elizabeth Bay, still a little queasy from the bouncing ferry, she regretted inviting Martin for dinner. She needed the time alone. She would have liked to wander by herself around Noah's rooms, to sit in his armchair and peer into his secrets. The annoying woman was in the garden, scooping leaves from the swimming pool and extracting them with finicky care from her broad plastic net. Evie nodded as she passed. When she entered the flat, closing the world behind her, she felt once again the chill of her father's absence. It was not just the death, she told herself; it was the questions, the Italians, the police. It was the wider mystery of things gone missing so that a private matter might be exposed, so that she and Martin could be called upon to attest to their father's worth, when he was still inside them and not yet resting in peace.

Evie found a bottle of gin in a side cabinet and poured herself a shot. She sat in ochre half-light sipping and looking around her, and then she rose and began to inspect more closely, rifling through papers, lifting objects and pulling open drawers. There were the two icons she knew to be semi-precious antiquities—a Madonna and Child, their earnest faces set together in a field of flaky gold leaf, and a dour saint, possibly Jerome, since he was Noah's favourite. Both had crazed lacquered surfaces and a supernatural glow. Each head bore a halo, picked out in starry dots. A map print of early Venice, foxed and water-stained, prestigiously faint, hung above the icons. On the desk stood a faded photograph of her parents in the seventies. It was not one Evie had ever seen before, and it was this artless relic that gave her pause. Noah had lanky hair and a gormless smile; her mother, Katherine, looked attractive in the manner of that time, kohl at her eyes, hippie hair parted in the middle, a tame, placid and faraway expression.

Evie stared into her mother's face, seeking her own. Her memories were only of the astonishment of not finding her there, of searching the rooms of their cold house, of crouching in corners waiting, of listening to her own breathing, the barest rhythm, in case stillness might summon her mother back. She could not recall crying, though certainly Martin did. Only this waiting, this watching, this disbelieving search.

They left the house soon after, moving to London for a few years, then later back to Australia. Her mother drifted into a state of complete erasure. Evie's memories were of shaded domestic spaces and inadequate heating, of the dank gloom of the bedroom she shared with Martin, of the small electric heater they leaned towards, eating toast and flicking the crumbs to sizzle on the element. Once, they scorched the corner of a blanket just for the stink of wool burning, and for the brazen amusement of something soft and accessible destroyed. Noah was upset. They could have burnt down the house, he said; they were naughty, both of them, he was afraid he would return from work and find them burnt to a crisp. He removed the electric heater from their bedroom and their punishment was the cold. *Burnt to a crisp* became a joke between them: Martin used it as a warning, to be cheeky, and to entertain her; she as funny wordplay, riffing on crisps.

She'd always considered her forgetting of her mother a deficiency of her own character, as if she'd not paid attention, or cared, even as she witnessed her brother weep. But she'd been old enough to know something drastic had happened and that there could be no return or restoration. She'd looked at her tear-stained brother, already exhibiting shame at his lack of self-control, and felt a helpless concern. He'd wept so piteously she had no choice but to practise self-containment. She'd touched his cheek and he'd withdrawn. Even then, she felt older.

This was when Evie began forming her lists. She discovered later that Noah had thought her a child savant, but for her it was a simple, reassuring skill: to commit to memory indiscriminate details from life or from books, to order things according to dates, or acrostics, or the first letters of objects. She started with the names of sweets, of streets, of comic-book characters, but, having no sense of boundary, moved quickly to adult topics. Later, at school in Adelaide, she had the novelty value of being an English girl without a mother, but she was also set apart by her mad and vigorous talent. A provincial whiz-kid, arrogant, with glittering eyes. When she was eleven, her teacher told Noah she was a disruption in the class because she liked to talk to herself, sometimes chanting her lists aloud. As other girls played skippy or hopscotch, she would be perfecting twelve unusual flowers starting with S, or looking in the library for kings' names that repeated through history, or types of igneous rock that she could place in alphabetical order. There was no logic to her selections, just a will to know everything, and have it under her control.

Impressed by his little sister's eccentric behaviour, Martin now and then asked her to perform for his friends. She obliged with the names of cars—since boys liked this kind of thing—or a list of nautical knots. They thought her commendably crazy. Yet she understood that the world was full of patterns and connections. The globe itself was wreathed by ornate organisation, just as it was by networks of roads and cities, by flight paths and shipping channels. When she lay, a motherless child, staring at the ceiling above her bed, it was a relief to think of the world with so much movement going on, somewhere and everywhere. Her mind caught at words flowing by that would establish these connections, and though she knew the remoteness of her method she was still reassured. Rational systems—alphabets, webs, logical associations—these offered the simplicity of something solved and evidently indubitable.

Evie stared at her mother's face and felt the old urge for alphabetical order. Everything submitted to alphabetical order. Her compulsion, she reasoned, was harmless enough. The photograph was a lamp in the dusk; it glimmered and flared out at her. How humble this understanding, that she had never mourned her mother. She'd been a self-enclosed and peculiar child, ardently attached to her father and brother, and without a cluster of girlfriends or the rituals they carried with them. She liked boys more than girls, she liked adult books more than schoolbooks. She was expelled from school at sixteen, and went to university late, at twenty-two. No woman's advice had been sought and she'd grown up withdrawn, and inward. This mother, this unfamiliar woman from the past, would have found her a stranger.

So Evie stood before the photograph of her parents and knew a double bereavement. She had entered her father's rooms, and found there an image of her mother. All her ordering and alphabetical confidence fell away. She moved to the window. She could see the edge of the swimming pool, extending its shining trapezium into the leafy courtyard. Ripples, ordered as lists, were swept by a breeze over its surface. Not wishing to envisage her father, she thought of Nina swimming there, diving deep and surfacing, lifting her wet child-limbs, triangular, into the fading silver light. It took an effort to imagine, and not to imagine, but what does one do, she asked herself, faced with his liquid grave, confronted at each leaving and returning with the container of his death?

When Martin arrived, she'd not even begun to think of dinner, nor, she confessed, had she remembered to buy food. He found her hanging around, staring at nothing in particular. She felt she'd travelled a long distance and was in the confused lag of another time. He hugged her and left to buy a Thai takeaway. When he returned, he rattled around in the kitchen, set the table and spoke very little. They ate together from the greasy plastic cartons in silence, companionable in all that remained unsaid.

Evie understood and appreciated his effort of control. Martin didn't ask about Angela and Nina, he didn't ask what she'd found in the flat, he didn't ask her again to come with him on an Italian journey. All that he'd been meaning to say to her over dinner was wisely stored away and he ate, in any case, as if already preoccupied. It was his first return to his father's home since Noah's death. Perhaps he too had been driven to a more solitary remembering; perhaps he too had baulked at the swimming pool and known he must repress his imaginings.

When Martin stepped out into the porchlight, sounding a soft goodbye, Evie was pleased not to have been alone, but also pleased to see him leave. She watched him walk around the edge of the pool, bend to pick up a bloom of frangipani, then stride down the bright driveway, and disappear into the night.

8

NOAH GLASS ARRIVED in London determined to refashion a self. His old one was tainted. He had been at university in Perth, for four long years, and conceived there an ambition to become someone else, to fill his head with old-world imagery and the wisdom of other generations. He was not a scholar, or brilliant, but desperation made him conscientious. He was a snob, and wanted his snobbery endorsed. He found his lonely life intolerable, Australia more or less barbaric, and no amount of fantasies of exile made the situation better. He imagined England the magnificent exemplar of all cultural aspiration, and under this gorgeous miscalculation aimed his life there. He boarded the *Marconi* and waited the entire sea journey, gazing from the porthole, reading in his stuffy cabin, for the coming revelations.

The imprecision of his imagining became a source of distress. When Noah arrived in London in January 1971, hoping to find work before he went up to Cambridge in September, he found the monotone streets oppressive, the chubby blokes in the pubs boorish, the dingy bedsit that he rented a temptation to despair. The cold spiralled inside him like a virus unwinding, and his woollen coat, for which he'd laboriously saved, was both unfashionable and inefficient. Noah walked around the National Gallery, taking meticulous notes, registering line by line his self-improvement, missing almost nothing, but then had to traipse the long, inartistic road back to his room, shivering all the way. There was rubbish in the streets and a low, murky sky. Londoners walked with their heads bent, as if in a city of penitents. And though the newspapers were all about swinging Carnaby Street and the Beatles and scandalous music and fashion, the place seemed to him essentially bleak. How could they live like this, in this ash-coloured city? Sometimes he entertained the idea of heading home to Australia, but it would have been a humiliation and an admission of failure.

Eventually, predictably, he found a job at a pub in Earl's Court, serving tepid beer in sloshing jugs to other expats, all united in their loud disdain of the Poms. In the overheated, slightly nauseating atmosphere of the pub, in which all men's faces looked the same, swollen like toads and glowing with an alcoholic blur, Noah felt he was somehow camouflaged and safe. Spivs in kipper ties and over-the-top accents whacked him on the back with an assumption of team spirit. He practised endurance. He was stubborn, apart. And though Noah hated the work, this was also a hole he might hide in, while he saved up money for the new Noah Glass. He learned that living in cheerless London-in-winter was not his crowning achievement. It was a time linked inextricably to the sound of a shilling falling through the metal guts of the gas meter in Soho. The chink chink epitomised his sadness and his dislocation. In the future certain coin sounds, heard in unconnected circumstances, would recall the terrible pang of those early weeks.

Noah feared he was becoming a kind of buffoon, a man locked outside his own fervent ambitions. But a few months after his arrival, and in the leafy promise of spring, he found his vocation in the National Gallery. He saw at last a painting whose singular majesty moved him, and was reminded why art history was worth pursuing. Piero della Francesca. The *Nativity*. 1470s. He'd had his fill of block-faced holy babies and drowsy Madonnas, of lurid martyrdoms and rapturous ascensions, by the time he paused before it. There was a ruined old wall that stood in for a stable, five ordinary-looking angels singing their praise, and a kneeling Madonna, very lovely, very simple, who had her baby set down before her, lying on her blue robe. Baby Jesus had no crown or sausage limbs, no divine particularity or glorious election, but was reaching just as babies do, human and set apart. There was a magpie sitting high on the roof of the stable, there was Tuscany in the background, there was the artist's home town, Sansepolcro, visible in the distance. For all its cramming of faces and animals, while Joseph sat, apparently bored, with his foot on his knee, like an ordinary bloke looking for a thorn, to Noah this picture seemed to possess a rare distinction. Images local and from afar enigmatically coincided. The mundane and the divine, he told himself, in seamless coalition. Afterwards, saner with his decision, he realised that it was the singing magpie he loved most of all, and the touch of the commonplace, and the thin baby set apart on a field of blue, reaching.

Noah went outside to take a breather. In the chilly drizzle of Trafalgar Square, it occurred to him that he might go to Italy, that if he were to take up his scholarship at Cambridge in September, he might one day travel to Sansepolcro. With this artist, he could find things to say and matters to investigate. He felt pragmatic, reasonable, but also drawn to something from his boyhood that lingered at the fringes of his consciousness. He could not have articulated his sudden choice. It was less scholarly than romantic, less considered than a whim. He smelled wet wool and exhaust fumes and cigarette smoke intermingled, the streets were coated in the sky-shine of recent puddles, he was cold and alone and a foreigner in London, but he also felt an astounding relief. It was almost joy, a joy such as he rarely felt again looking at a painting in a gallery. When he met Katherine a year later, and described this moment to her, he wondered whether it had actually been so, whether he could have been so sure and so open, even for one afternoon.

Katherine White was an Australian from Adelaide studying literature in Cambridge, at Girton. This much he knew. She possessed a composure that made others reticent. She was softly spoken, intelligent and introspective, but she also wore thick eyeliner, miniskirts and knee-high boots. Noah thought her dazzling. He had seen her at parties with her English boyfriend, a lethargic, limpid fellow who wore neck-scarves and smoked with his head tilted backwards, like a man in the movies. He was also studying literature, and had published poetry in small journals with oddly artful names. Noah despised him. He discovered over time that Katherine preferred the Stones to the Beatles, Dickens to Austen, Labour to Tory. She was an Anglican, an only child, and hoped to become a writer. Her postgraduate topic had something to do with the comic novel.

When her boyfriend dumped her, Noah asked her out, and to his surprise she agreed. After enduring a cacophonous concert by a no-name band, she took him to her room, made love to him and then cried in an unseemly gush over her old boyfriend. Noah was besotted. As she wept, he held her in his arms, hardly believing his luck, but already fearing that he would soon lose her. His hand had come to rest on her thigh, warm and damp from their lovemaking. He snuffled at her hair, which was scented with chemical lavender; he felt the shape of her body, slightly pulsing with her tears; he knew her sumptuous perfection, even as she was thinking of someone else.

They married six months later, James turning up to perform the role of best man. Katherine's parents, Norman and Margaret, made the long journey from Adelaide and kindly paid for their honeymoon in Italy. Noah felt happy for the first time in his life, and Katherine, too, seemed wholly content. He was to remember her padding across the carpet in black stockings and no shoes, waving a few pages of a story, newly typed, with the bright hills of Umbria in the window behind her. Her thesis work ceased, but she was focused on her fiction, and busy. When they returned to Cambridge, they rented a detached, leaky cottage with bad plumbing on the outskirts of the town. Katherine read chapters of Noah's thesis and fixed his grammar; he in turn praised her writing and worked part-time in the local pub.

When Martin arrived, early and unplanned, it had at first seemed a calamity. But both parents looked down upon their son, flapping his rosy limbs, staring up at them with such abundant trust, and felt amazed at how feasible their married life now seemed. Noah thought of Piero's *Nativity* and recalled a phrase from somewhere: *the tiny, not the immense, will teach our groping eyes.* In the fuzzy, milky mornings they stayed in bed together, heating each other with their bodies, chatting in soft voices and cooing nonsense to the baby. Noah scratched at the yellow cradle cap that encrusted his son's scalp, leaned over, sniffed at the small dangling head, and felt at last that he had become an adult. Any doubts of their life together faded. Their hasty marriage had been substantiated. Here between them, wriggling, hiccupping, leaking and burping, was the new being to prove it.

Parenthood altered their sense of time. It raced and it stalled; there were wearisome nights and accelerated days. Their capacity to withstand sleep deprivation increased, so that they swung between heightened delight at the baby, a surprising elation, and dire exhaustion. But both kept working, each on their project. Both were smitten with Martin and found in him a lucid focus when neither could see the other clearly.

When Katherine had her first short story published, Noah bought a bottle of Chianti, nesting in its straw basket ('called a *fiasco*', he instructed), and toasted her success.

'To more *fiascos*!' Katherine shouted.

This was another moment that would stand in later for fleeting accord, for the time he felt able to seize her wrist, and pull her towards him, and know that some spirit and desire had been reciprocated. Mouth to mouth, his lips on her neck, the feather-feel of her breath entering his ear. For all her complaints against him, and her essential dissatisfaction, he knew enough to cherish those occasions when she fell into his arms. He was the wrong man, she announced to him more than once, and though told he was wrong, and a substitute, he nevertheless adored her.

Katherine kept writing but with little acknowledgement, and when Evie was born she became depressed. Noah visited her in the clinic, handing over his baby daughter with trepidation, thinking his wife might drop her, or fling her away. But her attention was on picking fluff from her nightgown, while the baby swept its arms around, wailing, finding no mother. When at last Katherine came home, she was little changed, and from time to time went to bed, as his own mother had, leaving the children to fend for themselves.

Once Noah returned from work to find four-year-old Martin attempting to bathe his one-year-old sister. Evie was gasping for breath and deathly cold.

He was frightened, then. Frightened by fatherhood and his apparently unknowable wife. Frightened to lurch forwards for his squirming baby, blue from near drowning, and scare his son, who was already sounding an offended howl. A kind student, Sally, was installed as the home help. She was happy to be dignified by the title 'nanny', and agreed to keep the children alive.

What stage was that, he would wonder, in the summary of his life? His children endangered, then saved, his anxieties almost perpetual. It had marked a shift in him, to see his children on the edge of disaster. Noah had by now secured a junior teaching post at a provincial university. Once a year he went to Italy, taking his family with him, and they all began to yearn for these luminous times away. They ate together in trattorias, they hiked up mountains and swam in lakes, they lingered in ruined and picturesque places, Katherine and the children standing on paths of small stones, or waiting in the shade of umbrella pines while Noah took notes in the sunshine. He dragged them to galleries and churches and lectured them on frescoes and paintings. His world had a bossy authority they could not resist, and his interest in Piero supplied images that became a language they shared, as other families shared television, or tales of cheery outings.

From the outside they looked like a happy family. But when Norman and Margaret visited a year after Evie's birth, they sensed something amiss and whispered of it to Noah. He didn't tell them about the bathing incident, but he hoped Sally's presence would reassure them. Together they holidayed in Florence, the grandparents doting, impressed by Martin's beginner's Italian and his little sister's charm. Katherine tried her best, but with news of James's death in a car accident later that year, she again subsided. Noah's own grief was put aside as he dealt with Katherine's gloom. She slid away once again. She became unreachable. He knew then, instinctively sure, that solace lay with his children. And it pained him to realise that he had not made her happy—indeed, that he had married an irredeemably unhappy woman. Katherine was never restored to his original vision, from a time when she was with someone else, aloof, and scarcely acknowledged his existence.

She died of cervical cancer, three years later. The world closed in on them. The sky collapsed. Noah went quiet and Martin wept without restraint. Evie hid herself away, under the table, or a bed, or in a dark corner somewhere. It was a shattering Noah could never have prepared for. He felt abandoned and worn out, and could hardly bear the cruel spectacle of Martin weeping. If he neglected Evie at that time, it was because Martin, like himself, could barely stand up with the weight of losing her. The sight of her hat on the hallstand was enough to set them off, and the scent of lavender she loved—her hand creams and soaps, the disintegrating sprigs she had left everywhere in cupboards and drawers—became intolerable. Together father and son began eradicating signs of her existence. Evie, too little to understand, watched bewildered as they made bonfires and bagged clothes and packed away photographs. They agreed, for the time being, not to speak of her, and this became a pact between them, a shrewd and practical repression, so that Noah and Martin conspired unwittingly to unmake Evie's memories.

At Christmas they bought their customary Italian panettone. Noah and his son faced each other over the enormous spongy cake, tears in their eyes, without any appetite, trying to maintain just a semblance of family ritual. Evie stuffed herself, oblivious, and then wanted more.

After the loss of their daughter, Norman and Margaret begged Noah to move back to Australia, and a few years later he did, bringing the children to Adelaide. His job in art history at the university was not in his area of scholarship, and it was harder at such distance to contrive their visits to Italy. But this was family, now, the grandparents and the children, and this was his city, now, though he thought it vacant and severe. Its grids of white light disturbed him; nothing in it spoke of connection. It was Katherine's place, not his. Walking up North Terrace, his face in the hot wind, Noah felt stranded on another planet, almost choking in the wrong air.

Colleagues at the university were helpful and kind, and Noah managed to teach, once a year, a course on quattrocento paintings. Cycling to work through the parklands, listening to the call of corellas and wattlebirds, seeing the flash of light through the trees, and his own skin mystically dappled, he felt halfway himself. He looked down at his freckled hands gripping the handlebars and knew he was able and modestly strong. He felt his legs pump him in and out of patches of shadow, pushing him forwards. There was something to be said for humble endurance. Perseverance is all: it could have been his slogan. But he was forty years old and felt his life almost over.

Even then he knew he had inordinately gifted children. Martin, by now fifteen, could draw images with preternatural skill, and Evie had a freakishly retentive memory. Noah persisted for them. Only for them. It was his children's attachment to life, their rigorous vitality, that saved him. Of his own parents he knew little. His father wrote a curt note on the event of his marriage, but they'd not resumed contact. Noah sent his Adelaide address and phone number, but received no response. The gulf between

76

them remained, and neither party was inclined to cross it. How disproportionate, this severance of feeling. For each it may have been both a punishment and a mutilation. Occasionally, Noah dreamed of his father as he dreamed of Maggie, waking in fright like a child, relieved they were only figments, and gone.

One day, walking on King William Street, he met Sister Perpetua. She strode towards him, instantly recognisable—the flap of her white habit, the austere air of stability—and he felt his old life circling around him like a noose. This accidental return filled him with ambivalence. They made small talk, then went to a teahouse for a more serious conversation. To Sister Perpetua, only fifteen years older than himself, he described how the leper colony had deformed him, so that fear made him exaggerate his own importance, and become vainglorious and alienated from his family. He had used Francis, he had neglected his parents. He told her of his life with Katherine, and of her and James's deaths, of the talented children, and of his love for them. He spoke shyly of his despair and more securely of his scholarship. And finally, bravely, Noah confessed his sense of worthlessness.

When he encapsulated it for her, it seemed indeed a paltry life. Holding herself apart, Perpetua offered a predictable response. She reminded him of Christ's love and the force of prayer. She recommended self-denial and submission to fate. One of the mysteries of time, she added, was reparation.

Noah withered under Perpetua's impersonal slogans. For all her concern, she was following a remorseless script. She'd become orthodox, and forgetful of the place and time in which they'd met.

Then she asked, 'Your painter. What's his name again?'

Noah described the *Nativity* in the National Gallery. He'd last spoken of it years ago, trying to seduce Katherine, and then in lectures to students who were too discourteous to disguise their boredom. And now here he was, describing it to a nun. He was revealing that moment when, like a panicked saint, he'd come alive with inception and changed the direction of his life. He was speaking with passion of an image, and the timeless call of images. He might have had flames coming from his body, or a blaze of blood in his eyes. In this moment of disclosure, heart to heart with his past, he understood how art had made his loneliness endurable.

9

AFTER THE THAI meal with Evie, Martin walked back to his home in the suburb of Alexandria, threading through the streets of Kings Cross, up through Surry Hills and across Waterloo. He was sober and alert. The sky was clear. He thought of his sister, there, in his father's rooms, touching his things, looking about, experiencing time alone with Noah as in a private communion. He felt envious and troubled. He wondered if she might take something he cared about and store it away for herself. It was an irrational resentment, born of their silence. She had not wanted to speak and he had felt he was intruding. At home he went to his studio, brewed a coffee on the small portable gas stove he kept there, and sketched late into the shiny, obsidian night. At dawn, noticing as if stunned the change in the light, he went exhausted to bed, brimful with images.

After the Thai meal with Martin, Evie felt a sexual yearning. She considered walking into Kings Cross to pick up a man at a bar, something she'd not done for at least ten years. But instead she took a bath in Noah's rather chaste-looking bathroom. Lying there in clear water, she thought of Martin's question about de Saussure, and recalled the sky chart and its neat gradations of blue. Looking down at her own body, she remembered Condy's crystals. When she was a child, her father sprinkled them in her bath to relieve rashes. The crystals leeched in runnels and swirls so the water became violet, then fuchsia. Noah had swished the bathwater with his hand, evenly dispersing the colour. She'd thought it beautiful. Her own limbs, a trembling purple. The specificity of this memory still surprised her.

Evie dried herself and pulled her nightie over her head. She lay in her father's bed, not feeling at all transgressive. Almost immediately, made tranquil by memory and bathing, she fell deeply asleep.

PART TWO

10

HOW HIS HEART leaped up. The descent into Palermo airport was terrifying, sliding past a jagged mountain and pitching down near the sea. There was turbulence and the plane seesawed like a toy, the mountain and the sea tipping and rising. When Martin stumbled onto the tarmac, he almost fell. He found his way to the airport bus, parked in the centre of a building site surrounded by barbed wire and palm trees with no palms, and hoisted his luggage into its belly as the driver stood apart, smoking with a sneer and pretending to ignore him. On the long ride into town he watched the coast flash by, then the new high-rise apartments on the edge of town. In the old centre, at the train station, he gathered his bag and set off with a barely legible map, printed from the internet.

Crossing near Piazza Giulio Cesare, he was almost killed by aggressive traffic. It was not a good start. A car mirror bashed his elbow, which began to throb as if fractured. An angry face shouted out a Sicilian obscenity. In pain, Martin dragged himself up noisy Via Maqueda to discover that the small hotel he'd booked online claimed never to have heard of him. The large man behind the counter waved him away. After twenty-four hours of travel from Sydney, Martin felt deranged. In the lobby a man approached him, offering alternative accommodation, a spare room in the place he shared with his mother, in a little backstreet not far from the Ballarò market.

'Tommaso Salvo,' he announced. He did not extend his hand.

It was a cold greeting. Martin noticed his discreet nod to the man at the counter. *Where was he from? How long would he stay? What was he doing here?* To the last Martin answered, 'Tourism,' and Salvo seemed satisfied, while also making clear that he didn't believe him.

In Palermo, almost at once, Martin sank into stopped time, as if held under glass and fixed for inspection. He told himself he was following his father's footsteps, but his motions were already those of a man lost in the world. His elbow flared to a purple plum, then deflated to a black and yellow bruise. Twisting his head, he examined his injury in the speckled mirror on the wardrobe in his room; the discolouration, *pied*, was an omen of bad luck. Each day it rained, heavy and cold. He'd come from rainy summer in Sydney to rainy winter in Palermo, and walked with soaked boots and a hunched body to explore the city.

It seemed reasonable to begin his inquiries at the art history department of the university. He told the female voice on the telephone that he was a bereaved son, in search of his father. He wanted sympathy and his mission recognised, but she was curt and practical. Yes, the Australian man, *Noah Glass*. Yes, he had been here. Martin was given the name of another art historian, Antonio Dotti, who she said had been a friend of his father. For a short time, apparently, Noah had stayed with Dotti in Palermo and once co-authored a paper with him. This man, of whom Martin knew nothing else, would perhaps explain why his father had visited Sicily and what he had discovered here. Dotti would return to work in a week, maybe two. The voice said not to call again, that Signor Dotti would be in touch with him when he returned.

In the meantime, having no company, Martin made an effort to befriend Tommaso Salvo. A blunt man with a look of perpetual suspicion, he nonetheless enjoyed having an ignorant Australian to educate. He was about the same age as Martin, and lived with his mother, Maria, a thickset triangle in black, who rarely left the kitchen. She nodded to Martin once, impressed when he formulated an elegant compliment to her cooking in his competent Italian, but never spoke in return. He'd heard her argue with her son, but she was silent when he was present, as if speaking might release something that could harm or diminish her.

Martin's room, though on the first floor, was dark and cramped and held a view into a brothel across the street. From his room, uncomfortably close, Martin could see women leaning out of the windows for a smoke or hanging their underwear on a looped line. He heard Sicilian, Italian and what could have been Albanian. Once a woman called out to him, but he ducked behind the curtain, and then heard a wave of derisive laughter. After that he kept the thin curtain drawn, not wanting to seem too curious, and wishing to indicate respect.

Martin discovered that Tommaso liked to be asked questions.

'The palm trees,' he said, puffing out his chest like a politician, 'have been eaten by a red weevil. All Sicily is destroyed.'

Tommaso took a sip of grappa, pausing so that Martin understood the gravity of the situation. 'All Sicily. It was the *turchi* that did it,' he added. 'The *turchi* from the docks brought with them the red weevil.' He mimed an energetic spit onto the kitchen floor.

It took a while for Martin to discover that *turchi* referred to any black men, usually North African. The palmless palm trees had troubled him since he arrived, and it was good to have an explanation, even if the human culprits were non-specific and possibly fictitious. Everywhere the palms stood, fat poles with no fronds, dark presences, ostensibly dead and left behind.

The old centre of Palermo had a ravaged look; buildings were crumbling, or boarded up, or in a state of disrepair. The shells of houses bombed during the war still remained amid piles of rubble, often with sprawling plants growing among the bricks. There were garbage and graffiti everywhere; a bloated dead cat, its eyes extruded as if its head had been stamped on, lay in the lane behind Martin's room. He had to avert his gaze each time he made a short cut on that route, and was relieved when suddenly the grisly mess disappeared. At the end of his street stood a church—'*Sconsacrata*,' said Tommaso—its door blocked up with concrete and its windows plain slabs.

There were many such deconsecrated churches. Martin was moved by the ancient 'Church of the Three Kings of the Orient', its massive wooden doors tagged and defaced. His father must have found this saddening, and wondered what frescoes might be inside, or what flaky baroque images clung in darkness to the ceiling, what blessed saints still hung there, lonely and unregarded. It gave the city an air of secrecy, Martin thought, to have so many buildings with concreted windows and padlocked doors.

For something to do, for a kind of purpose, he walked the

streets looking for *le chiese sconsacrate*. In a dismal catalogue, he began to photograph the churches and write down their names. When the weather improved, he decided, he would return and sketch them. He might make an artwork, he thought vaguely, on the topic of deconsecration.

One day he walked in the direction of the port, heading down Via Alloro and across to Via Cala, and on his return was pelted in a freezing hailstorm. Thunder boomed loud as Etna, the sky opened with weapons, and he rushed along the slippery footpaths, skidding sideways on the ice, afraid he would fall. He stopped to watch a curl of cloud from the bay and admire the viciousness of the hail. He pulled the hood of his coat close under the stippled sky.

A sucker for pied beauty; was that what Noah had said? He remembered a hailstorm in Kent, when he was a boy, how he'd run outside in a thrill to feel its roil and shock. He gathered the hailstones and piled them into latticework lines on the lawn. Noah ran to claim him, but he'd resisted his father's grasp. They battled together, Noah pulling at his elbow, until the pattern was accidentally kicked, and destroyed. Did he cry? He was such a crybaby as a child. Noah dragged him inside and scolded, but there was a quiet time in the evening when, reconciled, he told his son about pictures made entirely by dots and flecks. His father made a lesson of their conflict, and found an art-historical example. Because they had fought, each spoke and acted with especial care. Long after the hailstones were liquid, he remembered the word *pied*.

By the time he arrived back at Salvo's, he was blue with cold. Maria, taking pity, heated red wine and lifted his sodden coat from his shaking shoulders. She passed the mug with a maternal nod, shook his coat, spraying drops, and hung it by the fire. She kept her back to him, as if abashed by her own fond actions, and

87

he wondered then, at that moment, touched by her kindness, what he was doing there, and why he had come. Why he had been wandering the melancholy lanes of old Palermo with no idea of what he wanted to know about his father. It was some folly that had driven him, or he was proving a point to Evie, who suggested in a casually mean moment that he was running away from his grief. Martin sipped the hot wine and felt an impulse to write to her. They had parted in argument: he called her unfeeling, she claimed he was self-centred and trying to find a way to possess his father. Why, she'd demanded, could he not let him rest in peace? He thought her remarkably superstitious for one who claimed to be an atheist, and told her so. Divided in their mourning, they'd insulted and hurt each other.

By the time the call came, Martin had almost given up. It was exactly a fortnight, but felt much longer when Maria handed him the telephone and he heard for the first time the voice of Antonio Dotti. A meeting place was agreed—a café in a street Martin had never heard of. He felt nervous that night, and could not sleep. He was aware of the business going on across the lane, and sexual loneliness added to his disquiet. He felt, though it was foolish, like a man newly widowed, a man who might never again sleep with a woman. One of the women, half-undressed, had called out a word to Martin that he didn't know. Tommaso told him it was Sicilian slang for 'handsome', a term they probably gave to any potential customer. He had practised the word in his head, too embarrassed to say it aloud.

In the rainy morning Martin set out for what he already thought of as the 'other' city, the wealthy city. He left the dereliction of the old town and walked up the broad boulevard towards the Via della Libertà, past the opera house, past the colonnaded Politeama concert hall, topped by rearing bronze horses. Tourists descended from cruise ships and walked or rode in decorated pony carts to the shops in this area: Gucci, Prada, Rolex, the disciplined clean spaces of international affluence, the polished enclosures that merited spending and souvenirs.

On the wet street, barely sheltering, an old man with an accordion was playing the *Godfather* theme. Screen faces returned from teenage years: Marlon Brando, Al Pacino, Robert Duvall, all fatigued and backlit, shadowy as fossils. Remembered images from old movies were oddly consoling. They were the confirmation, it seemed to Martin, of his own stringent inwardness.

Women wore furs and stepped high-heeled from expensive cars. Restaurant touts held up plastic menus on falsely ancient scrolls. The buildings were new and air-conditioned. Martin had become accustomed to the old city and the poverty of the market area; this district was rich and seemed a contradiction. He hurried to the address in his map feeling ill at ease and out of place.

When Martin collapsed his umbrella and pushed the door open, he knew that the man alone, curved with a book in the traditional bad posture of a scholar, was Antonio Dotti. He was in his early fifties, thin, bald and with the profile of a predatory bird. Martin immediately thought he would like to draw him. They greeted awkwardly and ordered espressos. They chatted about the bad weather, the palm trees and the length of Martin's visit. At some point the tone changed, as if both had decided it was time to discuss Noah.

'They mentioned at the university that your father had died. I am sorry for your loss,' Antonio said formally. 'He was a good man, your father.'

Martin mumbled something, accepting the new manners that now attended his father's name. He told Antonio of the death in the swimming pool and the accusation of theft.

Antonio straightened up. 'Vincenzo Ragusa? I heard something of this matter.' His tone was remote, impossible to read.

'Do you know of this artist?'

'Of course, a famous Sicilian, but outside my area. A sculptor.'

Martin waited.

'Not the kind of artist your father was interested in. You should speak to my colleague, Dora Caselli. She also knew your father. She knows about Ragusa.'

He seemed reluctant to say anything else. It may have been professional etiquette, or rivalry. They had their areas, these scholars. Their professional withholdings. Something in Antonio's reticence implied that he might, in other circumstances, have more to disclose. He changed the topic.

'When the rain stops, you should go to Mondello, to the beach,' he said. 'You should go to see the cathedral of Monreale.' It was what one said to tourists. He sounded bored by his own suggestions.

Martin listened to these names thinking only of his father, whose pallid face, like those of the movie stars, had vividly returned. He may have sat in this very seat, sipping coffee and talking art history to this bird-profiled man. Martin wanted to say: *I am not a tourist, I am not here for sights, I am here to follow my father and understand what he was doing in Palermo.* Yet he was struggling to define his own purpose, even to himself. Less true investigation than the grip of a selfish confusion. Less proportionate mourning than defect of character.

Martin realised he had waited two weeks for this meeting and learned nothing at all.

'We will have dinner,' Antonio said, as if conciliating. 'On Friday. This Friday. We will talk some more.'

He scribbled the name of a restaurant on a paper napkin, rose, grasping his book and umbrella, and left.

Martin looked around at the smart café and felt immensely weary. The glittering surfaces, the glass tabletops, the Sicilian cakes revolving, tier on tier, in a cold plexiglass cylinder: they all oppressed him.

He walked out into the relentless rain and headed back towards his room, back to what seemed to him the authentic city. The *Godfather* accordionist was having a cigarette break, huddled in his coat beneath a dripping awning. Martin nodded in his direction, as if he knew him. Then from somewhere behind he heard a man loudly whistling. Whistling. What property of optimism, what crazed lightheartedness, might one need to whistle loudly in cold and rain? Whistling was spiritual indemnity against hostile weather, or unreasonable sadness, or outrageous fortune. Or a reassertion of the child. He should learn to whistle. Afraid the man would stop, he didn't turn to look. The whistle drifted and thinned.

Martin was feeling wintry again, longing for sunshine, and disconsolate at the prospect of yet more waiting.

11

WITHIN A WEEK of arriving in Sicily, Noah Glass met Dora
Caselli at the University of Palermo. Escaping the heat, seeking
Antonio, he had walked through an old portico and into the dusty
hall that served as an antechamber for the art history scholars.
There she was. It was his birthday and hers; they were exactly the
same age. Somehow Antonio had discovered this coincidence and
insisted they meet. Both were congratulated; both encouraged by
the festive levity of others who had joined the surprise luncheon
arranged in their honour. They ate caponata and seafood and
drank Moscato di Noto. Toasts were made comparing the brevity
of life and the longevity of art. Voices upraised in a jesting release.
It was a memorable celebration. Towards the end of the meal,
watching her laughing, her manner open and heedless, Noah

caught Antonio's eye and blushed for what he was thinking. They all walked together back to the department, but did no work that afternoon, too inebriated and cheerful, too reminded of physical life.

Later, after Dora invited him to her apartment, she made a joke about their advanced age and the unseemliness of their celebration. He looked at her dozing on the bed in the late afternoon light, her brown skin aglow, her face flushed with lovemaking, and could not recall a better birthday.

The swift intimacy of this beginning established the intensity of their connection. As if a filament ran between them, there was a quality of light that flashed in her, or seemed to spark in shared voltage when he exchanged glances or approached. He felt her detachment, but also her wish to attach. It confused and excited him. There were her bare feet, touching the cold tiled floor, her hands, reaching for her discarded underwear, her sturdy stride into her skirt and her arms reaching backwards for the zip. She dressed with what seemed to him astonishing speed. Slim, elegant, she tugged on her blouse and buttoned it, looking away, recovering a solitude that might have been judged severe.

It was Dora who told Noah about Vincenzo and Eleonora Ragusa. In her sitting room was a fine charcoal sketch of a young Japanese woman. The hair was drawn up, and her shoulder and breast were exposed by a casual gape in her loose-flowing garment. Her face had a calm expression and her features were smooth and youthful; clearly, Noah thought, this was the work of an artist in love with his subject. For his own part he was feeling as he hadn't for years, that intensification of hope that comes with the body's pleasure, the belief that the woman he was with would enliven and save him.

This was a preliminary sketch, Dora told him, for a famous sculpture, Vincenzo Ragusa's portrait of his wife, Kiyohara

Tama. She told him the history.

In the 1870s the Japanese government decided it needed foreign expertise in areas of arts and technology, so it enlisted teachers from around the globe to give instruction and advice in Tokyo. Vincenzo Ragusa, from Palermo, then in his mid thirties, was chosen to teach sculpture to the Japanese. He arrived in Meiji Japan in 1876 and stayed in Tokyo for almost six years, introducing Italian artistic traditions: casting in bronze, forms of ceramic construction, different approaches to carving in wood. He had his own studio and produced a series of remarkable sculptural portraits, including a commission from the emperor for a statue of Napoleon I.

In Tokyo he met the family of his future wife—the father was an expert in lacquer ware, the mother an embroiderer—and in 1882, when the Japanese school was closed, he brought them with him to Sicily. Their daughter, Tama, was a painter in oils, Dora added, a distinguished artist in her own right. When she married Vincenzo Ragusa, she changed her name to Eleonora. They set up an art school in Palermo, the Scuola Superiore d'Arte Applicata. The parents returned to Japan, but their daughter stayed on, only going home and reverting to her old name in 1933, six years after the death of her husband.

'Very romantic,' said Dora. 'A love story. An art story. Two nations connecting.'

Her field was Caravaggio but she had begun researching Vincenzo as a kind of hobby, and then became fascinated by Eleonora, split between countries, living in Palermo, forgetting her Japanese, because there was no one who understood her. When Eleonora died, half her ashes were kept in Tokyo, said Dora, and half returned to lie with her beloved Vincenzo in Palermo.

Noah was charmed by this story, but he did not expect the

names to ring through the remainder of his life, or to see how Dora might be compromised by them. In the first days, still naive, Noah learned that Ragusa had trained in ivory sculpting—those small, devotional objects he had often inspected with a magnifying glass in art museums. Then he'd become a soldier, joining Garibaldi's forces in the fight for unification. Ragusa was also a discerning collector, and Noah agreed to visit his collection of Japanese art, housed at the Museo Preistorico in Rome. He and Dora would go together. They would stand before works neither had seen before, and be filled together with passionate stories.

There was so much light, that summer. So much sensual bounty. And, with Noah in the condition of falling in love, everything connected to Dora Caselli became enchantingly irradiated: he thought of the uranium glass his mother had briefly collected when he was a small child. In those days it was still called 'depression glass', coloured mostly yellow-green and glow-in-the-dark. She owned a swan of depression glass, which, being so unnatural, he particularly treasured. This came to him later, this colour, this haphazard connection. He wondered what became of the yellow-green swan, a kitsch object whose only distinction was that it sat on his mother's dressing table, swimming in the white lace pond of a doily, the unlikely focus of her son's attention. It disappeared when they moved to the leprosarium, leaving so much behind, sold or in storage, to inhabit so different a world.

Now, in Dora's city, he understood its appeal. Palermo was fantastically complicated, a puzzle of styles and peoples. Africa was here, and the Arabs, and the energy of ages intermingling. Noah loved especially the port area of the old town, its stern buildings, the branch-shapes of moored fishing boats, spiking a curved bay, and the tangy, fierce winds that blew in from the ocean, and infiltrated the irregular streets of Kalsa. Somewhere in there Dora had shown him a cathedral with no roof: 1509. Not bombed, but splendidly, audaciously, unfinished. Gazing up at the blue sky, arched outlines blazing, Noah felt shyly grateful.

In the ten weeks he was in Sicily, they spent most days together. For part of that time it was the summer break at university and Dora was free to show him her city. They made small excursions as if on a honeymoon. At Monreale cathedral, whispering, they looked through binoculars at Old Testament mosaics and located the seven panels on the life of Noah. High in the shadows of the south nave, an old man composed of tiny squares shone out, as if manifest just to them. Noah leaned from his ark, arm extended, greeting the returning dove with a sprig of olive leaves in its beak. Peeping out of ark windows were his three sons and their wives. Two drowned men, their faces upturned, sank in stylised waters below. Upon the exposed chest of one of the drowned stood a raven, pecking.

Noah saw above him the formal beauty of the disastrous blessing: some few might be saved while so many others drowned. Some might be unharmed, upheld in the grace of flotation, while others flailed in floodwater, elegantly submerging. He had always hated his name, bestowed as if he would fulfil a religious vocation. Beside him Dora, in a pale blue cotton sundress, stepped backwards and bumped into him. Gazing intently, she had forgotten his proximity.

'*Scusami*,' he exclaimed spontaneously, feeling always at fault. The drowned and the saved; this was all that he knew.

'There, Noah's drunkenness,' she directed to the right.

He moved his focus. The last panel depicted Noah naked and prostrate in a drunken slumber. Poor Noah, he thought. Who could blame him, bearing the heavy load of his fate?

He lowered the binoculars and turned towards her. Byzantine

gold seemed to shine on her skin. There would be no moment more complex than this, doubled by namesake, made meek by her presence, caught in artful admiration. The fabric and illusion of noble sentiments was less than her skin, and his knowledge of it, her shape, and its claim on him.

Sensing his attention, Dora also lowered her binoculars. 'Poor Noah,' she said to him, and ruefully smiled.

In the fiery *mezzogiorno* beams of that last summer, Noah told Dora the story of his life. Her small balcony overlooked a private courtyard, and they stretched in canvas chairs talking and reading, the sweltering light an almost primitive assault. Below them a single lemon tree shimmered in the sunlight, hung with white bridal stars and new green fruit. Just as Sister Perpetua had listened to him speak in sorrow, now Dora listened to the kind of truth-speaking that came with joy. He told of his detachment from his parents, and how much he regretted it. He told of Francis and *Ben-Hur* and his own deplorable arrogance. He spoke tenderly of his children, boasting, praising, but also relating their particular sufferings and grief. It had taken sixty-seven years to understand proportion, he said. Against the shameful recollection that had been ever-present in his life, he had gradually understood emblems, signs and wonders. Initially, a sense of marvel only fuelled disbelief. But there were people, paintings, the humility of limits. Gradually, he'd gathered an intelligence founded on art.

'And now I am lecturing you,' he said. He knew how pompous he must sound.

She leaned over and kissed him quickly. 'Yes, you are lecturing me.'

But he was forgiven. He had never said it before, never spoken before in this wanton manner of affirmation. This was what Dora

Caselli had made possible, this announcement of a personal faith.

Dora was more ironic, more guarded, claiming she was a *tenebrosa*, that she didn't believe in lights coming on, or occasions of sunstruck revelation. Sicilians understood this, she told him, the mesmeric pull of the darkness. The Caravaggio that she saw every Sunday as a child, the nativity that used to hang in the Oratory at San Lorenzo, had taught her, she said, how shadows might beautify a face. Not his best work, she insisted, not at all. But *ours*. It was *our* Caravaggio.

It was one of those moments in which all one has learnt of a new love coalesces. He knew then that Dora, like Katherine, would remain inaccessible to him. That she would retreat, and that he would probably lose her. He was in love, but she less so, or perhaps not at all. Perhaps she simply tolerated him, or saw him as a novelty encounter, the coincidence of birthdays an aspect of amusement. As the day darkened and the twilight fell as in a dream, they moved inside, back to the shade of their bed. Noah wanted to tell Dora about the yellow-green swan. He was not sure why recall of this object seemed to connect them. It was possibly an attempt to find something in his past to stand in for emotional magnification, or imply a wished-for continuum of self. He'd loved the depression glass, and even the name, his name. But in some instinct of privacy, perhaps, Noah changed his mind. He did not mention the swan on the doily, nor did he describe himself as a boy, in short pants, bashfully avoiding his reflection, standing at attention before the swan on his mother's dressing table.

12

PALERMO SEEMED TO Martin to be full of South Asians. They stood shivering on street corners, trying to sell cheap Chinese umbrellas. They had modest stalls at the markets, displaying trinkets and scarves. They hung around the cathedral and the central piazzas, with handfuls of plastic cigarette lighters, or small selections of postcards. They had poky little stores and ran internet cafés. Some had more substantial businesses, a restaurant on Via Dante Alighieri, a small goods store in the Vucciria. Martin felt, if presumptuously, a sincere kinship with them; they must also be missing the sunshine, missing the south.

When he entered the internet café, four Indian men sitting in a row at computers stared up at him. Martin felt self-consciously foreign and tall. '*Scusatemi*,' he said.

It was a facility, he realised, for their own community, one of those places where there are phone booths for international calls to families in tropical countries, and lines of out-of-date computers, boxy as panettones, with gummy keyboards and antiquated systems. He spoke Italian, but a tall man answered him in English. Yes, he could Skype. It was nine-thirty a.m. in Palermo and seven-thirty p.m. in Sydney; Nina would be waiting in her pyjamas for his call.

When he summoned Angela with the cheery ringtone, Nina appeared almost instantly, her pearly face illuminated and too close to the screen. He signed hello and she signed back, and they performed a miming ritual in which Martin acted out rain and hail and sucking up a bowlful of pasta. He made her laugh. His daughter, glistening in weird light thousands of miles away and tucked into her silence, was in a humorous mood. She held up a drawing she had done for him, a self-portrait surrounded by flowers and asterisks that might have been stars, with an ebullient NINA printed at the bottom. She pressed it against the computer screen so that she disappeared behind it and he saw her smiley child-world billow and enlarge. When she dropped the drawing, she tilted her head and crossed her eyes, and Martin crossed his. He made himself fish-eye, touching his nose to the screen, and watched her recoil, palms upraised, in mock-horrified amusement. Eventually Angela leaned over and said that was enough. She asked how he was doing, but didn't want a reply. She had clicked off the signal before he could blow a second kiss to his daughter.

Surfacing, glassy, from this far-fetched meeting, Martin saw the tall man smiling down at him.

'I too have a daughter,' he said. 'I too use the Skyping.' He jogged his head in a double verification. 'Next time you must remember to turn on the sound.'

Martin pushed back his chair and was pleased to see that the others in the room were ignoring him. But this stranger, this father, wanted a connection.

'Veeramani,' he said.

'Martin. Pleased to meet you.'

The man shook hands as if meeting an old friend. Martin was moved by his assumption of paternal pride and the implicit solidarity of his handshake. He said he was a visitor, from Sydney, Australia.

'So next time, Mr Martin, we shall speak of the cricket, yes?' Veeramani laughed.

On the overcast street he felt glum and solitary. It was the image of his daughter's face sucked away into darkness. Martin resisted the intimation of mortality. Another thing disappearing, her presence come alight, otherworldly, then shut down with an electronic chime. He had written simple emails to his daughter and sent her photographs. Still, she seemed almost tragically distant. Veeramani's impulsive friendliness was tingling on his hand, but it was not quite enough.

Around the corner from the internet café Martin spotted a cinema, the Orfeo. It was nocturnally dim and uninviting, and he wondered if it was closed down. He crossed the road to peer in the glass doorway and saw that it screened only pornography. There was a dingy foyer, wholly vacant, with one or two salacious posters. Full ashtrays were dotted around the room. There was no one to be seen. A movie, he thought, might have been distracting, but not at the Orfeo. Later, he would ask Tommaso for cinema advice. Turning away, obscurely disappointed, he hastened his stride in order not to yield to his feelings.

Within a block he came upon a poster for a circus. He stopped in his tracks. A huge lion's head, a copy of the MGM logo—and

Orfei in curly script across the lion's open mouth. Orfeo, Orfei: the world of signs was confusing him. Martin stood before the poster, took a photograph with his phone, and emailed it to Nina. They both loved the fatheaded MGM lion—Angela loved it too—and here it was, a bold replica, yawning on the streets of Palermo, seeming to manifest his own sense of images misplaced.

His listlessness hung upon him. He thought again of the European sky chart and idly wondered what colour-number today might be. There was Prussian blue in the heavy clouds, and a streaky undertone that was almost turquoise. There was a tint of verdigris, such as he had seen in Sydney skies. A certain automatism commanded his movements; he headed off in the direction of his rented room. Passing the empty shell of a building, strewn with rusticated stones, Martin had the sensation of his face being lightly touched. The rubble reminded him of something he could not recall or identify.

Cutting back through Ballarò market, he met Tommaso and Maria, shopping together. It touched him to see Tommaso guiding his mother's elbow, and carrying her bags. Martin told them he had been talking on a computer to his little girl, and he heard his Italian shift to Sicilian in Tommaso's mouth. Maria repeated *picciridda*, little girl. She did not look him in the eye, but it was the first time she'd spoken in his presence. He felt given a new esteem, as he had briefly in the internet café. They walked together, the three of them. Tommaso introduced his friend from Australia to some of the hefty men standing at the stalls. There were few women stallholders. Maria hung back, and at some point disappeared, so that the two men were left wandering the narrow aisles, each carrying some shopping.

Everywhere trestle tables under red canvas were heaped with food, and Martin was reminded that he would like to paint the market. Goats' heads hung suspended above huge trays of offal.

Swordfish were displayed in an arc, balanced among gigantic pink octopuses and rows of lustrous fish. Blood oranges, cut open, forests of emerald broccoli. The loaves of Monreale bread, which he now recognised, being sold from bakeries or from the boots of cars. The damp underfoot made the market both lush and slightly foetid; everything left over becoming slime and organic life, the blood and guts from the fishmonger squirted into a general slush. Martin's shoes stank. He bought a plump mound of ricotta for Maria, since he had seen how she loved it; Tommaso told him it was an excellent choice.

Martin enjoyed the subdued murmur of the market. Perhaps it was the rain. But, unlike Naples, where everyone shouted, where, as a child, he remembered being afraid, the vendors in Ballarò did not harass customers. Patient boredom seemed almost a point of honour. Some played cards, scopa or briscola, when custom was quiet. And, being with a local, he felt less an outsider; Martin had the impression Tommaso was well liked and respected. He decided to ask for a cinema recommendation.

'Orfeo,' Tommaso said. He gave a conspiratorial smile. 'There you will find what you need.'

Martin explained it was another kind of movie he was seeking.

Tommaso looked sceptical and disappointed, but also persisted. He confided that he did not use the women across the lane—they were too expensive. He liked best the Nigerian women in the Parco della Favorita, or the whores who stood after midnight in front of Giulio Cesare, near the station. Then there were the transsexuals at San Domenico, very late at night. Double or triple fee for 'unprotected'.

Martin had no idea how to respond to this information. Nigerian women, possibly refugees, coerced and unfree. He felt a moral shudder and thought Tommaso both boastful and irresponsible. But what to say? He hesitated, caught in the conundrum of mixed feelings and a wish to have Tommaso remain a friend.

'And my mother would know,' Tommaso added, 'if I went across the lane.' His rumpled face smiled again. 'That is our way,' he said. 'Perhaps you have your way.'

The next day, returning from his walk, Martin discovered that a television set had been placed in his room. Tommaso had decided his guest needed some entertainment. Flicking through the networks was a dispiriting affair—dubbed American crime and sitcoms, repetitious advertisements for push-up bras, or bling, or impossibly beneficial mattresses. There were mawkish soap operas from Argentina, and blowsy women and bulky men in star-spangled gear singing sentimental songs to elderly audiences. There were live broadcasts of some sort of religious festival in Catania, and a woman telling fortunes to hapless viewers who called in. Martin had almost given up searching when he caught a station that was entirely pop classics from the sixties to the nineties. He watched Prince performing 'Little Red Corvette', then Thelma Houston, riveting, in a white costume and turban, singing with a jaunty spirit 'Don't Leave Me This Way'. He realised that if he did not begin to paint or draw he would go crazy. He could hear that the rain had started again; there was an echoing drip-drip at the casement window and the sad patter of drizzle.

For dinner that night Maria served an unidentifiable meat, possibly horse, in a dark, gluey stew.

'For your sexual problems,' Tommaso whispered. He tapped the side of his nose with his forefinger.

Maria looked steadfastly at her plate.

'Don't Leave Me This Way' tumbled in Martin's head. He finished his meal, grateful that nothing more was said, and that he was excused, like an errant child, as soon as his plate was removed.

Alone in his drab room, Martin remembered. The shattered building. The rusticated stone. The fragment swelling into recall with its own song-like momentum. Somewhere on the Appian Way his father was lecturing him about the meaning of the word 'dilapidation'. It came, Noah said, from the Latin for stone, *lapis*. It meant a scattering of stones. Not just any run-down wreck, his father insisted, but stones, only stones. Martin had made the mistake of describing a wooden hut as dilapidated, hoping to impress Noah with a big word. His father felt obliged to admonish and correct him, aloof in his own knowledge and insensitive to the boy's hurt. Martin played in the gravel to show his grievance and contempt. He'd been dirty, hateful; he'd been a slave rebelling against an emperor.

Martin would email Evie, and she would corroborate. She would remember the disgrace and Noah's tyranny. He recalled more: she wore a red dress that day. There it was—a sundress with pinprick sprigs of yellow that tied in petal-like bows at the shoulders.

13

DORA WAS BORN, like Noah, in 1946, a year before her father was killed in a May Day massacre of leftists by mafia bandits. Eleven died, and many more were injured, when machine-gun fire pierced the crowd that was celebrating a minor communist victory in the local polls. Four children were among the dead. Her mother was not at the rally, so did not see her husband fall. His brother Vito, Dora's beloved Uncle Vito, appeared in her doorway, stiff with shock and covered in blood, his palms open in the universal question: *why?*

'This is how I see it,' she said. 'Vito with his palms open. My mother at first expressionless, uncomprehending. Then *svenuta*, like the Madonna—a fainting collapse. I've spent my whole life picturing it, the moment she heard the news.'

Here Noah waited, not sure she would go on.

'I cannot imagine my father. So it's Vito and my mother, telling and hearing the bad news, assuming artistic postures. I've condensed my father to this moment. I've made him a story.'

Noah remained honourably silent.

'I am telling you, so you will know what side I am on. Many Sicilians of my age have violence somewhere in their history. And anyone who tells you there are no sides now is a liar.'

Noah could not fit what she was saying with the elegance of her apartment, her paintings, her interest in art history. The bowl of pomegranates, rosy, on the table before him. The embroidered cloth beneath them. The fine Sicilian linen. He knew she was more political than he; she spoke of refugees, the EU, the various Middle Eastern conflagrations. No doubt she considered him naive: Australianness, she'd implied, was a condition of ignorance and innocence, corrupted by good luck. He suffered from her condescension, even as he was blessed by love.

'Do you have siblings?' he asked.

'I had three brothers. Two were trade unionists who were killed in the *mattanza* of the early eighties. Their bodies turned up, mutilated, near Bagheria. The third, my favourite brother, Guido, was an anarchist and a writer who disappeared about the same time. We never saw his body. We still don't know what happened. Uncle Vito is the only one now still alive from that time.' She paused. 'And me, of course.'

'The *mattanza*?'

'It's the word we use for the annual tuna killing. Migrating tuna are trapped in nets and harpooned from boats. The sea turns red. In eighty-one and eighty-three it was like that, we say. It was like the *mattanza*. The mafia decided to round up their enemies, including the politicals, and exterminate them all in one big operation. We do not like to speak of it. It embarrasses and shames us.'

Noah remembered something vaguely, in a film somewhere. He cast about for an English title, a relevant scene. He did not know what to say.

'I know what you are thinking,' Dora said. 'That we are a brutal lot. You are thinking *The Godfather*. Don Corleone. You are thinking clichés.'

Noah was surprised by her anger, which he felt he'd done nothing to provoke. 'No,' he said, half-lying. 'I'm wondering how, from all this, you grew up to be an art historian.'

'It is what we have. It is our compensation. Everywhere in Italy you will find the marvellous preserved in old images. I chose Caravaggio because he knew how these elements went together, because he was a man of violence.'

This was a conclusive statement; the subject was closed. Noah was learning that Dora liked to have the last word.

She walked out onto the balcony and lit a cigarette. Noah did not follow her; her mood forbade him. He did not want to bungle this moment, to utter false reassurance, or to pretend that he knew how she felt. He sat with the wine she had given him and thought how he ought to have discovered her history before he told her of his own. Nothing at all connected them, but the coincidence of age and art. The birthday thing was no more than an illusion of accord. He'd confabulated a connection; he'd needed complicity.

Her silhouette was beautiful: *woman smoking*. She leaned forward, her arms on the rail, her cigarette at an angle. She peered down into the courtyard. He did not know what she was thinking. She did not know what he was thinking. Yet he considered her silence hostile and felt ignored, stranded.

He cleared his throat. 'I'm sorry.'

It was meant to express sympathy, but his voice was forlorn. Noah thought at once that he sounded like a little boy.

~

108

Against these episodes of distance, they practised kindness together. It was Dora's idea to accompany him to Syracuse. She would teach him, she said. He might know the island better with her informative company. She smiled. She was already in the habit of creating his expectations. Noah saw again the promise of her attention, wanted her smart conversation, needed her hand upon his forearm and the graze of her skin, her body open beneath him. He imagined unbuttoning her blouse. He almost felt the rocking sensation that absurdly reminded him of lifeboats. If she had asked then and there, he would have been ready.

Noah became interested in Caravaggio after his retirement, the year he saw *The Crucifixion of St Peter* in Rome. It was three years since he'd stood in dwindling light in the Santa Maria del Popolo—at a bad time for viewing, everyone said, too late and too shadowy—and with his euro coin lit the dim chapel to pull the image from obscurity. Here was the vision of the old man, crucified upside down, and three burly men trying to heave him into place. St Peter was bald, with a white beard, and furious at his crucifixion. Though he'd seen it years ago, Noah now understood, for the first time, the tribute of Caravaggio's heresy: to make the man so physical, to up-end authority in this way, to invent an agony of reversal.

'Pissed-off St Peter' was how Martin had described it, when Noah showed him the postcard.

They'd laughed about it then, but his son seemed to understand what he had glimpsed in the brown light of that Roman church, with the dust filtering down, the clotted groups of tourists departing, and a sense of how thin, how unmuscular, his own ageing body had become. When the bells rang and the church closed, he had hurried back to his conference, just in time to hear the final paper of the day. It was a talk on the chemical

109

composition of Baroque pigments, and it sent him to sleep.

In Syracuse Noah and Dora stayed in a cheap hotel in a hard-to-find street in Ortygia. Their room had white linen curtains, open-worked in a pattern of daisies, and the hotel offered a breakfast of bread rolls, lemon cake and bitter coffee. Both were happy, knowing this afterwards, realising only in retrospect how very easy it had been, still exultant during the first weeks of their affair. Dora was always instructing him, and refining his Italian; he in turn found her presence exciting and her manner charming. All the components of his life, he reflected, had conspired to lead him to her, to this Syracusan room. The lonely anxiety of the last few years was as nothing in her presence.

He liked to watch her dress in the morning, the way she looked like a Degas dancer, elbows out, closing her bra; and the vigour with which she brushed her mid-length hair, then pinned it back, not looking, with plastic combs. He felt like a younger man. He felt something had returned to him. When they made love, they took their time. When he could not, when he urged his body but nothing happened, she embraced and reassured him. His own naked thighs seemed no longer contemptible. The immodest look of an unmade bed was now a sensual motivation. The sunlight streaming through the daisies, falling in a slanted row of petals, failed to incite their derision or irony.

He had come to see Caravaggio's depiction of the burial of St Lucy. She was the patron saint of Syracuse, and her church, Santa Lucia alla Badia, stood exactly where she was martyred, or so the story went. Noah knew the various accounts, how her eyes had been gouged out, then miraculously restored, how she was undefiled though condemned to a brothel. Eventually her throat was cut, and she entered eternity. The relics of her body were scattered all over Europe, her saintly head coming to rest in Rome. Martin and Evie liked to ridicule their father's addiction to saints' tales, but Noah knew they also loved their holy-roller excess.

The church was simple, fifteenth-century, and the painting was from 1608, when Caravaggio was briefly in Sicily, on the run from the law. It was a dark, soiled image, inept in some ways, and distinctive in the prominence it gave to the gravediggers. They were labouring giants, not unlike the massive blokes lifting St Peter's cross, and took up the entire foreground. They had bulky legs and buttocks and formed a kind of barrier one had to look past in order to see Lucy, horizontal and attractively dead, awaiting her burial. Dora reminded him this was an example of *pentimento*—that Caravaggio had originally painted the head severed from the body, but then reattached it when his image was considered too grotesque. A thin red line showed the cut to her throat.

They stood in the church longer than Noah expected. Dora could see something in the painting that he could not. She did not disclose her thoughts. She was alone in her own world of contemplation. Noah sat in a pew and flicked through his guidebook, quietly unable to interrupt or to hurry her.

At last Dora turned and led the way into the uninterrupted sunlight of the piazza. 'Campari, now, don't you think?'

In the geometrical shade of a café umbrella, they drank to St Lucy, looking back into the light. The façade of the church stood before them, the larger duomo to their left. The sky was cloudless, indigo. A handcart festooned with multicoloured balloons in the shapes of cartoon characters was steered into the piazza and parked in front of the duomo. Mickey Mouse and SpongeBob SquarePants flashed their wide smiles. The balloon seller, an old man, extracted a cigarette and lit up, his hand cupped against the wind, his head inclined as if he were a priest, straining to listen to a whispered confession. He stood patiently smoking, the balloons

111

with their simplified faces shivering and squeaking above him in the breeze from the ocean. Later, this memory would have the quality of a dream. Later, Noah would wonder how they could have been so effortlessly happy.

And afterwards, lying beside her, he casually remembered. He said, 'It was *Stromboli*, the movie. In *Stromboli*, Ingrid Bergman witnesses the *mattanza*. It's a terrible scene—she is splashed with water and blood from the killing of the fish.'

Dora did not respond.

Noah felt miserable. A movie. He had ruined the luxurious repose of their afternoon with one untimely sentence. He imagined then, in the severity of her silence, in her refusal to engage, that he had now fulfilled her lowest expectation. He had no real cultural knowledge and must reach in his naivety for cinematic models.

She was turned away from him, impatient perhaps, and in another time. She may have been thinking of Uncle Vito, long ago, Uncle Vito with his bloody hands open, standing in shadows at a doorway.

14

ANTONIO STOOD AS Martin entered the restaurant. Again, he was the early one. Martin half-expected the Italian double kiss, but instead they shook hands and sat down. The restaurant this time was a trattoria in the old town not far from Tommaso's; it specialised, said the sign, in *true* Sicilian cuisine. There were bright overhead lights, a sideboard piled with antipasti, and a mountain of bread, already cut, stacked in straw baskets, daintily balanced for distribution. The tables were covered in thick plastic cloths. Relaxing with the expectation of a good meal, Martin ordered the wine, a Nero d'Avola, and prepared himself for what Antonio would tell him.

After the inevitable small talk about the rain, for which Antonio apologised with an obsequious smile, he guided Martin to the antipasti and recommended the *neonata*—newborn whitefish cooked whole and conglomerated in a fritter. The tiny black eyes of the whitefish stared up at him.

'You must try them, the season is very short,' said Antonio. 'This is a delicacy.'

He heaped Martin's plate with the whitefish, then with artichokes, mozzarella, olives, tomatoes, salami. Martin tried to be a good tourist and accept his recommendations. The pile of eyes was disconcerting. When the *secondi* came—they both had *pasta con le sarde*, pasta with sardines, breadcrumbs, fennel and pine nuts—Martin was wondering if Antonio would ever speak of his father.

Antonio waved his fork. '*Mangia! Mangia!*'

He commented that the cook had forgotten the sultanas, but nevertheless ate with undaunted enthusiasm. Martin watched the spaghetti twirled and sucked and flicked into his companion's mouth. He could not match the alarming rate of consumption. He'd never seen a plate of pasta disappear so quickly. Only when the main meal came did Antonio relax. By then both had drunk several glasses of wine, and Martin had ordered more.

Over braised goat Antonio leaned forward, his lips shiny with olive oil. 'It is Dora, you know. Her family was wiped out by the mafia and she has always wanted revenge.'

Martin had no idea what he was talking about. 'Dora?'

'The mafia trade in stolen art. It's not as lucrative as drugs or arms, but a handy little side business. And good for collateral. You know they stole Caravaggio's *Nativity* from San Lorenzo, just down the road from here? In 1969. Never recovered!' Antonio stabbed at his meat in emphasis. 'Never recovered,' he repeated.

'What has all this to do with my father?'

'Art theft is the biggest illegal trade after drugs, arms and people-trafficking. Less than ten per cent is recovered. About

twenty thousand art thefts are reported in Italy every year.'
Antonio took another mouthful, chewing hard, and then
extracted a tendon string from between his teeth. 'So why do
you think the Carabinieri would have followed up something as
minor as a Vincenzo Ragusa?'

Martin began to think that this man, who had seemed a
mild-mannered academic, might be slightly unhinged. 'So tell
me,' he said.

'Because it is personal. Because of the connections. One of
the capos here is well known for his interest in Ragusa, and has
some connection to the Tokyo yakuza.'

Martin sat back in his chair. He watched Antonio wolf down
the last of his meat, then mop at the plate with a torn piece of
bread. His own fish meal was barely touched.

'You don't believe me?'

'I don't understand,' said Martin. He was thinking: yes,
unbelievable, this man is a nutcase. What did any of this have to
do with his father?

'A mafia boss loves his Ragusas. He has a private collection.
The Jap sees them and wants one. All those Japanese faces, here
in Palermo: *miracolo!* The boss finds out that Dora is the expert,
and gets her to steal one from the museum. Noah is a convenient
distraction. Easy to blame. That simple.'

'You're telling me that crime bosses collect art, and that this
woman named Dora was responsible for a theft.'

'Art is a trophy, like everything else. They like to think they're
cultured. Here, look at my Monet. Here, look at my Ragusa.
What? You haven't heard of him? The great Italian genius of
sculpture after Michelangelo? The great Sicilian? What a peasant
you are. What an ignoramus. *Idiota! Cretino!*' Antonio was
warming to his topic. 'So this capo, see, he wants to impress this
Jap. Offers to have a nice piece stolen for him. But then, presto! It

never arrives in Japan. Who but Dora?'

Martin was nonplussed. How did he know these things? Antonio poured each of them another generous glass of red. 'Dessert!' he commanded. He waved his arm like an emperor. '*Tiramisù!*'

The more Antonio drank, the more he repeated his story. Dora had stolen a Ragusa sculpture from a museum and Noah had been blamed. There were still mafiosi in Palermo, still Cosa Nostra. But not, he insisted, like in *The Godfather.*

'It's easy,' he said drunkenly. 'A few years back a ten-kilo Dali sculpture was taken from a museum in Bruges. Just lifted up and walked out the door. No alarm. No nothing.' He smiled. 'I've thought of it myself,' he said. 'But steal from a capo? Never! It was meant to be delivered in Japan, see? But Dora didn't deliver.'

Antonio's beaked nose looked enormous, leaning so close. His neck was all columns and his eyes had narrowed into stones. Martin had now begun drinking more rapidly. He must meet this woman, Dora. But he thought that Antonio was a bullshit artist. He was tempted to say so.

'There's no way,' Martin began, 'that Noah would be mixed up in anything criminal.'

'Ah, but he might be mixed up with a woman, yes? They went on a holiday together.'

Antonio looked pleased with himself. He ordered coffee. They drank in silence. Then he ordered Strega, and Martin endured another version of his speculations on underworld connections and missing art. Antonio had his own theory about the missing Caravaggio, which also involved a Japanese connection.

By the time Martin asked for the bill both were stupidly drunk, swaying like seaweed as the room washed fluidly around them. Everything Antonio had claimed now sounded entirely credible.

Antonio had done a special course in art theft, he explained, a famous course run annually by Interpol, in Tuscany. He hoped eventually to retire from the university and become a private investigator of stolen paintings. 'Big money,' he said, rubbing his fingers with his thumbs.

Antonio bestowed upon Martin two sloppy farewell kisses, and disappeared unsteadily into the night. Martin stood on the corner in the cold and realised it was not raining. He wished he'd brought his camera. There was an eerie loveliness to the city night, long shadows falling in fractal patterns, pools of street light in quivering reflections. The old church nearby, grimy in daylight and clothed in an air of neglect, now recovered in its looming form a colossal spiritual ambition.

He lurched off through the dark, glossy streets for Tommaso's, took a wrong turn and almost immediately became lost. Somewhere in a laneway in Kalsa he felt afraid; a man in shadows called out to him, something obscene. Sober, Martin would have shouted *Vaffanculo! Fuck off!* But drunk he felt vulnerable, and hurried away, stumbling over broken flagstones, almost colliding with a motorbike that came roaring from nowhere to menace and scare him.

When he found himself at a night market, Martin saw how lively the late city was, how many people were out and about, and what a spirit the place had, of feasting and unity. The noise he noticed first: squeals and shouts, both men and women, and booming loud laughter. His sense of dreadful isolation was acute. He was the only man in the city, it appeared, standing alone. The scene ought to have been cheering, but the hanging lights looked jaundiced and compressed into hard knobs, the faces had a quality of crude exaggeration, the food on display in the stalls made him feel nauseous. He recognised a local specialty, spleen boiled in lard. Men held it caught in bread in their chunky fists and ate it with vigorous greedy thrusts. Its mushy texture revolted him.

And he'd lost not only his way, but also his equilibrium. He began to shiver uncontrollably, and felt sure he would fall. Lurching like a drunken tourist, ready to be robbed, Martin saw how outside community he was, and how worthlessly foreign. He'd begun with an artful gaze, an appreciation of the night, but was now exposed as a mess of a man. All around was the sputter of threatening motorbikes and imminent danger. In this, his own darkness, he had no idea how long he was lost. Eventually, he happened upon a major road, Via Vittorio Emanuele. It was nearby all the time. He almost wept with relief. Using this street as a landmark, he found his way home.

Martin hadn't been so hungover since the morning of his father's funeral. He experienced a wave of self-disgust. He calculated he hadn't drunk much, certainly not as much as he did in his youth, when he went through a stage of getting smashed on straight vodka with his mates. Perhaps he was losing his tolerance for alcohol.

In the kitchen, with Maria waiting, Tommaso presented him with a double espresso loaded with four teaspoons of sugar, and wanted to know exactly what he had eaten and how much it cost, and what kind of family this Antonio Dotti was from, what district he lived in, how much he earned. Martin was surprised by the interrogation and became evasive, which in turn spurred Tommaso to ask more questions. It occurred to him he might confide in Tommaso, tell him of Noah's death, of Antonio's theories. But he felt overwhelmingly tired and ill. His knees ached. He felt weepy. He wanted to sink.

Martin decided he would Skype Evie. He would tell her how isolated he felt here, how he wanted to leave, but could not, about his attraction to the city and his sense of being lost. Evie would understand. Evie would listen. He would describe to her the palmless palm trees, and she would know what it was he found so compelling, the melancholy of the place, the suggestion of plight, and of undercurrent, and of something important gone missing.

15

NOW THAT HER job was starting, Evie hesitated before knocking. She thought, for the first time, how old-fashioned it was, like being a servant, perhaps, or an indigent companion. She stood before the dirty white door of the terrace house and realised she had pictured something wealthier, more formal and more admirable, more suited to a barrister. She had seen the advertisement pinned near the door at the Cinémathèque in Paddington: *Assistant wanted for blind movie viewer. Descriptive audio. Must be movie enthusiast.* ·

The advertisement asked for a three-hundred-word biography. Nothing more. Evie had composed a florid and somewhat metaphysical note, which ended: 'curious about the invisible that lies beyond the visible'.

She liked the corny internal rhyme and the oblique sentiment. She deleted, on reflection, the quote from Spinoza. The composition had been a pleasant enough exercise. A phone call said she had been chosen from five applicants. Her commitment was to watch the movie herself before viewing it with her employer, and her job was to describe the movie during the pauses in dialogue. There would be a trial period of one week, fully remunerated, during which two movies would be described. The client, said the woman's voice on the telephone, was a fifty-year-old man named Benjamin who had become blind almost five years ago from something called retinitis pigmentosa. He was a man of means and a devotee of cinema. He had been a barrister and was particularly fastidious about detail. Evie had wondered whether the voice meant 'neurotically fastidious', whether this was a warning, or advice, or an instruction as to her method of description. Lots of detail, presumably.

She tested this out, speaking aloud to herself over the gaps in movies on television, and realised 'detail' could only mean precise vocabulary, since pauses in dialogue were often brief, and periods of silence in movies mostly occasional and random. She'd imagined retelling a story, or describing characters' appearance with assiduous care, but realised that some things must be said before the movie began and ran to its own persisting rhythm. It would seem like chasing silences, in order to fill them. They would be sitting in the dark, perhaps, with only the silver blaze of the screen before them.

From behind the door Evie heard the deep custodian woof of a large dog, bounding up the hallway. It was a labrador, she was sure, and not a well-behaved guide dog. The door opened and a bulky black labrador swept forwards, bumping her with its head in a friendly greeting, sniffing under her skirt, weaving around her legs. An attractive woman of about sixty roared at the dog,

'Rocky! Down!' but it took no notice. She bent over and seized its collar, dragging it backwards. 'Uncontrollable, hopeless,' she said. 'Sorry about that.'

The dog looked up at Evie, entreating a release. She passed her hand over its hard, bony head.

'Don't encourage him...'

The woman introduced herself as Judith, Benjamin's sister, and led Evie up the dim, cool corridor and into a spacious living room. This was one of those Sydney terraces all renovated on the same model: the back wall knocked down and replaced by sheets of glass, the kitchen incorporated in an open plan, the ceiling cut up with rectangular skylights. It was without shadows, far too bright, and almost crackling in the summer light. Already, she missed the sensations of Melbourne enclosure. She missed the plaintive high screech of a tram rounding a corner, its green and yellow form disappearing into a delicate cool mist. And her own apartment, poky, with mildewed walls and forties beige and an air of bohemian degradation.

Rocky padded over to sit at the feet of his master, and Judith moved to stand beside his armchair. It was as if they had assembled themselves for a portrait in oils. Judith was undeniably the older sister. They had the same long faces, the same full lips and dark brown eyes. Her hair was grey, severely pulled back by a band, his still mostly dark and worn a little long. As Evie played this in her head, she realised how commonplace it might sound, that she would need to convert faces to words with much more authority and precision.

Benjamin stood and walked towards her, unhesitating, his hand extended. They shook, and he invited her to sit.

'Well, I'm off then!' Judith was already gathering up her handbag, kissing her brother on the cheek with a swift scuff, and rushing away. The front door slammed. The dog immediately lowered and settled its head between its paws.

'Now we can relax,' said Benjamin. 'She means well.'

She saw his body unstiffen. He turned towards her. His expression was neutral and his bleary eyes strayed a little, like the slide of distant, miniature planets.

'I hope you don't mind the absence of dark glasses,' Benjamin said. 'I know some people find it a little unnerving.'

They began like this, civil and impersonal. Benjamin was testing her out. He mentioned that he liked all genres of movies, including action and thrillers. In these, he said, there was much more to describe, since car chases, fight sequences, inevitable suspense scenes when heroes moved stealthily through forbidden territory—these never had dialogue. There was an app for blind viewers, but it was mechanical and unimaginative. Now he wanted to try a human, he added wryly.

Evie pondered how she would describe bashings and fisti-cuffs, and police cars hurtling in elastic slow-motion twists as they crashed. Men running through seedy backstreets. Murders. Conflagrations. The way the hero and heroine charge to the foreground as the world explodes behind them in a golden fire of satisfying immensity.

'Art-house movies, too, have long silent periods.'

Evie felt that now he was condescending. She did not respond.

'But you know that, of course.' There was a note of regret at his blunder. 'Forgive me, I should have offered you a drink. Tea? Coffee?'

And so Evie and Benjamin, both reticent and private, both wretched, in some ways, with the experience of loss, began to speak to each other. The candour of their meeting was unex-pected. Benjamin told Evie of his late, but rather sudden, descent into blindness, how he had believed he would be brave and philosophical but was instead fearful and miserable. It was almost two years, he said, before he accepted his condition and re-entered the world. He hated his weakness and lack of autonomy. He could not come to terms with the loss of his career. His wife had left him. His daughter worked abroad. He said he missed above all the distinction between night and day. He had been an early riser, in love with the dawn; now there was only a slight shift in his perceptual darkness, a tiny cinereous gradation when he stared at the sun. Omnipresent night had once seemed a death, he said; only now was he learning how it could be an alternative life.

For her part Evie told him that her father had died five weeks ago. She was encouraged to say more because Benjamin could not see her; he could not see how her eyes began to swim and redden, how she looked down, how she had trouble controlling her unruly expressions. It was a relief to speak from a position of invisibility. She said she felt remote from ordinary life and things. She was staying in her father's apartment, surrounded by his possessions, and had not yet packed them away or disposed of them, as was her duty. It was a difficult situation to find herself in, but she was unable to resolve it. She was not sure how long she would stay in Sydney, but needed work in the meantime. She'd been part-time for three years now in the bookshop and her funds were depleted.

Benjamin asked what work she had done in the past and Evie said she had trained as a philosopher, but found university life unphilosophical.

'It's a peculiar vocation, unsuited to institutions. Elucidation when the system wants obfuscation. Clarification when it prefers darkness.'

She wanted to retract; perhaps he heard it in her silence.

'It's okay. I'm used to it. No one prefers darkness…'

They were careful then, curving around words that seemed to speak too directly of her or his condition. Evie was aware of her attraction to metaphors of sight and light.

'I wrote a paper once,' she said, changing the subject, 'on *acheiropoieta*. It's the idea of miraculous images, things made without hands, just appearing. The Shroud of Turin, Christ's face on Veronica's veil. Or the Virgin turning up as an image on cheese, or toast. When I was a child, I thought of movies like that. I couldn't imagine people making them: they were just there, huge visions mysteriously unfabricated. It was a kind of natural magic.'

Benjamin remained silent. She was encouraged by his evident attention.

'Anyone who looks at a photograph,' she went on, 'intuits this mystery. Then, as an adult, it occurred to me we might read the natural world in this way: patterns in rocks, the clouds, the secular iconic...'

Evie became self-conscious. She blushed. She had not spoken like this for a long time.

'Go on.'

'It still interests me. Our veneration of images. Our wish to see them as impromptu, and separate.'

'This may be difficult to sustain when we're watching *Die Hard*,' Benjamin said. 'Not much veneration there.'

She liked his attempt at humour. She liked his hands, veined purple, and his low, soft voice. And she wondered too how she would deal with this unusual job, whether she would mind being the eyeball, rolling along in movie-time. Whether the act of finding intervals into which she might stuff a few explanatory words would seem rude, even violating. She didn't mention her reservations; she needed the work. And she needed, even in so strange a manner, to begin to talk to people again, to return to the world. Benjamin sent her away with *Marnie*, a Hitchcock movie, for their first session.

~

In the evening, Martin Skyped. Evie had left it open each day, as he had requested, and there he was, ringing in the morning on the other side of the planet. His voice boomed into the apartment, teleporting his vivid quasi-presence along with it. Evie was struck by how efficiently he filled the room, how his voice resonated, conducting him from Palermo to Sydney.

When his face came into view, she thought he looked rather tired, but he dismissed her inquiry about his health by saying he'd been out late at dinner. She was unpersuaded. He had the brainy pallor of fluorescent lights, and the moist, febrile look of one who had just risen from a sickbed. She guessed he was hungover. She felt a surge of love for him.

Martin began speaking in a falsely jovial tone about the life of the city, but soon changed register to a surrealist ramble. He spoke of palm trees without palms, of the ruins of buildings in the old centre, untouched since the war. He had seen two street kids, tough-looking boys, wheeling a family of five puppies down Via Roma in a pram; he had seen churches, deconsecrated, with concreted windows; he had seen a row of goats' heads hanging in the Ballarò market, and, beneath them, a tasty bowl of glaucous eyes. He was trying to entertain, to convey the narcotic oddity of being a stranger in a new city, delighting in the non-PC fun of tourist primitivism. But he was also desolated, she saw, and not coping well.

'Just a late night,' he said again.

'Noah,' Evie insisted. 'What about Noah?'

Martin paused. She could hear him formulating a response. He told her about a man named Antonio, whom he had met and distrusted, but who had known Noah. A colleague. He'd claimed a link between the sculptor Ragusa, who had worked in Tokyo, and international art smuggling. Martin's story was unclear. Evie

126

anticipated clarification. But instead he said, 'Conspiracy theories! Don't you just love them?'

Evie waited in frustrated silence. 'What, Martin? What have you actually discovered?'

'Not much really. There is a woman, called Dora. Antonio said she was the thief.'

Martin was only half-convinced; she could hear it in his voice. But Evie was filled with questions.

'Later, later,' said Martin. He was planning to meet this woman, then he would report back. There was no point chiding.

When it was Evie's turn, she gave Martin a nonsensical version of her new employment. She would be the voiceover, she said, in a new kind of cinema; she would not allow any silence to go unchallenged. Something her employer said reminded her of an early eighteenth-century scientist called Johann Wilhelm Ritter, who was interested in the subjectivity of seeing. He fitted a contraption to his eyelids to hold them open so that he could expose his eyes to direct sunlight for up to twenty minutes at a time. The consequence was that for days afterwards—or so he reported—the fire in the hearth was a wondrous sulphuric blue, and blue paper appeared to be fiery red. So there are men like de Saussure, she said, who wanted to calculate the blue tint of the sky, then others, like Ritter, who revelled in the instability of vision. The childish bloody-mindedness of pressing on the eyelids or staring too long at the sun.

Martin was curious and they talked on this topic for half an hour. He wanted to know more about Ritter. Evie mentioned Purkyně and Goethe; she taught him the word 'phosphene'. She resisted making an alphabetical list of eighteenth-century philosophers preoccupied with vision.

Then suddenly she felt the need to disengage. Evie glanced at the clock and saw that it was not even ten, yet somehow it seemed later. The energy of her talk had infected Martin. He looked revived now and ready for a much longer discussion. He smiled and made jokes. As if it were a machine for invigoration, the Skype screen had opened a current of words, iotas, semes, sparks, pulling her brother back to life as she herself subsided. When she said goodbye, he made her promise they would continue their discussion. He had a plan for a series on deconsecration and needed to think about the colour blue.

'Blue,' he said emphatically. 'I need to think about blue.'

Evie slept badly. In her father's double bed, she tossed and turned. A dream transformed her into a woman composed of particles, streaming like electricity through circuits and systems. She'd been hijacked in sleep by movie special effects, of the type favoured in sci-fi dashing and lit transmigrations. Noah, it seemed, was present in the dream. His voice was there, speaking in bass tones, but his image and body were not; his image and body were gone. Untimely, as dreams of the dead inevitably are, but also partial, mostly missing, just an acoustic ghost. He sounded like the wind, her father, like a straining wind. He had no substance at all, and no holy afterlife.

16

HIS FATHER, JOSHUA Glass, died of heart failure.

Towards the end of Noah's first year in Adelaide, he received the news by phone from his uncle Luke.

'It was his heart, Noah,' his uncle's quavering voice declared. 'They said it was his heart.'

The repetition of 'heart' dismayed him. Still, he could not imagine his father's heart. His first thought was that he had not seen Joshua for many years, and now would never see him again. His second thought was for his mother, Enid. He had not seen her, either, and wondered how she must be coping, why she'd not called him herself, whether she would need help with the funeral arrangements. His mind turned on these wearying practical matters, in which guilt and grief and relief competed. He had become detached from his parents. He had not cared enough to keep in touch. He was a bad son.

Noah flew to Perth for the funeral, leaving his children with Norman and Margaret. They had never met his mother; now was not the right time. He thought he was managing well. But the sight of his mother, shrivelled and demented, being wheeled into the chapel by a uniformed nurse, and the look of Uncle Luke, his eyes brimming, so resembling his father, as he bravely shook hands, these signs of broken family filled him with regret. Noah felt a gagging at his throat and by evening his rash had scalded and spread. It fanned open, scaly, and exhibitionist as a flag. He was aware he displayed his guilt for all to see: the unprodigal son, ever the boy, pleading implicitly to be an orphan.

He sat in the chapel between his mother, who did not recognise him, and his uncle, who was heartbroken, listening to a man he didn't know spin a story of his father's life. Joshua was devout, devoted, selfless and saintly. He had given his life to the poor Aborigines of Western Australia. He had brought them the light, when they were lost in leprous darkness. He had served afterwards on committees and was a leader of the church. A local politician spoke of how Joshua was a 'pillar of the community'. A torrent of banalities swept over and swamped everyone.

Somewhere else was Joshua with a bloody chicken tucked under his arm, fearful and strange. Somewhere else rose the sharp stink of kerosene as his father turned a metal knob to extinguish the light. And somewhere was his voice, not yet dead, still full of commands, and his tenacious refusal to make peace with his son, and his son's equal refusal to repair their estrangement. Death was no end, thought Noah, but the continuation of these remnants, and these failures between them.

Then Luke rose, and gathered his shaky voice. He told of

how his older brother had returned in 1945 from a prison camp in Burma. He was a hero, said Luke, already a doctor, and a survivor, already a good man. He married his childhood sweetheart, and was blessed with their first son, Noah, in 1946.

From the platform, framed by twin vases of wattle blossom, Luke looked down on Noah with no hint of reproach. Joshua had rarely spoken of his war experiences, but Luke knew, he said quietly, how much they had affected him. He had chosen a Higher Cause. He had served his God. He was proud of his two sons—here Luke indicated Noah to the congregation—and devastated by the death of his youngest, James. His wife, Enid, had been his loyal companion of many years—here Luke indicated Enid, who had fallen asleep—and she had staunchly accompanied him on his life's mission.

When it was Noah's turn to speak, his throat was so constricted he felt he was choking. He looked out across the congregation, a small cluster of grey heads, one or two Aboriginal faces, and croaked a few platitudes. It was difficult to speak. He quoted from a Methodist hymn his father sang, even in the shower, and in a scarcely credible tone described him as 'sturdy'. He reached into nowhere, failing, for truthful feeling, and could not bear the sound of his own weak voice.

Afterwards an old black man, whom he could barely remember, came forward to say how much he had loved Joshua Glass. The man had been one of the drivers who brought stores from Derby to the leprosarium; he wondered if Noah remembered the jeep. Often, he had let him and Francis sit in the jeep, the man said. Back in them old days. Back when he was a kid, before the city time. 'Long time, now. Long time.'

Noah stared into the man's face and saw Francis there. Yes, Francis was his nephew, Maggie was his sister. This man had taken the job to keep in touch when they were sent to the colony. They were his family. This man had been the emissary of another world, bringing tea chests of packed goods, tobacco, flour and condensed milk, bringing the rumour of a freer, healthier place. The jeep, of course Noah remembered the jeep. He asked after Francis and was told he was doing well. He was a qualified mechanic up in Derby. Had his own business and a family, four little girls. James had helped him in the early days. Good boys, Francis and James.

'My boy Francis,' the old man said. There was a pride in the announcement—he could not conceal his feelings—and a claim of success.

Noah had missed the man's name when first he spoke and now it was too late to inquire. But this old fellow was the guardian of part of his life. He remembered each of them, Noah, Francis and James; he had preserved, and even cherished his memories of each of them as children. The man held a brown felt hat and stood turning it by the rim. A bushman's hat, Noah saw, with a spray of goldfinch feathers arrayed in the leather band. Large hands, scarred, black, capable. They shook hands, in the end. Noah calmed his own trembling fingers in the old man's firmer grasp.

In a stinking bar in East Perth Noah watched his uncle, whom he remembered dimly as a man of moderation, drink too much beer and tell stories about his brother. They were propped at a table ringed with stains and the burn marks of cigarettes.

The younger by five years, Luke had hero-worshipped Joshua. His own war had been spent in Darwin, and the family believed that Joshua had died in a prisoner-of-war camp in Burma. It was a shock to everyone when he returned, more skeleton than man, dreadfully thin, his civvies ill-fitting, his hat pushed back, to greet their shaken and disbelieving stares. Luke felt ashamed, wanting to be the only son. He'd not wanted his brother to return from the grave.

At some stage in the halting narration Noah understood that his uncle was confiding in order to seek forgiveness. He'd wished Joshua dead. He'd wanted his skeleton brother gone. Luke's liver-spotted hands reached out and clasped his, and Noah played priest for a while, reassuring his uncle, mentioning the scriptures, speaking of the ambivalence between siblings and the need to sense one's own life confirmed. Luke hugged him and manfully held back his tears. Noah called a taxi and saw his uncle fold into it, brotherless and blurry and bending like a doll. An arm shot out, flailing, as the taxi pulled away.

Back in his room, in the Criterion, a hotel in the centre of the town that had seen better days, Noah still could not recall the old man's name. The window in his room looked out onto a solid brick wall. He sat on the orange nylon bedspread, staring at the garish primrose decor, and again felt his throat itch and complain. He had nothing to do. He had no wish to walk around the dehydrated streets of Perth, or to ring anyone, or see friends from the past he was striving to repress. Everyone faces such a moment, he thought, alone, in a hotel room, caught in unmeasured time. This was his. He heard slurry words through the wall; a couple making love, perhaps, or the stifled labour of hotel workers. Others had wholesome, amiable lives, but he felt unclean, like the leper whose wounds were tended by dogs.

He thought: *now I am fatherless.*

Caught in a confusion of remembering and forgetting, Noah tried to recall his father. His images were shallow and dubious, a petty frieze of snapshots. So much had been pushed away, or crushed tight like the holy Lazarus card. He removed his shoes and lifted his feet onto the bed, and gratefully began to slip into a vague light sleep.

At some indeterminate point between waking and sleeping,

he thought of Luke in the taxi, his elderly body flopping, then remembered his father screening a Charlie Chaplin film at the leprosarium. Former missionaries had left behind a small cache of silent movies and Joshua had managed to retrieve and fix the vintage projector. On the whitewashed wall of the shed that served as their church, Joshua sent flying to its surface the stiff little fellow with his jerky mechanical gait, his facial tics, his gimmicky existence. The bowler hat balanced and tipped off the end of his walking stick; he hid his permanently surprised face behind it; his hat rolled like a ball that had its own volition. Everyone laughed.

Rubbery Charlie Chaplin, jelly Charlie Chaplin, Chaplin accident-prone, and sweet, and nervously silly. Noah remembered his father transformed: it was a wonder to observe him undone by laughter. For so serious a man, for someone habitually humourless and temperamentally solemn, the man who had chided his sons for moments of ungodly merriment, something had lightened inside him. He could have floated away with the puff of his own snorting laughter. Francis was there, and James, and Maggie—they all saw it too, a man changed as if by revelation.

Noah opened his eyes. A hideous light fixture of seventies vintage hung above his head. Faceted tangerine plastic in a halo of cubes. His throat was painful. He thought of his children. He thought of his father. He had missed his chance to know his father. They had never reminisced. Neither had explained the choices they made, or practised even a tentative intimacy. The inner man had gone forever, as stereoscopes had gone, and silent movies, and depression glass. And then it occurred to him. His mother, too, had now gone.

17

IT WAS THE second time Martin had seen street people with an old pram. This time, there was a single dog tucked into the pram, its angular black head alert and affable. The owners, or the family—for that's what they were—were a twinned punk couple, rough-looking and filthy, with spiked hair and grimaces. The dog peered out beneficently at the passing world, and the couple walked with purpose, as if late for a business meeting. Martin was thumped on the pavement, a kind of shove with the shoulder, to tell him to move aside. He moved aside. There was a trace of dope smoke and stinky living, and the sour hiss of contained aggression.

He was uplifted in spirit by the long Skype-talk with Evie. It had helped to tell her of what he knew; it had helped to hear her crazily specific knowledge about seeing and colours. And once he got her talking, they converged; they discovered areas of alikeness, even as they chimed and competed with wisecracks.

Dora's apartment block looked massive, grimy and forbidding. On its wall, in a smeared ejaculation, the graffiti read *Carabinieri assassini!* Martin rang the electric bell, and no one answered. Then he rang again, waited a while, and heard a faint serrated crackle from the perforated speaker attached to the wall. He announced himself, and a hidden lock clicked open. It was a heavy door, set in a recessed frame, so that he stepped over a threshold to enter the courtyard. There was lightly crazed paving and a sense of enclosure. Martin looked around and saw a figure gesturing from a balcony. He climbed the outside steps, and then the apartment door opened.

He guessed she must have been about his father's age. She had mid-length grey hair, held by plastic clips, and the slim, nervy elegance of attractive Italian women.

'Good afternoon, signora,' said Martin. 'I believe you were a colleague of my father, Noah Glass.'

It was peculiar to say his father's name aloud in this way, but he sensed the need for formality, and to give this woman a chance to divulge, as slowly as she might wish, her knowledge of Noah. According to Antonio she had stolen a sculpture, and somehow his father had been blamed. What might he discover?

A strong scent of coffee wafted in the room; there was a plate of new-moon-shaped biscotti at the centre of a low table. The woman who greeted him seemed calm and self-possessed.

'Colleagues, yes. I am sorry for your loss.'

There it was again: there was no more capacious cliché.

They were in a large, high room, with white walls of flaking paintwork. Green shutters were open to the courtyard, revealing a grey square of cityscape, blurring into the distance. There was heavy dark furniture, covered in lacy cloths and antimacassars, and a wall of bookcases, untidily stuffed. Papers lay in irregular piles on the floor.

Dora looked out the window, as if searching for something. For a moment or two she seemed to forget he was there.

'Please sit,' she said, businesslike. 'How can I help you?'

They sat opposite each other, he on the scrolled couch before the plate of biscotti, she on a hard chair that required her to pose uncomfortably straight. She poured the coffee into fragile cups and mentioned that Martin resembled his father. Now he felt like a boy, needing to give an account of himself.

And then Dora said, 'So, what has Antonio told you?' She rose and moved to a small sideboard, reaching for a cigarette.

Martin blurted out a garbled version of the story, and Dora frowned. It had begun badly. He could tell that she was suspicious of him. He heard himself say that he knew of course that the mafia story was nonsense, and that he simply wanted a sense of what his father was doing in Palermo.

Dora watched him attentively.

He began again, hoping to elicit clarity or confession. 'Antonio says that you stole a sculpture from the museum.'

Dora held herself firm. 'Antonio is a liar and a fantasist. Your father came to Italy to see the Caravaggios, and passed through Palermo. Not many here, of course, but my field is Caravaggio, so naturally he consulted me as a colleague. That is all. Nothing more. Antonio is right: I have a special interest in Ragusa, but more in his Japanese wife, Eleonora, a painter. This has nothing to do with Noah. Nothing at all.'

Dora inhaled deeply and sent a stream of smoke to her left. There was something seductive about the way she held the cigarette pointed behind her, some cinematic gesture.

It was a wasted visit, thought Martin; Antonio had spun him

a line and he fell for it. Or Antonio knew a truth, or a partial truth, that Dora needed to deny. Or the whole story was irretrievable, since one never knows one's parents.

'So you've not heard of the accusation? Against Noah?'

'Antonio will say anything,' Dora said ambiguously, neither confirming nor denying. 'Your sister, is she here? Noah spoke of you both. I have read two of her articles.'

She had already changed the subject. It seemed to Martin that Dora had hoped above all to meet Evie, and was disappointed. She said almost nothing more about Noah, but suggested Martin should visit Mondello beach when the weather improved. A charming spot. They have a windsurfing festival. A delightful bay. And had he been to Monreale? The mosaics were incomparable.

Martin knew by now this was what people talked of when they did not want to talk. He murmured something about being an inept tourist, and how he hoped, while here, to base some artworks on churches. Some caution prevented him using the word 'deconsecration'.

'We have so many churches,' she said, 'not all of them still in use. Perhaps you should see San Lorenzo, where the Caravaggio *Nativity* once hung. I used to look up at the painting as a child; not his best, by far, but it meant a great deal to me.'

This was the closest Dora came to revealing anything personal. She asked if he had been to the opera house, the Teatro Massimo. It featured, she added gravely, in *The Godfather, Part III*. 'Perhaps you recall the death-by-cannoli scene?'

Martin could not decipher her tone. Was she mocking or attempting a weak joke?

'Have you yet tried our famous cannoli?' Adding insult, as if this had anything to do with his visit. She pulled an ashtray towards her and stubbed out her cigarette.

Martin glanced around the room. A few paintings, a silver

reliquary of a hand. With a small shock of recognition he saw a faint prefatory sketch of the Ragusa bust. Dora possessed an image of the stolen artwork; how could she not be involved? But he saw too her composure—she'd not hidden the sketch, she'd seemed direct, and confident. Unlike Antonio, she had no hint of duplicity about her.

She followed his gaze. 'It would be wise,' she said casually, 'if you were to stop asking questions. Someone might get the wrong idea, inquiring about a robbery.'

Martin heard a vague warning. He was about to ask who the someone might be, when she added, 'Let me know if you need any sightseeing advice.'

So this was it; he was dismissed as a tourist. It wasn't worth disputing, or finding the right question. Dora was incurious about him and his artwork and had thought him boyish and gullible. She had disclosed nothing about his father's stay in Palermo. Martin accepted a paper bag of biscotti as he left. He might have been visiting a doting aunt. He felt foolish, and immature. He wondered whether, had Evie been there, Dora would have spoken differently, or revealed something new, or something more. Whether he would have been taken more seriously.

When Martin returned to Tommaso's, he found Maria had a gift for him. They stood in her kitchen, in which the tiles shone like mirrors and smelled of ammonia and sick flowers, and Tommaso ushered her forward, like a child presenting a school project. Maria had wrapped the gift in white tissue paper and tied it with a white ribbon. She handed him the parcel on her palms held together, outstretched, as in Muslim prayer.

Martin accepted, and unwrapped the offering with slow and finicky tearing. It was a small pair of ears, made from silver-plated tin. In response to the inevitable questions about family,

Martin had mentioned to Tommaso that his daughter, Nina, was deaf. Tommaso had told Maria and she had purchased the ears so that he could present them as a votive offering at the church of Santa Rosalia, on Monte Pellegrino. Maria would take Martin up the mountain, Tommaso said. They would go together on the bus. They would pray together. The saint would cure his terribly afflicted daughter. With due reverence for their curative magic, Maria had already polished the ears with a silver cream she purchased in the Ballarò market.

'She has cleaned the ears,' Tommaso announced, without the hint of a smile.

Martin looked across at Maria, who nodded encouragement, and patted her bulky black bosom, as if to say he had her heart-felt support. After avoiding him for weeks, she seemed to have decided she liked him, and that he needed her help. Perhaps, at some stage, she might even speak to him. But it was impossible to say to Maria that he felt his daughter didn't need a cure, that she was complete, and perfect, and impeccably herself. There was no defect that needed correction. Her appointed loveliness had been there, evident and ratified by adoration, from the very beginning. He'd often argued with Angela on this matter. She too wanted a 'cure' and thought him deplorably callous and selfish when he argued against a cochlear implant. This difference between them had never been resolved. And now Nina was scheduled to have the operation.

Martin thanked Maria and said in his most formal Italian that he would be honoured to accompany her to Monte Pellegrino. Her face bloomed like a pansy, round and darkly tender. She wiped her hands on her apron, accepting his thanks, and turned away. He felt a leaden hypocrisy descend upon him: all his artworks, his ambition, his women, his drunkenness, his selfish and irresponsible living were nothing compared to the extravagant purity of his love for his daughter. But he would go with Maria to the mountain, and he would think of Nina there; he would consider how blessed he was, in this fucked-up world, to know the singular joy of his daughter's existence.

They arranged a date, the next Monday. Maria turned back towards him and beamed. She was a woman, he could tell, of shrines and offerings, one of those believers one sees everywhere in Italy kneeling in churches, ignoring the effusive muttering of heathen and chatterbox tourists. Someone for whom the world of incense and invoked presences mattered. Monstrances with edges frilled like fried eggs, figures floating on curved ceilings in hallowed deportment, side chapels ablaze with electric candles, images of ghoulish tortures and savage crucifixions—all these held for Martin a complicated history. Noah had taken his children to churches, to study artworks. He and Evie, with rebel hearts, needing a piss, feeling a centuries-old pensioner chill in the inky blue light, endured his lectures on quattrocento art, trefoil windows and the use of tempera. He told them which were the miscible and immiscible painting formulas. It was one of his words: *miscible*. He named disciples and saints, placed faces within stories. He unlocked symbols and made a game of revelation. Martin still remembered when Noah first told them that the pelican was a type of Christ. They absorbed more art-historical knowledge than either would admit. He'd seen so many old women, like Maria, on their knees, in the pews. He secretly admired their endurance, and the solidity of their faith.

That evening Tommaso was drunk. Martin was not sure why. At about ten p.m. Tommaso knocked on his door and invited him into the kitchen for a rabarbaro, the bitter rhubarb liqueur Martin found rather sickly. Tommaso was by then already unsteady on his feet, oscillating like a toddler, his face red as a baby's. He grabbed Martin's forearm and suggested they should speak as men do, of manly things. In Maria's gleaming kitchen they sat at her spotless table, the shot glasses filling and filling again. It had been only last night that Martin was hopelessly shickered with Antonio, so he was wary and slow in accepting more drink. He didn't want the brooding misery of another hangover, or the ignobility of his body sickened and out of control.

Tommaso was not entirely sure what masculine meaning he wanted to impart. He boasted a little about a Nigerian woman with whom he had a 'special' relationship, a whore, certainly, but with a heart of gold. (Martin couldn't believe anyone still used that expression.) He would rescue her sometime, and take her to Malta when his mother, God bless her soul, died. Then he entered a monologue in a soft, confiding tone.

'When I was a child,' Tommaso said, 'there were the many killings in Palermo.'

He was hunched over the table, head down, clasping his small glass in a manner that allowed him to hold his own hands.

'The mafia left bodies around the city. Just to show. You know, just to show what they could do. I was ten, it was 1981, and I found a headless body in the lane behind our house. Just out there, just behind us. I can't ever go out there now without remembering it.'

Here, grievously weighed, Tommaso gave a buoyant little laugh. 'I didn't run away—that is what you would expect, isn't it, for a small boy to run away. I just stared and stared. Mamma came, and she screamed, and she pulled me inside.' Tommaso took another sip. 'You heard stories, of course. Everyone at school had a story about a corpse in a lane or a car bomb on the corner and bits and pieces of bodies blown everywhere. Brain matter on a lamppost, that was one of them.'

Martin looked into his glass, not sure what role he was being called upon to play.

'It was a young man, that headless body. A teenager maybe. Not much older than me.'

Tommaso began to giggle. His mouth became lopsided with spilled drink. He had the distorted face of one accepting physical punishment. 'You don't have nothing like that in Australia, now, do you?'

Martin was being asked to contribute a story. 'Every country,' he began lamely, 'has a history of violence. Every big city...'

Tommaso ignored him. 'I was ten years old,' he repeated. 'It was the time of the *mattanza*.'

Martin was unfamiliar with the word. He didn't ask. He drank alongside Tommaso, wondering if he should put an arm around his shoulder, or allow him to weep, or say something more about his life as a child.

Tommaso giggled again. Then he pushed back his chair, unsteadily, almost tipping over. 'Bedtime,' he declared. 'Enough talk of happy memories!'

He lurched upwards, upsetting what was left in the bottle. Dark brown liquid, rather human, spread in a circular stain across Maria's white tablecloth.

'*Porca miseria!*' he whispered. Another, higher laugh, more typically drunken. He put his hand over his mouth, smothering his desperate hilarity.

'It's okay. I'll get it.' Martin was already righting the bottle and gathering the cloth in careful bunches. 'Go to bed, Tommaso. I'll clean it up.'

Tommaso didn't object. He leaned against the doorway, saluted *goodnight*, and left. Martin lifted the cloth towards the kitchen sink. He turned the taps and, using Maria's dishwashing soap, scrubbed at the mess. He was fussy, impatient, his conduct

143

determined by his inability to deal with so gruelling a story. Martin made the stain a little paler, but it wouldn't disappear. For ten minutes he rubbed the linen between his hands without much visible effect. At last he left it there, soaking, like the guilty sign of a botched crime.

18

HAD MARTIN ASKED HER, Evie would have conceded she enjoyed thinking about her new job. Connecting sound and image, the consideration of time in cinema, imagining—did she dare it?—a blind man's world, all linked in unexpected ways to her past philosophical studies. Noah had told her once that Piero della Francesca spent his last months, or even years—so little was known of his life—completely blind.

Her father had been very moved by this detail. He'd mentioned it in the context of a casual remark about age, and she knew at once that he wanted to say more. He began listing dates, this or that scholar. Who believed Piero was blind, who did not. Before or after the publication of his mathematical treatise. Evie made an affectionate joke about how Noah's mode of parenting was the lecture, and he had clammed up. Her own method of communication, he responded crisply, was the lecture. Resorting to abstraction when she might have been more simple and direct. Talking of ideas when she might have expressed emotions.

'We're alike in this,' he conceded. It was a flippant remark, but to the point.

Embarrassed, both had backed off, not wanting further to hurt the other's feelings, or to say something that would remain as a corroding insult.

Still, she remembered it, and knew that he was right. And she should have understood that her father was afraid of ageing and of blindness. She should have offered comfort.

Evie was beginning to feel less like an intruder in his apartment. It was her duty to bundle up Noah's life and to dispose of his possessions, but she had removed very little. Those things she assumed would be easiest, like his hairbrush and his shaving gear, still lingered in the bathroom, pushed to the back of a cupboard. These were intimate objects of daily use and, though easily disposable, retained his fingerprints and bodily traces. Other things, the furniture, even the paintings, she might quickly sell. Martin would inherit the golden icon of the Madonna and Child, she, the dubiously identified saint. They made the decision in one of their shapeless and desolate encounters around the funeral, when each was both more and less themselves. She would keep Noah's two monographs but his books she would give to a university. It was a scholar's library, eccentrically specific and only professionally useful. All this word-and-image paraphernalia of mind. She thought in a slogan and almost dispassionately: the disappeared mind of Noah Glass.

When Evie opened her email, she found a message from Martin, asking her if she remembered their father lecturing them—that was the term he used, *lecturing*—on the meaning of the word 'dilapidation'. It was somewhere outside Rome, on the Appian Way. She remembered the sunlight and the confrontation and smart-alec Martin's humiliation. He'd thrust his fists into the pockets of his shorts and walked off in a sulky huff. She'd been competitive and smug, and grabbed her father's hand as though it was a trophy. She also remembered how excited she'd been to learn that words could work in this way, could have objects inside them, and archaeological histories. That day they ate pistachio gelati, rode on wonky bicycles and visited the catacombs. It was an unusual childhood, made more so by Noah's pedagogy.

Evie emailed back that yes, certainly, she remembered that day. Pistachio, bicycles, *dilapidation*. And did he also remember the little phoenix with a halo in the catacombs that Noah had pointed out to them? Did he remember the tall poplars and the lizard they saw? And the fat woman at the pensione who pinched hard at their cheeks?

She closed her email and set out to walk to Benjamin's. Walking stimulated her mind; it was the balance she loved, the motion of the world before and behind and on either side, the sanity of each deliberate step. She trialled a new route, and listed, trivially and for her own pleasure, the names of seashells of the South Pacific. It was a list made years ago, in thrall to her passion for swimming. She was a woman in a floral dress, straightening her shoulders, breasting the wind, already at cowries and already at E. *Egg cowrie, eglantine cowrie, eroded cowrie, eye cowrie.* There was no point to her skill: it existed only as a token of order. Yet in this it had a beauty, it had marvellous elegance and rightness. Her lists took the rhythm of her walking: she was a mobile poem.

As she approached Benjamin's house, she faltered. *No further,* she thought. Wild now, unalphabetical. She was conscious of her body.

Evie could hear Rocky again, bounding up the hallway towards the front door. When Benjamin opened it, Rocky once again wove around her, his tail thumping against her legs with the throbbing enthusiasm of a dog in want of a walk. He ducked beyond into the small front garden, sniffing, all-alive, his head shovelling at the overlong grass, and Benjamin called him back. Evie could offer, perhaps, to walk the dog; she saw in his muscular ripple the thrill of an old-fashioned romp.

The house seemed quieter, somehow. Benjamin greeted her and indicated that he again expected to shake hands, and Evie did so. This formality surprised her. Benjamin turned and led the way down the corridor into the over-bright sitting room, his dog now reconciled to staying at home and springing ahead. This time she noticed certain details of his life: the sensitive portrait of a boy in oils that was surely him as a child, the little bust on a side table that might be of Garibaldi, or indeed one of any number of bewhiskered nineteenth-century men. There was an expensive sound system, and a collection of glass paperweights on the desk, next to the computer. There were paintings by various Australian artists whose work she recognised. Above the computer—yes, unmistakable—was a picture by Martin Glass, one of his early drawings in a series called *Nature Opened*. She owned a drawing from the same series, of leaves of grass.

'So, what did you think?' he asked, feeling behind him for the armchair.

'It's trash, but I suppose it's interesting trash.' She was hoping to provoke him.

'I've only seen two Hitchcocks, *Vertigo* and *Spellbound*, so I thought this might be an easy place to start. I have a vague idea what to expect, but it will be a good test, I think.'

'Of me or of you?'

Benjamin smiled. 'We will have an intermission,' he said. 'And a glass of wine. We should finish by six.'

Before the movie began, Evie described the main character, Marnie, played by Tippi Hedren. She is pert and meticulous, with hair the colour of champagne, swept back in a neat bun, slightly beehived, exposing an unusually high forehead. She has flawless skin and a doll-like uniformity of features. She wears rose-pink lipstick. Her posture suggests strenuous repression: she holds herself firmly, clutches her handbag as if it were a lifeline, is prissy, classy and exudes a tone of chilly boredom. All her clothing comes to the neck, all her sleeves are long. There is a hint of perpetual sneer, especially towards men.

Sean Connery, Benjamin knew. He must remember Connery, Evie said, as he was in *Goldfinger*, made the same year, in 1964. The same macho mannerisms, tilting his head as he measures up a woman, a determined and pugnacious setting of the lower lip, a square way of standing that suggests barely withheld violence. He plays Mark, a widower and the wealthy owner of a Philadelphia publishing house. An ever so slightly hip element is introduced with Mark's former sister-in-law, who wears tight sweaters and riding pants and is clearly in love with him. The soundtrack, Evie advised, is heavy and intrusive, and these are the main points at which she would describe the special effects and wordless action on screen. Might she pause if she needed and lower the sound a little?

Benjamin handed Evie the remote. Rocky settled his head on his master's feet and dozed.

The opening shot focuses on a canary yellow handbag, being held by a dark-haired woman, who is walking away from the camera. As she recedes into the shot, she is revealed to be walking along a train platform; in her other hand she holds a suitcase. The shot plays again soon after as the same receding woman walks up the corridor of a hotel, preceded by a bellboy, who carries shopping bags and a new suitcase. Alfred Hitchcock himself, his profile blobby, pendulous, steps into the hotel corridor, glances at the camera and disappears. There is a scene of identity changing that involves Marnie washing her black hair and emerging instantly as a blonde, the first time her face is shown.

And so it went on. Evie described the gambits of exposure and concealment, inserting description where there was only music, trying not to reveal her understanding of plot. Every time Marnie sees something scarlet-coloured—blood, ink, the spots on a jockey's uniform—the camera focuses on her face, and the screen turns bloody with a dread, expressionist glow.

'Blood red,' said Evie. 'Marnie is afraid of blood red. Her look is one of anxiety and terror, mouth slightly open, her eyes wide, her head flinching away.' She resisted commenting: *bleeding obvious!* Such a clunky device.

When the movie was over, Benjamin and Evie drank a chilled white wine and ate green olives. They had forgotten their intermission, being both caught up in the action. Benjamin enjoyed her narration and thought the movie better than Evie had suggested. He liked the twist at the end and the voices of the actors. He liked the intrusive soundtrack and was fascinated by the contradictions in the characters: Marnie both brazen and timid, Mark a sexual predator and capable of fond concern.

There was no obligation to stay and talk, but Evie was pleased to do so. A languid comfort descended, the dreamy aftermath of their movie absorption. Benjamin was feeling expansive and relaxed. He talked of his childhood love of James Bond and how he'd made drawings of Bond's gadgets. The word 'revolver' entranced him and he'd imagined owning one. Curious, he said, how lucidly he remembered the opening sequences, the silhouette of Bond half-kneeling to shoot through a camera aperture at the audience, the veil of blood dripping down, the morphing shapes of naked women, all inevitably doomed. This was the high point, he said, of a befuddled adolescence. Not his expensive cello lessons, or his first place in physics, but diligent fandom of James Bond movies.

Benjamin became pensive. Possibly he regretted this admission of boyhood tastes, or was caught up in his own unspooling nostalgia. Possibly he had cultivated habits of self-enclosure. His eyes drifted and, for a second or two, closed, then opened. He heaved himself forward to place his hands on the coffee table.

Evie watched the careful way in which Benjamin poured the wine, testing with his fingertips the rim of the glass, listening for the point at which he should stop pouring. Blindness, she thought, must be a world of cautious precision, all movements, even tiny ones, being so consequential. It must be pure space, pure prudence and pure attention. She saw his unseeing eyes slide away from her. There was a moment in their conversation when Evie felt an inclination to touch his arm, but didn't dare. His blindness made her feel shy, just as his manner inspired social diffidence. Yet Rocky, alert to their connection, seemed to notice her impulse. He cocked an ear, lifted an eyebrow, and gazed at her, his tail lifting a little, then falling with a gentle thump. Evie reached down and patted him, and he in turn licked her hand. It was a furtive complicity.

When she left, it was almost eight and dark. She decided against the bus, preferring to walk through the humid summertime suburbs. The terraces shone like mica, black and silver, their windows casting ideograms of light onto small gardens and courtyards. She heard the faint screeches of fruit bats high in the trees, and domestic sounds—a television, a child calling, the clatter of dinner dishes. There was a soft quality to the air, and an earthy scent. There was a mysterious bottle-glass shine she already associated with Sydney nights. All was peaceful, still. Caught in the spell of her own steady walking, she thought: later, it will rain. But for now Evie relished the heavy night air. For now she walked as if this were her city, not Martin's, and she could take pleasure here, as she knew he did.

She wondered about the memory of 'dilapidation', etched deep inside him. From somewhere she retrieved an image of the stoning of a saint: it was a fresco entitled *The Lapidation of St Stephen*, it was in Prato, years ago; and there was Noah, dear Noah, pointing to direct their vision. Even then she was appalled by how much torture appeared in religious art. St Lucy's eyes on on a golden plate, St Agatha's breasts.

Memory and consistent stride made her inward and serious. Martin's stony wound, persisting from that day on the Appian Way, was in part to his pride, and to the harmony of their little family. She remembered his flushed face, turning away, how he scratched an obscenity in the dirt with a stick, then erased it quickly when Noah stepped near. She didn't tell her father. Though triumphant, she felt protective and knew 'dilapidation' was a gift that Martin had offered. But she also remembered their father's hand, extending upwards, and his merciful teaching.

Something else. Something else returned with 'dilapidation'. It was Martin, with the same expression, in the heroin clinic. He'd succumbed in his early twenties, and again two years ago. She'd seen him dazed and disconnected, propped against a bank of pillows, Noah nearby and unmistakably distraught. The tang of diamorphine and cleaning ammonia and the light bleak and institutional. The tone of surly irritation. Martin's wrecked face.

And their joint history piling on top of them, heavy, like stones.

PART THREE

19

IN THE FIRST years in Adelaide they were a tight unit of three, the grandparents hovering, always available for a school-holiday jaunt to the windy beaches of Victor Harbor, or the comforting ritual of a Sunday roast. Norman stood as he carved a dauntingly huge leg of lamb. Margaret passed the mint sauce in a jug fashioned to resemble lettuce leaves and crossly told the children to take their elbows off the table. They commenced the meal by saying grace. The children were obstinately non-compliant but Noah joined in. They made small talk in lowered voices. They commented on the predictable or unpredictable weather. They ate in unison and complimented Margaret on her cooking. It was a semblance of what others called family life. But it was damaged, they all knew. It was incomplete.

There were the usual childhood complaints: measles, flu. After an outbreak of chickenpox, and ensuing panic at the school, Noah was reminded of his anxieties at the leprosarium, and he began dreaming of Maggie again, seeing at night her lipless smile and her open red mouth. His blatant fear, persevering, seemed ignominious. After his father's funeral in Perth, the dreams included Maggie's brother, whose lost name Noah still some day hoped to recall. In his dreams, this man was always driving a jeep, disappearing into a bulging cloud of grainy red dust. It was a scene possibly lifted from a movie somewhere. A black man appearing in the shape of a black man. A man remote, enigmatic, signifying something forgotten. This figure was a void in himself he could not name or even contemplate.

In Adelaide, Noah developed his ideas on Piero della Francesca and time. Piero was known for his mathematical mania in the development of perspective, his scrupulous lines, his fanatically specific axes and disappearing points, the calculation of which confirmed his faith. Most scholars wrote on Piero and space. So many compass lines and ruled verifications. So much that met golden means and mystical thirds and the artist's own conviction of the theological dimension of numbers and angles. But gazing at the familiar reproductions, Noah thought that the images might be more about the mystery of time. In *The Baptism of Christ*, Jesus is at the centre, radiant, hallowed, consecrated for eternity by a single drop of water, but behind him, looking awkward— indeed, it must be the most awkward figure in quattrocento art—is a man pulling his shirt on or off over his head. It's the amusing moment children instinctively like, when the head is encased, and elbows are jutting out, and the bare back is bent. He could be any man. He could be Christ himself, just after or before the baptism, so that the audacity of the painting would exist in imagining a man exceeding time. The insight realigned Noah's otherwise unconventional thinking; it made him wonder whether little flaws or inconsistencies might offer a second theology.

Likewise, he thought, with the famous *Flagellation of Christ*. Art scholars went on and on about the classicism and the over-defined architecture—but this could mean that the event was happening in present-day Sansepolcro, that a man's suffering for others is always contemporary. In this painting, Christ is in the far background, a manikin of torture, and in the foreground, separated in their own space, are portraits of two local men who were both known to be grieving their adult sons. This too seemed to make sense as a meditation on time. Might the death of a son issue in a temporal fold of some kind, so that the human and divine were radically continuous? Did God grieve? Was that a preposterous question? Did heaven tip upside down, like a body tumbled face-forward into a grave?

When he delivered his first academic paper on the topic, others at the conference listened with polite disdain. *Ahistorical. Decontextualised.* Noah was disappointed. But gradually his ideas began to seem less far-fetched, and scholars here and there wanted to support him. It was easy to argue that the famous panels on *The Legend of the True Cross* declared the loops of time—repetition, surely, must be a kind of temporal mystery— but *every* Piero painting, Noah believed, worked on a variation of this principle.

It was a small idea, not even original. But something in his contemplation of images had led him here, to see his own children in the figure of the man wriggling in or out of the shirt, to see his religious beliefs expressed in the way one body might look next to another body. And to see Christ as the body that was always in and out of time.

When Martin was a teenager, Noah tried to explain this to him. He struggled to insist on the sincerity of his meaning. Yet he'd made up his mind. He was convinced of his own ideas. They would be his own fundamentalism.

'For fuck's sake,' Martin said, in a bored whisper, half-admiring, half-critical, as sons of sixteen often are in the face of a paternal explanation.

Martin was rubbing his head with a towel, sitting on Glenelg beach. They were drying off, each watching Evie swim in the choppy water. She was always the last to leave the ocean when they had their swims. There were her churning arms and her small head, cresting and falling; there was her slight form asserting its shape in the dappled wavelets and foam. Every now and then she dived under, disappearing, flicking her feet upwards, and then returned, as in an ancient enactment. Martin saw it too, Noah thought, how Evie stood in for both of them as the body pitched against obliteration, as a declaration of energy. He understood that Martin only half-listened to his little Piero lecture. His son had entered the age of humorous contempt, and offered merely perfunctory or blasphemous observations. At length, to signal boredom, Martin pulled out his sketchpad, sucked at his pencil and drew Evie, a girl-form in a field of theoretical water, the warped triangles of waves, the deadly flatline of the horizon.

Sitting in silence, they could hear sea birds. Both noticed gulls hanging in a strange suspension above them. A cool southerly breeze swept over their faces. The birds lifted up on streams of air, tilted down, lifted again, their white wings flashing. Gradually, Noah and Martin made their peace. They were united by watching Evie strive against the might of the ocean. They were united by looking not at each other, but in her direction.

At Mondello beach, Noah watched Dora swimming, not too far away. He was sitting with a book, unable to read, under the

September sun. He was daydreaming, recalling his children. Somewhere near the centre of the curve of beach between Monte Pellegrino and Monte Gallo, he had bought a patch for a few euros and spread their towels to mark the boundary of their little claim. The beach was densely populated with noisy families. Noah noticed how loudly Sicilians spoke. Every voice seemed pitched in shouting and exclamation. Adults yelled, children ran, or cried, or ate pastries and gelato. A small boy beside him, whining, was having his naked body rubbed dry with unseemly roughness. A nonna was arguing with a nonno, abusing him in public. A small girl was singing to herself, something in dialect, about butterflies. Noah remembered the Italian command 'zitto!', a word his children had liked because it sounded like a cream for skin ailments, they said, or a fizzy drink.

Noah wanted the silence of the beaches in South Australia, in which the distance between bathers meant that the ocean was audible. He wanted the high singing wind, and the voices of birds crossing above. Here, with the human noise, he could not read or think. Australians take space for granted, Noah reflected; we extend ourselves because we can, and gain a physical confidence. He'd seen how, in the move from England to Australia, Evie had transformed athletically, as if by enchantment.

He watched Dora swim towards the horizon, then back again, buoyed and conveyed by the rhythms of the ocean. She had a still-slender body, encased in jade-coloured lycra. She looked towards the shore, bobbed up and waved. In some momentary confluence of admiration and lust, Noah saw how her body became the symbol of a hope he'd long harboured inside him.

She emerged from the water, glistening. She plodded up the beach and bent over him, blocking the sun, spraying droplets of water, then drew up and shook the sand from her towel. She rubbed first at her head, then her body, moving downwards so that her face was close as she rubbed dry her shapely calves. She had not spoken. When she lowered herself down, her hair ribbed and dripping, her face aglow, she said, '*Allora*, let me tell you my Mondello story.'

She was so vibrant to him then, her head glazed with seawater.

'I was strolling with a boyfriend, once, along this beach.' She smiled, as if teasing him. 'It was early evening, in June, and we were just getting to know each other. Very shy. Not saying much. The weather was clear, when red lightning appeared on the horizon. It was the strangest vision, flares of scarlet, a sense of something mysterious happening. It was Stromboli, of course, away to the north-east. This way.' Dora gestured across the water.

'You could see its lights from this beach. I've always wanted to see it again, the red of sprayed lava, the drama of a volcano over there, just out of sight. But I never have, though I've been here often. So I enjoy this memory, which includes a boy I didn't really like, because it was an accidental vision, because it was random, and lucky.'

It could have been a deficit of his sensual life, but Noah loved her most at this moment, when she told him a personal story. She lay on her chest and turned her face away, closing her eyes. She was sunbaking in her own past, smiling to herself with the memory of the boy she didn't like and the Mondello horizon lit with red flares. Noah restrained himself so that he did not reach over to kiss her. Her small revelation imposed an emotional austerity. He remained quiet. Solitary. He lay down beside her, covering his sunburnt face with the tent of his open book.

He was thinking again of his children. He was unable to say how being a father moved and engaged him, how Martin and Evie, even in times of estrangement, were his centred world. No hypothetical eternities, but their actual now. And the memory of them when little, dressing, undressing, pulling garments on and off their vulnerable bodies, the incandescent light falling like seawater over their small bent backs.

20

WHAT WAS HE seeking, leaning too close to the screen, his face broad as a moonstone and artificially shiny? What was she wanting, leaning back, distrustful of his imploring image?

'I don't understand,' said Evie. 'This woman is taking you to a shrine?'

'To cure Nina. She wants to help me cure Nina.'

'I thought you didn't want her *cured*.'

'Lighten up, Evie. It's folk wisdom, you know. I'm not really wanting a *cure*. Maria bought these cute little tin ears to place before Santa Rosalia.'

'Jesus,' she sighed. 'So, what else are you doing there?'

'Sketching. Walking. Watching Italian pop on the telly. There's a great performer, Jovanotti. Totally cool.'

'You sound like a kid, Martin.'

'*Grazie, mamma. Grazie mille.*'

'So what else?'

'Hanging around. It's a sad city, Evie. It gets to you. Gets into you. I feel things gathering inside me. Memories. Ideas.'

At his new tone she paused before formulating a retort. She heard Martin pause, too, perhaps not sure how to go on after what seemed the spilling of a secret. It was a moment in which both glanced away from the monitor.

'Noah,' she insisted. 'Anything more about Noah? What did Dora say?'

'Not much. She didn't want to talk. Antonio told me they'd been on some sort of holiday together, so I figure they were close, but you'd never guess it. Tight as a clam. A bit edgy. She has a sketch of the sculpture, but no real link.'

There was nothing to tell. No reliable information. Evie was disappointed.

'And what about your blind guy?'

'My employer, not my blind guy. Benjamin. It's going well, I think. I passed my week of probation. A Hitchcock: *Marnie*. And a Bertolucci, *The Conformist*. Good that he knows Italian.'

Martin was too near again, his face looming and inflated. There was a starry glint in his eyes that might have been the reflection of his screen.

'How about we turn off the vision and just talk?' Evie asked.

They did so and, returning each to their own world, their conversation calmed. What a relief the dark screen was—no huge brother-face to incite or command her.

'Tell me more about that Czech guy, the anatomist you mentioned.'

'Purkyně? What about him?'

'Anything, really. You're the smart one.'

'I thought it was Ritter you were interested in.'

'Him too. But I like the name: Purkyně. I wrote it down when we spoke.'

'You could just google him, you know. Jan Evangelista Purkyně, 1787 to 1869.'

'Yeah, right.'

'Okay. Subjective vision. He liked to experiment on himself.' She knew this would entice him.

Martin waited. 'Go on.'

'It's not really my field.'

'Indulge me, Evie.'

'Well, the story goes that as a kid Purkyně was fascinated by what we call entoptic images—like what you see when the eyelid is pressed against the eyeball. Shadows of blood vessels, dots, squiggly lines. You close your eyes and there are images, but they're not images of the outside world.'

'Right.'

'He ran electric currents into his own eyeballs and did little drawings of what he saw, diamond patterns, mostly, and lines that looked like filaments and zapping electricity. And he took various drugs to gauge the effects on his vision.'

'What drugs?'

'The usual. Opium. Camphor. Datura. But he also did experiments with digitalis, which is a poison. Lots of flickering of the eyelids and nausea and distorted sight. Under the influence he wrote about something he called his "shimmer-roses"—isn't that beautiful? Petals, concentric circles. He had the visual impression, like mysticism, of a many-petalled flower.'

Martin was silent. 'How come you know these things?'

'I don't know much at all. I'm a failed academic, remember? But since I met Benjamin, I've been thinking again about these guys, with their romantic faith in our bodies as intelligent organisms. Sightless sight. Images without screens. What it might mean to have visions. It's your turn, now. Who is this Rosalia?'

'Patron saint of Palermo. That's about all I know. I'll tell you more after I visit the shrine with Maria.' Martin paused. 'Shimmer-roses, I like that too. Was he a mystic?'

'Not as far as I know.'

Both became silent. The monitor stood waiting, the patient dark wormhole of their supernatural speaking. In Sydney, Evie could see faintly her own reflection on the dusty black screen. She imagined Martin sketching something indistinct that may have been a shimmer-rose. Perhaps he was thinking sideways, distracted, of the sexual appeal of lipstick. Evie was thinking distractedly of Benjamin.

'Is it still raining?' she asked.

'Yep, still raining.'

After her response to his question about Purkyně and his small flurry of interest, Evie heard Martin slide back into himself. He may have been falling asleep, or returned to the shell of his own imagining. He may have been staring in dozy inattention at an image he had just made.

'Let's talk again later,' she said, waking him up.

'Fine, sis. *Ciao, ciao. Mi fido di te.*'

'*Ciao.*'

Mi fido di te. I trust you. Why did he say this?

Their voices dissolved into the black passage between them.

She discovered later that Martin had quoted Jovanotti; the words moving through him like a passing spirit. Evie didn't mean to feel suspicious, but she didn't entirely trust him.

21

IN HIS SIXTY-SEVENTH year, musing on the surprise of falling in love, Noah Glass found himself walking past the architectural hotchpotch of the cathedral on Via Vittorio Emanuele. There had been no premonition of his Sicilian good luck. He was accustomed to meagre returns; at best an ardent encounter at a conference or a temporary fling in Sydney; at worst a feeling of hollowness and suffocation, as he looked into the placid ironical face of a woman he fancied, or made a gaffe, expecting interest where none was returned. It was tiresome and frustrating. It was a kind of emasculation. Dora Caselli was dignified and self-assured. Though she had never married and had no children, she was smart and sexual in a confident, even luxurious, manner, and wanted nothing of him beyond his intensification in her presence. There was no fuss or hidden agendas or double meanings. She met him as he was, and granted him the benefit of the doubt, that he might be more than he seemed in the simplified economy of appearances. At first it had looked like magical thinking or ordinary wish-fulfilment. But this supposition disappeared in her sun-warmed bedroom, in the slumbering ease that followed their lovemaking, in the jokes she made in husky banter, in the way she rose naked, unhesitating, to take up a floral dressing-gown of Japanese design.

In the courtyard, in front of the cathedral, a statue of Santa Rosalia stood on the stern of a boat. A group of Polish pilgrims had stepped off a rusty bus, and were taking photographs of her. They had their backs turned to the magnificently peculiar cathedral and were fixed instead on the wooden statue of the young noblewoman, pretty in a folksy way, with her flowing robes and garland of flowers in her hair. She was reputed by innocence alone to have saved Palermo from a plague. The pilgrims held cameras and phones to capture the saint's face. One carried a rosary. One or two bought postcards of Santa Rosalia's image from a poor Indian man lingering beside them.

As Noah passed by, the Indian man began following a young woman, the one most likely to be a sympathetic customer, and was thrusting his postcards at her. He was too close, or too insistent, and the woman looked frightened. From the bus stepped the large driver, who was built squarely and stiffly as though cast in bronze, like a Bernini statue, Noah thought. The driver seized the man by his collar, yanked him backwards, twisted him roughly to the ground and began kicking him. He had an appalling energy now that his body was a weapon. Noah saw the Indian man curl tight against the blows, and heard him cry out. No one came to his aid. The young woman began to whimper and pleaded with the driver to stop.

Noah stood only a dozen steps away, but did not move.

He watched in guilty fascination as the man became smaller under the boot, squirming, a figure of pain, his face bloated and contorted, his jaw working with no words. Blood spurted from his nose.

This was what was possible—the reduction of one man's life to bodily distress, time abolished in the crux of a spectacle. This knowledge made Noah hostage to his own paralysis. He had been thinking of Dora, and he had seen a man beaten. This was the truth of things—reversal of fate—and he did nothing to intervene.

Another pilgrim seized the arm of the enraged driver and pulled him away. The crying woman was ushered back into the rusty bus, the dazed remainder disappeared in dribs and drabs into the cathedral. Noah hurried along Vittorio Emanuele, ashamed of his cowardice and afraid to look back. His legs were trembling. He could have acted—he could have been the one to seize the driver's arm and pull him from the man turned creaturely with pain and submission. He could have remonstrated, or gone afterwards to lift the man back into life. But Noah had hurried to remove himself.

The city opened before him like a foldout map. He saw the landmarks and palm trees. He recognised certain storefronts and baroque façades. He squinted at the heat, and the city withered away in the glare. There was a shudder to the visible world that might have been the end of all things, a blackout, or worse. It seemed to Noah he was having a stroke, or a potentially fatal panic attack. He stopped on the pavement, his clogged heart pounding, and leaned against a filthy wall. Beside him a graffito read: *tutti i preti sono pedofili incalliti!* All priests are hardened paedophiles! It was the *incalliti* he noticed, *hardened*. Such a guilty word.

Noah was sweating and terrified. His legs could not support

him, so he slid down the wall, slouched over, his knees pressed close to his face. Passers-by ignored him. He stayed like that, blasted by outer or inner experience. He would die in the street, a dishonourable, foreign man. Stone, sun, the indifference of strangers. A stink, too; someone had pissed against the wall. He would collapse not only with this weakness, but in this reeking surrender.

When with difficulty Noah returned to his senses, his first sensation was of an immense thirst. He pulled himself upwards and staggered across the road into a café, where he bought a bottle of water. And so there he was, not a lover or an art scholar or a learned fellow from Australia, but some negligible figure, obscurely panic-stricken, pouring water down his throat like a man found wandering in the desert.

Two doors further down was a small hotel. Noah entered the lobby and headed for the toilets. There he dashed his face with cold water and, heedless, took off his shirt and splashed at his upper body. He saw his own deplorable reflection, shivery and tripled in the spotted mirrors. His face was yellow and held a doomed expression. He was not sure what fear had clutched him, what physical symptoms he had experienced. But in his muddled thinking he felt grateful to be hidden away. He entered a toilet cubicle and sat in its tangy, calcified confinement, looking into space and waiting for nothing in particular. He fingered his penis, as if checking it was still there. He felt old and ruined. He hated his shoes. There was a spray of pain at his throat.

Noah was late for his meeting with Dora. When he realised the time lapse of what he would later, in strict denial, call his 'funny turn', he was physically recovered, though still upset. He walked with fake confidence back out through the lobby— it was more modest than he had noticed on his way in, more two-star-cheery and down-at-heel—and a neat man at reception called out, '*Buongiorno, signore*,' as if he knew him. '*Buongiorno*,' he responded and almost ran back into the sunlight.

There was a handful of patrons in the café Dora had selected. She'd chosen a table in the far corner, tucked into the fiction of a private space. There were high slit windows, permitting a little grey light. Puckered, voile curtains hung in a sham-quattrocento symmetry. Strewn more unevenly were various Italianate decorations, candles and Chianti bottles, the banner of the Città di Palermo football team. These were comforting, Noah thought, these time-honoured decorations, along with the sound and the scent of coffee in preparation.

From the entrance Dora looked a much younger woman; in fact she seemed for a second like Katherine, a Lady Lazarus of his wife as she appeared when they first met in Cambridge, when they both possessed the assertiveness of youth. Then he saw an old man sitting beside her on the plush bench, and he too looked like a copy or a substitution. An old man for himself, secretly ancient, peering down a shadowy chasm towards death. Noah understood this was the dramatic after-effect of his turn. The mad logic of shock, the sight of damage to a face. He pulled himself together and strode towards her.

This man was Vito, her uncle, who had been sixteen years old when his brother had been slaughtered, who had turned up at her parents' house, distraught, his hands open like Jesus. This was the man Dora had spoken of not long after they first met, wanting him to know a small detail of her blood-spattered history. Vito had the sagging face of one who had truly suffered. His tired eyes were rimmed with red and his wiry hair was entirely white. Dora rose and Noah kissed her in the Italian manner, without indicating his feelings.

Vito greeted him warmly. His hands were on the table, giant

beside his espresso cup. He pushed a glass of water towards Noah, perhaps sensing the remnant need for first aid. 'So you are also interested in the world of art?' he said.

They were speaking Italian. Noah organised his vocabulary. He conceded yes, Italian art, especially Piero della Francesca. He expected the old man to snort his dismissal, but Vito leaned back and smiled.

'Dora took me one time to see his frescoes in Arezzo, *The Legend of the True Cross*. I liked the picture of the man asleep in his tent, dreaming of the angel.'

'Constantine,' said Noah. 'It's Constantine's dream.'

'And the wine. I liked very much the Sangiovese wine of Arezzo.' He smiled again, aware of the mischievous equivalence.

They were silent. Noah was not sure why Vito was with them, why Dora hadn't warned him.

'And you are Australian,' Vito went on. 'Kangaroos!' He performed a small leaping movement with his huge hands, self-amused.

Noah's coffee arrived. 'We have many unusual animals,' he said, making conversation. 'Platypuses, koalas, echidnas.' He sounded ridiculous, unsure of how to Italianise the nouns. Cartoonish creatures fled and scattered in his borrowed language. He dared not sound sardonic or catch Dora's eye.

'Platypuses,' Vito repeated, disbelieving.

Noah was still thinking of the hurt man, his face broken and bloody. He wanted to take Dora to a bedroom and pull her onto him, and then confess in a whisper his instinctive inaction and cowardice. All his life he'd had an urge to confess to women, to lay his soul bare in petition for forgiveness.

'Vito has a plan,' Dora said cautiously, 'and would like you to be involved.'

And that was when he first heard of it.

~

Vito's abridged version of their dilemma involved the mafia. Noah could hardly credit the narrative he was offering. Signor M, as he referred to him ('better you don't know the name'), wanted Dora to steal an original sculpture by Vincenzo Ragusa from a museum in Palermo. It was to be delivered to Tokyo. M knew of Dora's interest, and that she had twice travelled to Tokyo to research Eleonora Ragusa. She was the obvious art-mule. M knew of her history and he'd rung late at night, Vito said, and made explicit threats. Dora's job was to steal a Ragusa and smuggle it to Japan, where a third party would take delivery.

But Vito had his own plan. Dora and Noah would go together to Tokyo, but then Noah would continue on to Sydney with the Ragusa. Dora would return to Palermo, claiming that someone unknown, someone who must have been tipped off, had stolen the sculpture from her in Tokyo. Later she would join Noah in Sydney and retrieve the sculpture. She would be in the clear, Vito said. Dora would have stolen from criminals. Noah was unknown to them and they would never track him. They would be on the same flight, but not appear to be travelling together.

Dora had remained silent throughout this outlandish speech. 'It's still too dangerous, Vito,' she murmured. 'You don't have to be part of any of this, Noah. They threatened Vito unless I agreed. It's our problem, not yours.'

She sounded defeated, resigned.

Vito ignored her and pressed his case. This was a brilliant plan. They would trick signor M, fuck Cosa Nostra, and steal a national artwork. It might even lead to M's exposure, even though he had certainly bought protection. But times had changed in Palermo, Vito added, and it was harder for the older bosses to control the Carabinieri. Fuck them, he said again.

Noah stared at Dora. She would not meet his gaze. Was this

some complicated joke, some enlistment of mafia tales to remind him that he was a stranger in bad lands, so innocent and unused to violence that he might be shattered by seeing a single man beaten?

Vito was still insistent. He did not retract his ludicrous plan or change his story. He caught Noah's gaze and said quietly, 'This is serious, Noah. This will sound to you like the movies, but art theft happens here all the time. No one will be hurt.' He paused to offer a strategic explanation. 'Academics are not often approached, but in this case Dora fits well with the theft. If you agree to help, you mustn't tell anyone in Sydney of your relationship, not even your children. And you must be more careful from now on, until this is over. Maybe go to Rome for a while and spend your time there. It's a big city, easy to get lost in.'

Noah said nothing. He felt his throat constrict; he felt a sour panic rising. He could not believe Vito was calmly describing a crime, implicating his involvement, while Dora remained silent. She'd detached herself. She sat with him not in fondness but as if assisting a business deal. How was Dora involved? How had they been threatened? His mind reeled with confusion and genuine dread. But he didn't want more details, he wanted simply to flee. Vito offered a friendly grin, as if assuming Noah had already agreed to assist them, but in his sense of danger he thought again of the beaten man curled on the ground, his eyes closed, his tongue showing, the blood from his nose streaking his cheek. He might have been a saint, suffering. A face for Caravaggio, dark enough, and distinctive, shining with mute pain. Noah was a small-time art scholar, not a thief. In a moment of self-understanding, aware of his recent disgrace, he knew that he must refuse Vito's plan.

22

IT WAS STILL raining in Sydney. The high humidity of the past four days, which had given the city a ginger pall, had filled up the sky, and at last the rain fell. From the bus, on the crest of a hill, Evie saw the front sweep in, a veil before them, satiny and dense. When she arrived at Benjamin's house, having rushed from the bus stop with no umbrella, she was dripping and slick, but enlivened by her dash through the gusting weather. She stood on the doorstep catching her breath, listening for Rocky's greeting.

Benjamin seemed to know without touching that she was drenched, and the dog sniffed with excitement at the rainy world, his thick tail wagging, his fat head bumping in affection. Evie felt the kindness of their doubled greeting. Benjamin held out a towel, as if in tribute. He had placed it on the hallstand; he had anticipated the rain. He'd somehow known she would arrive on his doorstep wet and dishevelled. Evie stood before him, rubbing her hair.

'If you want to dry your clothes, you can change. I can offer a range of business shirts, white or pale blue.'

Evie looked into his face, which was turned towards her. This was an invitation, both subtle and open.

'Why not? Thank you.'

Benjamin walked as if seeing as she followed him to his bedroom. A large double bed, a print that looked like a series of eclipses. It was stylish, neat, with the strangely static mood empty bedrooms achieve. He opened his wardrobe, and Evie saw that his shirts, which were many, were grouped by colour: white, pale blue, and a row of assorted pinstripes. The uniform of the city. The robes of another life.

'Choose for yourself.'

So Evie chose. Benjamin left the room while she discarded her wet dress, and she thought this a coy and unnecessary delicacy. She realised that she'd wanted to undress in his presence, that she'd assumed, perhaps, a pretext for seduction on his part. There was a moment, pulling her clinging dress over her head, when she recognised the enchanted force of her own desire. She stayed for a few seconds thus, covered and uncovered, as children do. The hollow of her dress held her there, halted without words, shaded by the past. Then it was a swift change. Evie liked the touch of his cotton shirt, too large and flawlessly ironed, on her cool skin. In movies barefoot women in shirts express winsome sexiness. It was a formula costume. Yet, being unseeable, she was relaxed; she was wholly inside her own body.

Rolling up the sleeves of Benjamin's shirt in the stillness of his bedroom, with the buzz of his absence, the hint of erotic suspense, she noticed the scent of chemical lavender. It was all around her, sweeping into her face. Some unremembered event, some lost physical sensation, caught her unawares. She felt an irrational impulse to cry, but instead sat on Benjamin's bed, staring into space.

'Are you alright?' he called.

And Evie was obliged to say yes, and pull herself back, and meet him again, and make conversation. 'The scent of lavender,' she said, walking into the sitting room. 'It overwhelmed me.'

'Mrs Hamilton, my cleaner. She has a wide assortment of ozone-depleting compounds. Mistress of fluorocarbons. I've asked her not to use them, but she doesn't believe a room is clean unless it smells like industrial spillage.'

Benjamin smiled. Her mood had radically shifted. She looked at him and saw how he anticipated pleasure.

'Do you mind,' she asked, 'if we don't do the movie today? I'll stay until the rain stops, then return tomorrow.'

Now she saw his disappointment, and his failure to disguise it.

In a tone of grievance he said, 'You should have rung, and said so. You didn't have to make the journey here to say you weren't available.' It was almost a reproach. She could not explain why she wanted suddenly to be alone, slumped in on herself, and outside time.

'I like the shirt,' she said.

'It's yours. I'm sure you look great.'

'I chose white,' she added.

So they were bashful again. They sat quietly at each end of the sofa, far apart. In the vacancy that followed Evie was searching for a topic.

'It occurred to me I could walk Rocky sometimes.'

'I have a walker, a twelve-year-old. He loves Rocky and the pocket money. But if you and I walked him together, I would be grateful. He has way too much energy for an unaccompanied blind man, and I am also restless. I used to cycle, and run. It's been one of the most difficult things, changing my body.'

Both fell silent. Evie was still surprised by her swift reversal of feeling, the embarrassing grip of something she could not understand or identify. There was an intuition of remote, extra-sensory meaning. The dead language of a lost life. She thought of white swans on a cold river, and a frigid white sky. A curved bridge somewhere, in an English winter. Freesias, daffodils, and something skittish, apparently fleeing, in a nearby hedge. And the twinkle children notice, of distant water, of cars, of the condensation of breath on a pane. Nothing in this sweep of vague visions unlocked the meaning of her feelings.

'I've been wanting to ask you a movie question,' Benjamin said.

'Fine, go ahead.'

'Is there a movie made by a blind man?'

He was folding the towel. Evie wondered if he was one of those men who folded their clothes before making love.

'I'm sure there are several, but I know of just one. *Blue* by Derek Jarman.'

'What's it like?'

'There is just one image, a blue screen. It's a deep organic blue, such as that of cornflowers or delphiniums. But the sound-track is extraordinary—diaries, poetry, conversation. The sound of cafés, the ocean, a hospital, music. Images come into being, as it were, from the hypnotic effect of contemplation alone. Jarman was almost completely blind, suffering from AIDS, and nearing death. It's really very moving. It's about losing sight, but not losing vision.'

She waited for Benjamin's comment, but he made none. She could not read his expression. He might make a joke, or scoff, or suggest that such minimalism was pointless.

'Sorry,' Evie said. 'My father used to say I give lectures, not conversation.'

'I'm just thinking, Evie.'

They were quiet for a minute. She could have gone on, arguing the case, but it was an easy quiet, after all, and a coming together. There was a long opportunity to study his face, private even now, formally at rest. The telephone rang. Rocky leaped up with a yelp, startled from his doze. Benjamin rose and moved to the desk, taking up the handset.

'Yes, it is. Yes, yes. When? Does my sister know? No, I'll call her. Yes, okay. Yes. Thank you.'

He stood still for a few seconds, his back to her. He was shielding his feelings. When he turned, his face showed a weary sorrow.

'My mother. It may be a stroke. They are doing the tests. I have to go immediately to the nursing home. I'll take a taxi and can drop you on the way, if you like.'

He was attempting to cover something deeply personal and solemn. Benjamin waited as Evie returned to his bedroom to change back into her wet dress. She hung the white shirt carefully over the back of a chair. So they were strangers after all, Evie thought. He was preoccupied, wanting to leave. She felt herself a crass intruder in the private moment of a family she could not presume to know. Mischance and misalliance. The demands of others. Family. In the taxi beside her, not touching, he appeared to stare out the window.

Later, Evie thought how this day was a figure of life itself: a combination of happy glimpses and tragic possibilities, of interruptions, questions and answers, of desire and of defeated desire, and the rain, which was unceasing, as it was in Palermo, signifying some larger sense of the world beyond human control. There was an inconsequential meeting, slight conversation, and the rumour of art that might give the human condition a meaning. She felt the wet fabric of her dress as a kind of failure.

Evie asked to be dropped off at the train station, insisting it was easier for all. Benjamin was whisked away into the streaming rain, unable to look back. Evie bought an umbrella from a creaky rotating stand outside an enterprising newsagency, and decided on impulse to walk. Setting off down the shimmering road, she was visited by memories that may have been skeining backwards to the mystery of the lavender. These were of early childhood objects she had shared with Martin: a stamp collection, bearing emblems of flora, fauna, maps and politicians; matchbox cards that had once belonged to their father, series of sedans and vans, fire engines and ambulances; illustrated art books, with repro-ductions on glossy paper. Their father did not permit television, so these were the screens they'd peered into. And a doll she once had, with which both she and Martin had played, a plastic doll, dumb-looking and bubble-headed, with eyes that opened and closed with a click under a fan of stiff eyelashes. There was some more distant sense of their cold home in Kent, seams of blonde light slanted into a dusty room, the smell of burnt custard boiling over on a stove, the lonely adventure of sitting hidden under a cloth-covered table.

And now Noah. Evie had scarcely thought of her father all day. He would be the one with all the answers, since he had remembered her whole life, and known her forever. She had often been moved by the fine detail of his memories: something she had said when she was five or seven, some scrap of mispronounced wit or adorable behaviour. There was a solace in what he had preserved and told her. He had admired her savant talent for listing, and enjoyed her useless retention of facts. Now, imper-sonal death. No more questions, and no more answers. She was grieving for herself, for what Noah had taken away. As Evie walked beneath her umbrella, she began a silent list: it sprang up inside her like an affliction: *laburnum, lantana, larkspur, laurel, laurestine, lavender, lilac, lily, lisianthus, lobelia, lotus, love-lies-bleeding.*

23

IN THE DOWNPOUR Martin hurried along the uneven pavements, worried he would slip. There was the added hazard of soft dog shit, and broken umbrellas, and scaffolding, so that from time to time he had to step out into the wilderness of traffic to return to the pavement. There were Indian vendors with their wares indistinct under sheets of plastic, and a population reduced to dark shapes, hurrying, their intentions awash. In the market, which he passed through by way of a short cut, customers were few and the shopkeepers sat smoking or gambling under dripping tarpaulins. When they sold their fish or cheese, it was a bored and slow exchange. The sight of cast-off vegetable leaves in puddles filled Martin with despair.

'Don't Leave Me This Way' was playing with infuriating

insistence in his head. The same few lines. He must ask Evie how it was that songs do this; she was bound to know. When he boasted of having a genius for a sister, he really believed it; but somehow she had done nothing with her life, she was a drifter between jobs and partners, always broke, and unable to settle on one vocation. Things would be different, with Noah gone. They would see more of each other. He would be a better brother, and support her. If she stayed in Sydney, they might even share his house for a while, which was too empty and too lonely. He had begun formulating a plan.

In the internet café Veeramani stood as he entered, and stretched out his hand. 'And how are you, Mr Martin, in this splendid weather?' He grinned widely, pleased with his own humour.

'I would prefer more rain,' said Martin, as he shook his umbrella out the door and brushed water from his sleeves.

Veeramani laughed heartily and repeated the joke to the other men in the room, who were less amused than he. Tamils, he had told him: they were a community of Tamils. Martin was pleased to be doing a service. During his last Skype with Nina he had sketched her face, and Veeramani had seen his portrait and been impressed. In a nervous voice he'd asked Martin if he might sketch his two children when he Skyped them, so that he would have their portraits here, in Palermo. 'Real art is much preferable to photographs, don't you agree, Mr Martin?'

He would draw Veeramani's children while their father spoke to them in Chennai through a glass screen. The children had been told, and Martin had arrived with his sketchpad and pencils at the appointed time. The old computer had been lifted from its grubby booth and placed on a bench, before two chairs.

After Veeramani had introduced his wife, Amirtha, he summoned his children to the screen. Kavitha was about nine, radiantly excited. Her hair was plaited, and she wore large emerald ribbons on each side of her head. She leaned into the screen to say 'hello' to Mr Martin, the artist. Then her brother, Deva, appeared, seven, perhaps, quiet and shy, but impeccably turned out in a suit and a tie. Both had their hair brightened with coconut oil; they were smooth and flawless as electric angels.

It helped that they were not speaking in English. Undistracted by topics of conversation, Martin could concentrate on their faces. Each took a turn speaking to their father, and his animated jollity was clearly infectious. He was telling them jokes, engaging them in stories, commanding their attention by comedy and love. Martin had never drawn dark faces before, and enjoyed the challenge. His pencil was busy crosshatching and shading as he filled the outlines of the children's features with fine notations of skin, line on downy line to show their healthy round cheeks, their almond eyes, their slight expressions of amazement. Martin felt that something was being restored to him: this was what he was good at, and he was amusing this family and the proud father beside him.

Veeramani was thrilled. 'Oh, Mr Martin, you have exceeded yourself!'

He held the images to the screen and the children peered at their portraits. Kavitha clapped and Deva joined in, so that there were two children across the planet applauding his artwork in a pitter-patter that sounded like rain. Martin added to the ceremony by offering a little bow. They clapped again. Kavitha's perching ribbons somehow recalled Evie's. Had she worn them like this, like bulbous moths? The children's gladness prompted memories of his own affections: the stamp collection, a fluttery world, he had shared with Evie; and the scent of dried apricots stored in his desk at school; and the royal-blue cigarette tin he'd found, and in which he'd stored a collection of dead insects.

There was a dimension of tenderness to such things, prized for their secret associations and hidden value. Nina had reminded him of such worlds and, though he missed her now, he was filled with the images of Kavitha and Deva, densely observed, immaculate and effusive, as if they were his own.

Veeramani offered Martin tea and they sat for a while, talking. It was too late at night in Sydney to Skype Nina, but this small encounter had sparked Martin's spirit. Veeramani now knew of Nina's deafness, and Martin told him about his anguish, his arguments with his former wife, and his strong conviction of his daughter's perfection. There was more than one kind of perfect, surely? Veeramani had looked confused, and said that in India there would be pity for such a child, and that such a child might be said to have bad karma; and that a hearing child was, indeed, more perfect than a child who could not hear. It was a frustrating conversation. The internet café had no customers at all and Martin felt able to speak freely. But he failed to convince Veeramani that there could be sense in refusing a cochlear implant.

'She will perish without music,' Veeramani said gravely, averting his eyes, moving the zipper of his jacket up and down, evidently driven to restless fidgeting by Martin's perverse opinions.

Martin felt rebuked, and unsure. He had not had this kind of discussion with anyone but family, and was both touched and irritated by Veeramani's advice. It would haunt him, that sentence: *she will perish without music*. Another person had imagined his daughter's extinction when she seemed to him pledged to the future and full of immortal possibilities.

When Martin left the internet café, the rain had stopped. This was how he measured time now: *it is raining, it is not raining*. The air was heavy, submarine, and the light was grey from low clouds. He looked up and saw the vague glow of a lost sun, and felt a pang of homesickness for Sydney. He could be at the beach now, surfing. He could be flexing his body as waves surged like an embrace around him. He could be chatting up a woman in a bikini or building a sandcastle with his perfect daughter. Instead, he was meeting Antonio again, who had left a message. He was late for their appointment.

Martin hurried back through the side streets, through the irregular lanes and onto the main roads. Central Palermo was becoming familiar to him. After three weeks he no longer looked at street signs or read the names of buildings, but found his own ingress and egress, carried a city-shape inside his head, could move absent-mindedly and still find his way. It was a city subject to his intentions, marked privately by what he'd noticed, the particular wavelength of his impulses and interests. Idly, he fancied drawing the city by electrocorticography. Self-portrait in Palermo. There were still novel apparitions—a row of posters for the new movie *A Good Day to Die Hard* made him see for the first time the dying façade of the building behind it; the repeated words, the actor's appearance, were like the stamp of a *memento mori* on the face of the city. *Un buon giorno per morire* appeared everywhere. Each time he read it, he agreed that any day was a good day to die.

Antonio was rising to leave as Martin entered the café, but sat down again, annoyed. 'I thought only Italians are late. We are known for it, of course.' He gave an insulting shrug.

Martin apologised. Newly fixed on faces, he remembered how he'd wanted to draw Antonio's face. His bird profile was distinctive, a huge hooked nose and crevasses along his cheeks, handsome in a singular manner and reminiscent of spaghetti westerns.

'I need to go now,' said Antonio. 'But I have something to

say. I want to warn you to leave. They know you are here, asking questions.' There was no urgency in his quiet words, just an air of tense annoyance.

'Who knows I am here?'

'Better you don't ask.'

Martin felt the urge to make a dismissively ironic remark, but contained himself. 'Who told *them*?'

Antonio looked away. Martin thought him shifty. He waited for an answer but none was forthcoming.

'There is nothing to discover here. Your father is dead. You have stayed too long. Ask yourself what you are doing here.' His tone was growling, cantankerous. 'We have a saying here in Sicily for people who find nothing: *You've made another hole in the water.*'

Hole in the water. Martin could not fashion the words into an image. 'You're right,' he began. 'I've discovered nothing. Nothing at all. But now I'm working on a new art project.'

This half-truth, he thought, might placate or mollify. This was his own rationalisation for what had seemed futile roaming.

But Antonio was unimpressed. He pushed back the table, and took up his raincoat. 'I have to go. Think about what I said.' He headed for the door and was gone.

Martin ordered an espresso and sat with his sketchpad, disquieted, working on his vision of the city rendered in brain-waves. He thought Antonio Dotti fundamentally unreliable. Dora had clearly thought so too. Zealous, oddly gloating, seduced by imagining a dark crime. A sponger, a fool, who drank too much. Martin scribbled what looked like a seismological graph, then another, inverted. Even though he'd begun to know his way around, this was the quake of some inner disorder, the fault lines of his sense of disquiet in this city. It was a doodling image, such as one might make while speaking on the telephone. But Martin detected a patterning there, the jittery self that knew a place by nerve endings alone.

As he was leaving the café, Martin was shocked to see an old three-wheeler van, a vehicle that looked like it belonged in a fifties comedy, head unswervingly for a truck. There was the high sound of brakes and an ineffectual wobble of the tiny van, but it collided head-on, with a loud smack, and became crushed beneath the truck's wheels. How easily metal crumpled, like paper in a fist. What was remarkable was how little sign there was of a life extinguished. It was an accident magnified before him, but with no sense of drama. It was a hopeless termination where there should have been panicked activity.

The truck driver stayed up high, immobile, in his metal cabin. A few spectators edged forwards. A wave of sound grew. At first there was a kind of hiss of something atrocious having happened, an almost metaphysical disturbance in the air, then a blast of horns extending all the way up the street. It was an indecent cacophony. Shouts erupted, not of dismay, but of anger. Martin thought he saw an arm quivering beneath the crushed metal, and then become still. But perhaps it was not an arm; perhaps he wanted something explicit in so anonymous an accident, some ordinary sign.

He thought of the moment he identified his father's body. He could barely look. Noah's appearance: what was it like? It was like nothing. Nothing. Martin had blown his nose, he had flinched, he had looked away. Fearing the indignity of witness, aware of meaty stench and inner tremble, he'd focused instead on the white draped sheet, stretched taut across the body. A man stood behind him, resolutely silent. Martin recalled the high illumination, and wondering why, out of respect, the lights were not dimmed.

He wanted to get away and turned into a lane. There was

garbage, and graffiti that read *Liberi Tutti!* A dumped mattress had spilt its guts so that flock tumbled into puddles in mucky clumps. More boarded-up windows. A row of three shops, one of which, to Martin's surprise, turned out to be the workshop of a violin repairer. He could see the doll-like body-shapes of violins hanging on a wall and a man in golden lamplight, polishing wood. Such careful and tender touch: the rub of a plush muff. Next door was a bar, but without a single customer. A row of three unoccupied stools stood in a blister of light.

Martin went in and ordered a double malt, straight, and drank too quickly. He was a man who wished to be delivered from the present moment into the easiest of oblivions. *Hole in the water.* He felt vacant and irrelevant.

24

THE DAY AFTER Noah fled from the near empty café, unable to assimilate what Vito had told him, he found himself skirting around the cathedral, so that he would not recall the beaten man. It was a futile attempt. Two streets away the cathedral bells rang. It was Sunday, he realised, and bell-tone was falling in circles all around him, calling believers to mass. Everywhere now: the round sound of bells. Noah felt he should try to recover his dignity with a few hushed words to God. The sonic waves pursued him with their gentle lasso. And although he moved quickly, he could not escape their tether, and was obliged to think again of his cowardice and his fear, and to recall again the tedious collapse that had humiliated him.

~

Dora suggested a daytrip to Cefalù. She'd rung him in the evening, earnestly conciliating, saying she should have told him in advance that Vito would be there, he should have been more careful explaining their dilemma. And she understood, she said, if he did not wish to participate in the scheme, but she would like the chance to explain it once again, in a more personal context.

Noah was only partly reassured. In vague terms he mentioned the violence at the cathedral; it had rattled and upset him, and he'd not been in a frame of mind to listen to Vito's complicated plans. So they both tried hard to reconcile and agreed to meet at the train station. They were lovers once again, with a plan for a getaway and the expectation of an embrace.

North-western Sicily fled by, in a sequence of blurry vistas. Noah saw hills rise and fall, glimpsed patches of ocean, noticed the white farmhouses and the new freeway and the spread of orange groves. It was autumn, but still there were smudges of flowers scattered everywhere, asphodels, wild fennel, bright blooms he could not name in blues and mauves. Dora dozed, her face pressed against the window of their carriage. She was one of those travellers who slept at any motorised rhythm, and who somehow found in public transport a special opportunity to sleep. Noah envied what he took to be her capacity for relaxation.

Alone in her company, he could not view her objectively. He knew that, if she asked for his help, he would now instantly agree; he would be zealous and amenable for fear of losing her. He had a sense—which he'd felt only once before, on the eve of his wedding—that all his life was gathering in to this point, rucking in folds as though pulled by a drawstring. He was not immune, he knew, to romantic delusion, but knew too that such a configuration, which he imagined to be crimson and rose-shaped, might signify the point at which he must claim responsibility for his own life. On the rocking train he formulated it thus: this is the shape I have been placed within. What is gathered here contains me.

Dora's sleeping face. Last time, aroused but unable to perform, he had simply held her. This happened more often these days; his desire did not always match his abilities. He'd stayed limp and small, even with his cheek resting ardent on her naked thigh. She'd touched his wrist, then his forearm, then whispered, '*Tesoro*'— not a platitude, but a clarification of shared feeling. Her fingers in his hair, her reassurance. Against the cotton pillow, embroidered and lacy in the Italian style, her grey hair fanned, her face looked its age. They were both sixty-seven and not taking too much for granted. Both were absorbed by a quickened awareness of their own bodies, and by how they lay together, in that moment, intersecting. In the illusioned lives of men, so constantly aware of possible failures, there was not enough attention, Noah reflected, to the momentary gifts.

When they arrived, they walked side by side down the hill to the town. The old centre of Cefalù was a medieval coastal town in the shadow of a mountainous rock, from which, Dora told him, the place got its name—the Greek *kephalos*, meaning cranium. They would climb this bulky headland, she promised; they would mount the thick skull of rock and gaze at the city below. But first, the cathedral. Noah joked that he had resolved to avoid cathedrals from now on, but Dora insisted. So they found themselves arriving at the stately Norman building just as the congregation of a mass was dispersing.

Noah watched the well-dressed inhabitants, most older than himself, file quietly away. He had no wish to be here, in this space of antique celibacy. What he wanted was a bed and a room with a view. He was sick of art, and religion, and the adoration of yet more images.

They stepped inside and viewed, high in the apse, the Christ Pantocrator, a Byzantine mosaic from the second century. This Christ was unnaturally handsome, his colossal head authoritarian and glittering in gold. Noah tried to sound impressed. But somehow his folds, his gathering life, had already squeezed something away. He had seen it all before. Any number of Byzantine Christs and aerial spirits, concave faces removed from human pleas. He had a heretic heart. It was Dora he was focused on.

After lunch at a small trattoria, at which neither mentioned the conversation of the day before, they set off to climb the Cefalù rock-skull. Noah looked up at the steps and the rocky paths ahead of him and thought of his arthritic knees and his dodgy heart, but did not want to complain. Dora, clearly the fitter, slowed her pace to suit him, and Noah followed. He began the long haul, pulling his body up step after step, through steep walls of prickly pear and granite outcrops. At the remains of a Saracen fort, he took a photograph of Dora peeping through an embrasure, visible as just the slim stripe of a woman. She returned the gesture, and Noah too was just a stripe: they would be ugly photos. He was feeling dispirited and tired.

Further up, Dora pointed out circular walls and battlements and gave Noah a potted history of northern Sicily. Like Evie, she liked to lecture. But there came a point at which they stood still, opened up and, catching their breath, noticed the view. Noah was not sure of their height, but it was enough to convey elation. Wind in high gusts confirmed their sense of unworldly ascension. Below them lay the orange tiled roofs of the old town, the cathedral, the piazza, and beyond that a gently heaving sea, magnificently blue and blinking with sunlight; and further, on the horizon, rode container and cruise ships.

This simple shift in perspective seemed to cast off the

bitterness of the world. Noah felt the strong warm wind blowing into his face, he felt the contraction of muscles in his legs and the cooling sweat on his body, he felt returned to himself, somehow, after yesterday's grim disgrace. He knew it was possibly some endorphinous effect, the charging of the organism, as though there was a little brass dynamo churning away inside his chest, but still he cherished it: elevated and revved up, under blue heaven, standing beside Dora and looking with her at the wide sunny world.

She turned and kissed him. Caught up in his own thoughts, Noah was taken by surprise. He returned the kiss. It was one of those moments in which a newly proportioned sense of things makes the small gesture large. In the context of the skull-rock view, high above Cefalù, Dora's kiss was monumental, her impulse, not his, and her simple declaration.

They continued their climb. At the summit was a mass of grey stones representing a Temple to Diana; it was barren, windy, but enduring in its lunar isolation. The rudimentary cubicle of a long-lost faith. What endures, he wondered, other than stone? What is it that remains? It was an old question, possibly trite, that a pile of stones might provoke.

His knees hurt coming down. Once or twice he skidded. He was drenched in sweat and took regular rest stops. Dora seemed not to notice what he felt to be old-man tardiness. Nothing much had happened, a climb up, then a climb down, but somewhere in between there had occurred a transformation. Dora had shed yesterday's remote air. She was almost flirtatious now, reaching for his hand, grazing his face, leaning over to wipe his brow with the end of her scarf. She too had been affected by the elevation. When the angle of the path allowed, they held hands and walked side by side.

They ate blood oranges on the beach, facing the sea. They

washed their juice-sticky hands in shallow rock pools. They made easy conversation in quiet voices. Dora lit a cigarette and entered a kind of reverie. It was one of the mysteries of their relationship that he found the sight of her smoking so attractive, the noxious intake of smoke, the curls expelling, the way she inclined her head with each exhalation, or extracted, with thoughtless grace, a string of tobacco from her lips. Her wrist turned slightly to stub out her cigarette. She looked up at him, smiling. He felt her magnetic effect. The lure of brushed bodies in an elevator, heading to a dim hotel room. Sexual permission, abandon, the hush of a falling shirt, or skirt. Newly confident, Noah wanted to speak about his granddaughter, Nina. He would tell Dora of her deafness, her independence, her courage, how she'd saved his son, as children do, by being so alive to the world and so implicitly demanding. He felt he'd been granted a vision of the future.

Dora's cell phone rang. '*Pronto?*' She was listening, head down, in strictest silence. Noah watched her face slacken and then harden. An accident of some sort, a death, a catastrophe. When she snapped closed her phone, she said, 'Vito. They've threatened Vito again. I have to go.'

Who? he was thinking. Who has threatened Vito? Dora's face was cloudy. She was now tense, edgy, driven by the command of filial piety. Noah saw her rise, almost toppling in haste, and pull her leather handbag over her shoulder. Sand flicked in a tiny shower from her heels and her clothes. Her shadow passed over him. She was striding up the beach when he realised she was heading back to the train station and seemed to have forgotten him.

They sat together mute in the returning train. Dora was enfolded in misery. The late afternoon fled by in a sequence of reversed scenery, yellow now, and spoiled, in the thickening light. When at last the train arrived, she announced she would arrange the theft the next day. She would book a ticket to Tokyo, if they agreed to stay away from her uncle.

'Book two,' Noah said. 'Book two tickets to Tokyo.'

Dora did not even turn. She did not acknowledge what seemed to him an enormous commitment. She walked quickly from Palermo Centrale, crossing the dangerous roads around the Piazza Giulio Cesare without much care.

Noah rushed to guide her between the buses and cars taking the roundabout too fast. In the traffic he saw a group of five men, all African, carrying buckets and squeegees, and rushing to attack the windows of any car halted at the lights. They were precariously alive in the swift current of the traffic. They were abused and reviled. Occasionally one was paid a meagre coin for cleaning a windshield. Noah felt ill watching them, their flesh so exposed and defenceless. The migrant misfortune they carried. Each at risk, and imperilled. Their faces flashed towards him, another man in the traffic, another conspicuous foreigner, guiding a woman. He didn't wish to make eye contact, but somehow he did. One man stared at him, and suddenly smiled.

In the distress of the moment, in all that had happened and would happen, Noah was unguarded. He acknowledged, he smiled back.

25

WHEN EVIE ANSWERED the knock at the door, she was faced with an older woman who looked as if she had been disappointed by life. Her forehead was etched with a self-righteous scowl. She had the grey stubble of a slight moustache and her hair was the same colour, set in an unflattering coiled perm.

'Irene Dunstan, yours truly. Resident of number fourteen.' She stood her ground, expecting to be admitted.

Evie knew this was the woman who had found her father's body and wondered if she might need to express her shock, or grief. They had met only briefly, when she first arrived. Perhaps now she could offer her neighbour more time and show more compassion.

Irene Dunstan peered past her and noticed the gin and tonic on the coffee table, beside Evie's book. 'A little early, isn't it?' she said with wowserish scorn, but then added in a chirp, 'I'm happy to join you.'

So Evie found herself pouring a drink for this uninvited guest, who within minutes told her that her husband, Bill, a sales rep, had died three years earlier of cancer of the oesophagus, that she herself had numerous ailments of an esoteric female kind, and that her cat, Socksy, communicated with her by animal clairvoyance. 'We're like that,' she said, entwining her fingers.

Socksy. Evie remembered that Noah had mentioned the cat, and he had called it Strozzi.

She took a gulp of her drink. She endured hearing that her father was dashing, but reclusive, that he had fed Socksy, even though Irene had asked him not to, and that he didn't attend a single residents' meeting. Irene finished her drink and held out her glass for another. 'Don't mind if I do,' she said.

So in the late afternoon Evie, who considered herself a patient woman, found she was impatient with her neighbour who had nothing to say to her other than to list her father's shortcomings. It was a kind of persecution. She watched Irene finger the blouse straining at her over-large bosom. At the neckline sat a silver scarab brooch, and Evie focused her interest there, on the *Scarabaeus sacer*. She recalled a cartouche Noah had shown her in the British Museum as he bent beside her, explaining why Egyptians worshipped scarabs. In the midst of this woman's free-form complaint, Evie knew again that what her father had shown her had an imperishable aspect, gleaming through time.

'My mother's,' Irene replied in answer to her inquiry. 'I had it valued, but it's not worth much. Rubbish, really.'

The humble object held the attention of both women. Irene was doubtless thinking of her mother's faults, not least in bequeathing inexpensive jewellery, and perhaps also remembering her well-brought-up childhood, the lace hankies stuffed in her sleeve, the polished patent-leather shoes, the command to keep her knees together when sitting on the bus. Evie wanted to be generous, but found it impossible. She poured herself another drink, and, gesturing with the bottle, found that Irene was prepared to dash down her second to ensure a third.

Somewhere in their futile conversation they heard a loud splash from the swimming pool. Both gave a little jump.

'Well, I never,' said Irene. 'And not yet cleaned!'

Evie stood up. She had just noticed the time, she said. She was late for an appointment. She shuffled Irene Dunstan out of the door, and leaned against it, as if in a storybook illustration, holding the wolf at bay. Evie would feed Strozzi. She would not invite Irene in again. She needed to decide if, after all, she could bear to stay here, where her father had a history and relations unknown to her. Others did this, moved into family homes, 'deceased estates', appreciating what remained and establishing continuities. But this would not be possible. She would clear Noah's apartment and together she and Martin would sell it. Irene Dunstan, resident of number fourteen, had stirred her to become decisive.

To confirm her lie about having an appointment, Evie took up her shoulder bag and left the apartment. She made a point of slamming the front door, so that her neighbour would hear. It was self-indulgent, stupid. But she was shaken by the insolent liberty of Irene's criticisms of her father. She imagined him bending over the black-and-white cat, fondly offering a morsel, his hand cupped at its head.

A skinny teenager, about seventeen, dive-bombed the swimming pool. He leaped up, clutched at his knees and came down on the water as hard as possible, sending spray into flower shapes and flicking spurts. He was not swimming, or relaxing, but hitting the water with his body, again and again. There was a violence to his repetition, a wish to force his tight body into a kind of explosion.

Evie watched as he ran to the edge of the pool, leaped, curled and fell. She avoided the splash. This crazy kid was blasting the pool with his insistent force. He was almost delirious with what Evie considered a vicious enjoyment. She hurried away down the blue funnel of the plumbago-lined drive and headed in a swift walk towards the harbour.

There it was, Sydney Harbour, bombed only by sunburst. The great expanse of water opened before her, blazoned with small craft and the occasional ferryboat. Evie sat on a slatted bench and looked into the distance. Nothing was simpler than the way ruffled water pushed back the horizon and unfastened the known dimensions of space. She heard birdsong and mobile phones and the calls of small children. She listened to the wind across the water, feeling her senses refine. The world had explicit definition; she might have been wearing lenses or hearing aids from the future.

When her own phone rang, it was Benjamin. Evie pressed the phone open and heard the appeal of his voice. She had been waiting to hear from him. Since she'd undressed in his bedroom, since she'd seen the taxi carrying him away, she had wanted more of his presence. Benjamin's blindness seemed partially to conceal him, and Evie was unsure of exactly how she should behave. He greeted her warmly and said that his mother was resting, that it was not a stroke, after all, and that—there was a cautious pause—he was hoping she would be available for dinner in a few hours, not as an employee, of course, but as a friend.

Evie found a pen and wrote down the name of the restaurant he had booked; it was close by, on Macleay Street. She looked out across the water, saw a distant ferry rounding the headland, disappearing in a scintillation, and responded, 'Yes, eight o'clock.'

In the self-regarding confinement of her grief for her father, Evie had not expected the relief of a new acquaintance. When she met Benjamin, she had adjusted her sense of desolation; this was not a moral adjustment, the comparison disability inspires, nor was it the appealing peculiarity of her work, but something more to do with how they each moved through darkness of some kind. He possessed a mysterious coherence she envied. In his poised adaptation to his condition he appeared to her exemplary. When, over dinner, she shyly expressed this opinion, he responded that she was mistaken.

'Nothing so dignified, I'm afraid. I simply exhausted my despair, then accepted what was beyond my control. It was not a noble decision.'

After that they made small talk, wishing to avoid what most mattered. The intercession of a pesky waiter meant their conversation never settled. They fell silent as he burbled, then resumed in fragments. When Benjamin asked about her father, Evie felt a welling of emotion; she recalled the turmoil of Irene Dunstan's visit, and the boy bombing the pool.

'He was a scholar,' she began, 'of Piero della Francesca, 1415 to 1492.'

Evie had automatically cited the dates. She must be careful, she reflected, not to divulge a list.

Benjamin smiled. 'And?'

'And my father spent his career seeking answers and revelations. He was quasi-Christian, quasi-mystic. He was attracted not to Piero's mathematical virtuosity—as many scholars are—but to something mysterious about his arrangement of figures, certain anomalies in time and space. Eternity implied, that sort of thing.' She waited, then added, 'I suppose you think that is foolish.'

'Not at all. I've heard of Piero, but I don't remember his

paintings: you'll have to describe some for me.'

This was not the right time. Evie had no wish, over dinner, to try to describe Italian artworks of the fifteenth century. She thought of the altarpieces and the famous fresco Noah had shown them in Arezzo. Then of twin portraits, a couple, the Duke and Duchess of Urbino. The duke, her father told them, was blind in one eye, which was why he was depicted in profile, his destroyed eye hidden. The paintings were always hung so that the couple faced each other. Evie loved the carved nose of the duke, the insistence on the reality of a face.

'Another time, perhaps.'

She watched as he felt for his glass, sliding his hand across the table towards its stem. She watched him lift the glass to his mouth, then replace it on the table. She saw his hand uncurl. She realised again that she could stare at him as she wished.

'You're staring,' he said.

'How do you know?'

'People go quiet. They like to see if I'll knock over my wine. You develop a feeling for these things.'

And with that forgiving remark they relaxed again.

Evie asked Benjamin about his mother. He could hardly stand it, he told her, the nursing home, her failing health, the thought of her slow decline. Judith was better at dealing with it. Women are stronger, he added. Over panna cotta he described a visit to Italy when he was twelve, before his parents divorced.

'This is our connection,' he insisted, perhaps looking for a way to link them. 'Memories of being in Italy, as children, and with our younger parents.'

Evie had not mentioned her mother and realised Benjamin would assume she was still alive. Where to begin, with the disordered narrative of her life? How might they know each other but in interrupted stories?

'The scent of *tiglio*,' he added. 'It always takes me back.'

Tiglio: lime. She adored this word. It could have been a seduction.

Evie hoped he would ask her back to his house, but after the short journey to Elizabeth Bay his taxi dropped her off and sped away. There was no kiss, or hug, or an attempt to hold her hand. No welcome fondle or arm slid around her waist. She stood outside her building watching the red tail-lights of the retreating car slide out of sight. She felt querulous and lonesome. The dinner, though pleasant, had been like a false pretence. Was it her own fatigued youth and passivity that stranded her? She must avow; she must act on what remained of strong feeling. Pride or fright might have held her back. Or was it that she thought herself unworthy?

There were shell-shaped lights up the driveway, but the apartments were all dark. There was no wind at all, an extraordinary stillness. The swimming pool lay flat, a shiny black mirror.

Evie unlocked her father's apartment and stepped inside. She did not switch on the light, but moved into the shadows of an incomplete darkness. Irrationally, she sensed her father still there, drifting as a breeze might, in a ghostly tremble. The sound of the harbour rose up, a ferry passing by. A night bird, possibly an owl, let out a long, hollow call. The staccato sound of crickets; the tidal hum of distant traffic. There was a slight glaze at the window that could have been moonlight. In the mostly dark, Evie brushed at the air with her hands, swishing away blackness, feeling for her father's armchair. There. Here.

She lowered herself down and rested a while in quiet concealment, where he, her dead father, had not long ago rested. She allowed herself to whisper his name. *Noah*: her father, Noah.

26

MARTIN WOKE WITH an erection and a feeling of despair. He hated his body, so needful, so alone and unpleasured. He groaned at the banal variations of his gloom.

Bored, he stood in silence at the window of his bedroom. Across the lane he saw two men about his age linger for a while, looking suspiciously around them. One dropped a cigarette and crushed it with his heel. The other stroked lovingly his thick black moustache. Then they knocked on the door of the brothel. The woman who opened to admit them also looked around. She spotted Martin and sent up a cheery wave. He waved back diffidently, with just the hand, as monarchy does. He felt meek and exposed. For a moment he yielded to the fantasy of walking outside and crossing the lane, being led upstairs, undressing, taking the plump, round woman in his arms and entering her instantly. It was a dull, impersonal lust he felt, a drive to be discharged. It was also the sickened spirit of having witnessed an accident no one cared about.

The driver of the three-wheeler van may after all have survived. Martin could not know for sure that he had died. Perhaps he was now being tended in the electric world of a hospital room. A wife kissing his forehead, a child taking his hand. Or perhaps he had suffered terribly beneath the truck and was in unspeakable pain, hearing the cruel boom of car horns, scudding up and down the street, the final sounds, gross and tyrannical, before he died.

Martin retched a little in the toilet, pouring out a thin stream of stink, but still he felt ill. He wanted to sober up. It was important, he told himself, to sit quietly, to think, to make some decisions. Should he rent a studio here for the deconsecration sequence or start the Piero-Barbie piece? Should he keep trying to find out what his father had been up to? Maria would be downstairs, moving around in the kitchen or sitting with her crochet; perhaps he should talk to her. Martin paced the floor. He looked out the window, again, but there was no sign of activity across the street. It was a discreet establishment, one that admitted clients with a furtive check and then hid them away.

Martin could not think in a sensible sequence about his options or plans. He could not draw, or read, or compose himself. He felt ravelled and restless. His solitude oppressed him. He decided to walk a new route to the harbour and stare at infinity for a while. He would visit the ocean and he would drink no more alcohol. He noticed that the light in his room had changed colour with the advent of late afternoon sunshine. The streets were still wet, but charged with a baroque, brassy glow. It was more reason to go out, to see the changed city.

As he came down the stairs, Maria greeted him with a smile

and gestured to the light outside the window. It had rained for almost three weeks; now there was a cessation that was bright and clear. When Martin stepped outside, he felt his spirits rise. Shutters had opened, and even some doors; as he walked down the lane, he could see into the cramped lower floors of the ancient houses, into dim sitting rooms with plastic covers on chairs, and religious icons, and Padre Pio calendars hanging on the walls. There were many lives here, historical and inconspicuous. Martin had the sense of a whole population of women tucked away, recessed into the stony shadows of the old city. When he bent to look into a window, an old woman in a black headscarf looked back. She swore at him and let out an aggrieved shout. He'd frightened her, he realised, bending down into her world. '*Mi scusi! Mi scusi!*'

Like Dora's hidden courtyard, the trace of an Arabic seclusion, this face flaming up at him told Martin what he'd neglected to see, another kind of life, another kind of architecture, the passages and secret places he had still not encountered. Raising his gaze, he saw a small shrine affixed high on the wall, the painting of a blushing Madonna, blotched and flaking, and a jar of fake carnations on a ledge before her. He'd seen them before, these shrines, but now noticed them everywhere, as though they had proliferated overnight and the change of light made them newly visible. Martin took out his camera and kindly shot her.

Turning a corner, he saw a phalanx of five teenage girls, with arms fondly linked, walking towards him. They spanned the narrow lane as if they owned it. The girl in the centre wore a hot-pink hoodie covered with ornate silver script. It read *Abbracci, baci*. Hugs, kisses. Martin found it transfixing. *Abbracci, baci*: this was a chant he and Evie had shared as children, singing it in the back seat of their old Morris Minor or lying together on their parents' bed, staring up at the ceiling. Their mother had taught them; they may have been his first words in Italian, charming because they rhymed, because they sounded nonsensical, because they sang of the happy-family intimacy before she died. In this singsong was a micro-history of their emotional lives.

As the girls passed, they called out something in dialect that sounded mocking. Martin looked at them with the disinterested eye of an artist. He thought of the shape they created, a sculptured object, the way they broke into pods of three and two to let him pass, their swaggers, their posture, their sassy confidence. And he thought: I must find this hoodie as a gift for Nina.

Every now and then the sky clouded over, but mostly it remained clear. Martin could hardly believe it. The buildings shifted from grey to pale apricot; the streets were busy; pedestrians appeared everywhere. It was not yet warm, but it was a world renewed. These were, he knew, the Australian thoughts of someone who could not endure a European winter, or even a Mediterranean lapse into untypical bad weather. But the Sicilians felt it too—how bleak the world had become when all they expected was light. It was the first week of March. It was time for winter to be over.

At the Quattro Canti, the octagonal crossroads where tourists gathered to photograph the four fountains, and the monuments to four Spanish kings and four patronesses, Martin saw how rapidly the city revived. A Japanese woman made two-finger peace signs as her partner photographed her; a couple, who may have been Dutch, were consulting a map; enthusiastic Chinese passed by in a decorated pony cart. Marvelling at the holiday-snaps scene, Martin saw another man standing apart and alone. It was the policeman from Sydney, Frank Malone. Even idle fancy would have made his appearance unlikely. He gave a restrained wave and walked towards him.

'I wasn't sure there, at first,' Malone said. 'How long have you been here?'

Martin wanted to ask the same question.

'So what are you doing here?' Malone persisted.

'Is this an official question?'

'Jesus, I'm just asking. How about a quick beer?'

Martin suggested coffee. He led the way to the café he knew in this area.

There was a tension between them. His and Evie's mourning had been disturbed and somehow blemished by Malone. Martin remembered the interview in his office and the accusation of guilt.

'How are you getting on?' Malone asked as they walked.

It was a question Martin couldn't hope to answer.

'You know,' he responded.

Conversation dropped as they entered the café.

'It must be hard,' Malone added.

Martin could hardly believe he was having this daft conversation. With a policeman. In Palermo.

'It's a surprise seeing you, Detective.'

'Call me Frank.'

'Frank.'

Martin hailed the waiter, who he knew had a cousin in Sydney. Gino chatted for a while with Martin, excluding his companion. There was a satisfaction in seeing Frank at a loss. When Gino swept back with their espressos, finally they could talk.

Frank explained he was here only semi-officially. The blokes 'upstairs' wouldn't fund his travel, but he had wanted to get away for a couple of weeks from his fucked-up marriage, so he'd struck a deal that meant he could 'follow up his inquiries'. Leave without pay, but a little support. The Carabinieri Cultural Heritage Protection Agency was hosting him, but they didn't give a flying fuck, he said, about the Australian connection.

'Still, they're all hoping for a visit to Sydney some day. Scratch my back, I'll scratch yours.'

So he was an opportunistic bastard, Martin was thinking. Cynical, disengaged, probably on the take.

Nevertheless, Martin told Frank Malone what little he had discovered. It was good to speak of it. He described his meetings with Antonio and Dora, and realised how thin and vague it all sounded.

'So you think Noah was involved?'

'Dora says no, Antonio says yes. I wouldn't have a clue. I'm doing artwork, not detection.'

Frank asked for Antonio's contact details. 'He's the man,' he added. 'The side guy always has the goods.'

Martin smiled. It was time to go home to Sydney. A stubborn policeman was speaking in fatuous code. He felt ridiculous, not following his father at all, but pursuing a twisted story. 'No,' he said.

'No?'

'No, I don't think Noah was caught up in anything. It's art-world rumour, like Chinese whispers. Everyone has heard a snatched scrap of something. My father is dead. A sculpture is missing. So what? You want to impose a criminal reputation on my father? You want to impress your bosses? You want a medal?'

Frank looked chastened, like a schoolboy rebuked. 'Jesus, give us a break.'

He was probably lonely. Amped up in Italy. 'Lugubrious', Martin thought, was coined for the face of Detective Frank Malone.

'Changeable weather, isn't it?' Frank was trying hard. He indicated the sudden glare after a swift interval of gloom. A Cinzano awning flapped audibly outside the window. This was not the Italian holiday Frank Malone had expected.

Taking pity, Martin decided to invite Frank to join him for dinner. He'd introduce him to true Sicilian cuisine. And then they could check out the new Bruce Willis movie. They'd go to a cinema that didn't dub, where he could hear untampered English and ignore the subtitles. Frank Malone looked overjoyed; he might have been a passenger pulled from the *Titanic*. Martin saw his relief to be treated like an ordinary guy, stranded on a whim of escape. They had that in common, he realised. They were both fleeing something emotionally imprecise and freighted with familial danger. They were both enticed by the possibility of explanations and understandings.

He looked across the table, absorbing the implications of Frank's presence. In truth, he was unnerved. It was possible that his father had been lured into something, and felt unable to tell them. Or was simply himself, separate and mysterious as parents are, with his own adult complications, now irrecoverable from the void of his passing. Martin felt insulted by the easy presumption of guilt, by this detective's wish to pursue his father beyond the grave. But he too wanted the truth. Though sullen with the threat to the reputation of his father, he too wanted to know.

When they parted, Martin resumed his walk to the harbour. Three boys passed, dance-playing football with a plastic water bottle, which they sent flying towards him as a glittering missile. Martin took up the challenge and scooped the bottle onto his knee, then flicked it up and performed a header back in their direction. The boys let out a whoop of congratulation, danced again and were gone. He smiled to himself. Their innocence. Their harmoniousness. The sea wind was high. He took a few deliberate deep breaths against the vision of a man crushed beneath a truck.

27

NOAH HATED THE flight to Tokyo. Dora was seated in the centre of the plane, over the wing; he was right at the back, on the other side, in the shuddering darkness. Just behind him the flight attendants read magazines or gossiped as they endured the twelve hours of confined servitude. Occasionally they emerged from their hiding place to beam a flashlight and offer a plastic cup of water or a tray of ersatz food. In the strobe of their visits they all looked indistinct, the dark pits of eyes, the masses of hair. It was the scary effect kids like to create with a flashlight under their chins. Before him glowed a small screen of movies on a zombie loop; non-awake viewing, his body long forgotten. He could not read or think. He felt bug-eyed and needed both antacid and aspirin. This was how the twenty-first century felt, the anti-natural long haul of it, the exhausted otherworldliness, the sad experience of a shuttered sky.

He saw Dora rise once, to stand in line for the tiny toilet, but imagined she was sleeping most of the time. She always slept abnormally deep and still, like one trying out death. Once he'd shaken her shoulder in bed just to check, as one does with babies and little children. She woke with a start, and he could not explain to her what anxiety he was trying to allay. She'd immediately slept again, and he felt then as he felt now, almost annoyed at how easily she found her escape.

They had taken separate flights to Rome. Dora left a day earlier, and checked out where they would exchange their hand luggage. She texted him the details on a new mobile phone and then discarded the sim card. She carried the Ragusa, obtained, she said, by Antonio Dotti, and a substantial bribe to a guard at the museum. Noah carried an identical bag packed with her clothes. The Ragusa needed a duffle bag, not a wheeled case, and even without the plinth it was unusually heavy and conspicuous. Dora's contacts in Palermo had told her the bag would go through the X-ray detection system without any questions or trouble. She must arrive at the luggage screening at a certain time, look for a certain man, who would give her a certain sign, and join his line. Palermo would be easy, but Rome airport would be more difficult: she must find the right line and time her arrival so she met the bribed man in the last five minutes of his shift.

Noah had listened to these plans in fear and disbelief. The smuggling of Italian art treasures was not unusual, Dora reminded him. Workers at airports were paid handsomely not to notice items of interest. No one would be hurt. They would exchange bags, without seeming to, after moving through the security screening at Rome. Here Dora would buy duty-free items to bulk up her swapped luggage. They would not speak to each other or appear anywhere together. At the other end Dora would take a transit flight to Sapporo. It would still appear, of course, as if she was carrying the Ragusa. She would meet someone there, and would discover to her horror that the bust had gone missing. The bought men at Palermo and Rome would confirm she had carried it, and she would invent a robbery of the robbery somewhere at the Tokyo end. Meanwhile Noah would join a connection to Sydney.

'But won't my hand luggage be scanned in Tokyo?' he had asked.

Yes, Dora conceded, but there would be no suspicion: an Australian with a souvenir, an art object of no interest. Unless someone from Palermo informed on them, he would be passed through without question. In Sydney he would walk from the plane with his bulky bag, and settle back into his old life. After that, two weeks later, he would ring her at her flat.

Noah was initially unconvinced. Surely Vito would still be in danger if she didn't deliver? It was a risk, Dora agreed. But they were already entrapped and Vito had wanted her, urged her, to carry out the plan. He wanted the capo outwitted. He had talked to her of what it meant to outlive most of his family: he wanted to know that if he died there would be some loss to those who killed him. Dora would not speak of the risk to herself. She could handle herself, she said. Her main worry was Antonio Dotti, whom she did not quite trust. She had paid him most of her savings to stay quiet.

Noah could hardly absorb all this information. It was Vito he was thinking of. He realised that Vito possibly considered himself posthumous. His niece would act for him, but he was already in a remote and woeful heaven, already part of an impersonal design larger than himself, just as on the day of the massacre that included his brother's death.

In the plane, Noah felt a similar condition of nonentity. He was caught in some unidentified criminal's plan, even as he was hoping by proxy to subvert it. Noah had not even seen the sculpture, stowed above his head, but knew its form from the sketch in Dora's flat. It was the devotional figure of a Japanese woman, Vincenzo Ragusa's wife, Eleonora. Her kimono had fallen aside so that it revealed her shoulder and breast. It was a rendering of that suspended moment before one kisses the shoulder of a lover. Now she was stowed in the darkness, lying face-down above him, hovering as if for a kiss.

He felt spooked thinking of her there, a guilty, sexual object. A Japanese woman in Italy, longing for her homeland, trapped by love. Or obedience, perhaps, or parental command, or Ragusa's defining power over her life. This was the first time Noah had sincerely imagined the life of the figure whose work and image he had lifted, with some difficulty, into the overhead locker. The lives of artists, the persistence of their artworks in the real world, to be traded, or purloined, or venerated, or destroyed. He said to himself, *Vincenzo Ragusa, Eleonora Ragusa*. Their transnational marriage obligated him in a way he could barely acknowledge.

When Noah considered discovery, trial, ignominy and jail, he was overcome by dread. He could not allow himself to think in this hypothetical way, to move cause and effect forward. So it was a fictitious present tense he inhabited. The throb of the plane, the pitch and roll of its aerodynamics, the undeviating flight path around half of the globe: these were much easier and more impersonal thoughts. He might have cherished this negation of himself if he had not also thought of Dora nearby, of what he felt for her, and of what he would not relinquish. And his children, his adult children, from whom he would withhold this knowledge.

Noah walked up the aisle, between the toilets and back again, just to see her sleeping. She was wearing a small acrylic mask over her eyes. She was dead to the world. He said to himself: *Dora Caselli.*

When they arrived at Narita, Dora didn't look back. He saw her lower her bag from the compartment, balance it on the aisle armrest, then move off, following others, on the left side of the plane.

By the time he entered the walkway, she was already gone. In the crowd of international travellers, in the boom of high airport spaces, bouncing noise and relentless lights, she was nowhere to be seen. Noah knew they were both heading to Terminal Two for their separate onward flights: he might still catch a glimpse of her. He followed the signs and walked quickly. But there was no Dora, anywhere. In the peculiar stress of airport searching, Noah felt the labour of his heavy bag and the burden of his task. He turned left and right. He backtracked and deviated. He scanned again and again, but still he could not see her.

PART FOUR

28

THE VIEW FROM Angela's apartment offered an expanse of grass, across which children and dogs looped to and from each other in asymptotic curves. There was a cycleway at the perimeter and a path beside it, so that cyclists and walkers were perpetually streaming by, and, beyond that, the blue harbour and a smattering of small yachts. In all weathers, it was lively. There was just a glimpse of the ferry dock behind a clump of shrubs and figs. From Angela's window Evie felt she could see further and keener; through the silver light she could almost see the distant faces on the ferries, and the remote movements of families gathering for a picnic.

'It's that boy again,' Evie said. 'The boy who was blown from his bicycle.'

Angela moved to stand by her side. 'He's always there, that kid. Always alone. He must spend the whole weekend on his bike.'

Last time he had seemed in a kind of vaporous time warp, half Evie, half emblem, falling into the wild gusts speeding across from the water. Now he was a lonely child, pedalling stiff-backed, with his hands floating free. Sometimes he grasped the handlebars, but mostly he was making a point of his exceptional balance, riding as if daydreaming, as if his legs belonged to someone else. He may have been riding this way on the day of the wind, tempting the elements, expecting to be blown over.

Nina was standing beside her aquarium, tapping at its glass with her fingernail. Her two goldfish made insolent movements with their yawning mouths, and swam away. She bent down to attract their attention, making nonsense sounds of endearment. There was a plastic figurine of a diver, a minuscule treasure chest, and a pipe producing bubbles. Evie realised that Nina was talking to the diver, not the fish, which like all goldfish looked essentially unreal. Nina reached her giant's arm into the aquarium and lifted the doll-man out, gave him a little kiss, then pushed him back under the water. She had wet her sleeve. She turned around and saw Evie watching, held up her dripping arm, and let out a rascal yell.

'After the implant she'll have more friends,' Angela announced. 'I want her to be out there mucking around with other kids, not talking in her own language to plastic toys.' She gestured with a hand towel, and Nina made a drama of wriggling as her mother tried to dry her. 'Martin thinks I'm exaggerating, of course, but she's becoming too interior, too like a child shut away.'

'She seems happy,' Evie ventured.

'That's just what Martin says. Did he tell you to say that?'

'Of course not. She just seems happy, that's all.'

Angela wanted to insist on her daughter's unhappy isolation. She made a point of saying that it was unnatural for a child to spend so much time in solitary play.

As if to contradict her, Nina seized Evie's hand and dragged her into her bedroom. She threw herself onto the floor before her Barbie doll's house, retrieved from Martin's place before he went away. Evie saw now what he had seen, the arrangement of arches and pavilions that might inspire a story, the way the placement of a figure established human scale. In its simplicity it was not unlike a drawing Noah had once done for them, explaining perspective. Nina began chattering in her private language, apparently to Evie, but also to convey the enchantment of her doll's house. Such a tacky object, Evie thought, to create whole worlds.

Later, they ate sultanas on the beanbag, slumped in cheerful intimacy. They took turns popping them into each other's mouth. Physically, Nina resembled her mother more than Martin, but something indefinable, possibly her curiosity and a larrikin attitude, made her seem fundamentally more Martin's child. Evie was surprised to find herself thinking in this way. Too many holy families in her childhood, too much mystery around the parent who disappeared, too much attention from their father, trying to mother them and be omniscient. She bent over Nina and kissed her, making her lips pudgy and fishlike. Nina screamed in pleasure and with her two hands held Evie's face, distorted her own in a mirror of the fish lips, and returned the kiss.

Over tea Evie described to Angela her job speaking movies, making light of her attraction to Benjamin. She confided that she would ask Martin if they could sell their father's apartment. Yes, it was fine; but no, she wouldn't stay there. Angela told her of property prices and land taxes and the gentrification of the inner suburbs. She knew a great deal on the topic, and spoke

with passion. It was intolerable, Evie thought, this Sydney conversation, so riveted to home ownership and the endless imagining
of a better somewhere. Perhaps it was like this across the globe,
the subsumption of imaginative life into fantasies of ownership.
The dream of the room of one's own as a material asset. She was
wearied by it. They paused to watch Nina dismantle a biscuit and
place its fragments in a circle around her plate.

'You can't live like this forever,' Angela warned. 'No real job,
no real prospects.'

It had come out of nowhere. Evie didn't respond. Prospects.
What were prospects?

When she left, Angela stood by impassively as Nina waved
from the window. Evie waved back. Again, she felt her love fly
out to the little girl, up high, and, yes, happy. Nina jumped on the
spot. Her wave lasted longer than Evie expected. Children inflated
such moments, she thought; they knew their true importance.

When at last Angela drew her away, Evie continued across
the breezy oval, full of the dashing vectors of kids and dogs.
Then she saw the boy again, cruising past on his bicycle. This
time he carried a girl, a few years younger, sitting sidelong on the
crossbar, her skirt tucked at the panties, her pale legs dangling.
They looked remarkably alike. They were brother and sister. So
Angela was wrong: he was not a boy all alone, he was a boy with
a sister.

No real job, no prospects. But the afternoon by the harbour
was magnificently colourful. Another kind of prospect. Evie set
up a list: *azurite, carmine, cerrusite, cinnabar, cobalt, galena,
graphite, gypsum, haematite, indigo, lapis lazuli, limonite,
malachite, Naples yellow, orpiment, realgar, smalt, ultramarine,
umber, vermilion, zincite*...these were the fifteenth-century
pigments her father had taught her. She loved the words and

their associations; she loved the memory of her father speaking of plasticity and luminosity and the mineral constitution of images. His finger pointing to a detail. The way he peered both over and through his spectacles.

What was that moment at the manuscript room of the old British Library? Noah was showing them Byzantine manuscripts, featuring angels. They were remarkably well preserved, the ultramarine and vermilion of their garments, the scrolls of the borders, the elaborate penwork. But the faces of the angels were all jet-black. Noah began his lecture, explaining that in the nineteenth century hydrogen sulphide from gas lamps in the library had reacted with the flesh-tone faces and created lead sulphide, not a pigment at all, but a chemical blackness. Irreversible blackness. Pink angels turned black.

How delighted she was. How entertained. Martin was standing apart, having a bad day. He had his fingers in his ears and was chanting 'rhubarb, rhubarb, rhubarb, rhubarb'. Naughty, Evie thought then, with a degree of self-satisfaction.

Noah was exasperated, but emphatically ignored him. He lifted his daughter closer to the glass case and began explaining the general points of Raman spectroscopy, dating procedures and the detection of forgeries.

'And there,' he would say, 'that is gold leaf. That is lapis lazuli. That is malachite.'

He might have been reciting a poem. Evie peered at small figures, birds, black faces, exotic curly print. Martin continued his derisive and monotonous chant. She hated him then, but she also sensed her father's pride in her interest, and felt his warm whisper on her neck, his arms firm around her waist. In the subdued light of the Manuscript Room, in its fusty sepia hall, she felt his binding touch and committed to memory all that he told her.

It was not too late for a swim. The prospect of ocean. Evie

would take the ferry and bus back to Elizabeth Bay, then catch another bus past skyscrapers to Bondi Beach. She would ride through the sprawl of the city, full of longings and real estate and children and unspoken memories, and throw off her clothes and run headlong into the sea. She would swim far out, out of sight, so that the dark of deep water would slide leviathan-like beneath her. Then she would return to the shallows and splash in spray and dive under as the dumpers came towards her. She would find her other, aquatic life and float outstretched on her back, looking at the sky, listing the poetry of pigments. Drifting, she would imagine her face going black in the sunlight.

29

AT TERMINAL TWO, lugging the heavy Ragusa, Noah found he was sweating and anxious. He had rushed, and not even caught a retreating glimpse. There was a throb at his throat that he knew to be his rash erupting, and he found a seat so that he could rest. He settled the duffle bag between his legs and resisted the urge to check if the sculpture was there, to zip open the bag and examine it. He sat and waited.

He thought of his blood pressure and dicky heart, and imagined that he might collapse and fall fainting in a shaft of light among the rows of navy-blue chairs. Efficient women would run to attend him. A natty man in a cap and black suit would command that his body be lifted and taken away. In the commotion someone kind would collect his bag, notice its weight and discover the stolen sculpture. One of Noah's lovers had once called him a 'catastrophist', always on the lookout for disastrous consequences. He resented the comment at the time, but now it returned to him as a shining insight.

A Japanese woman, dressed in a crimson kimono and employed to promote sake, approached him with a tray of glistening samples. Noah took a tiny cup, thanked the woman, and downed it. The woman bowed, just a bob, and shuffled away to offer her wares to another man sitting nearby. She approached only men. No one refused. In this little airport drama of costume and free drinks, she was a welcome distraction. Noah watched as she went from man to man, bending slightly, speaking in a high pleasant tone. He wondered if Eleonora Ragusa would have moved in this way, in this erect, formal manner, almost cut in half by her obi and hobbling in white socks on her solid wooden platforms. Eleonora Ragusa—Kiyohara Tama—had returned and was serving sake at Narita airport. She had punctured time, risen from the dead, and come to offer him a drink.

It may have been a kind of creeping hysteria, but it was also guilt. Noah knew he must look exceptionally guilty. Each time anyone in uniform walked past, even a pilot, he broke out in another sweat and didn't know where to look. Dora, who seemed so resolute and courageous, would be truly ashamed of him. Noah hoped for more sake and considered his wretched condition.

He became aware, all of a sudden, of familiar accents circulating around him. The flight to Sydney: Australians. Soon he would be disguised in the passenger mass; he would enter the temporary community of the plane, all with their overweight hand luggage and loud end-of-holiday voices, all with their merry air of innocents abroad. Just as he had subsided into dull suspension on the flight from Rome, he could do so again, be blank again in the context of a more generalised entrapment. He was missing Dora, sensing her proximity but tormented by her invisibility. Soon they would fly in opposite directions, shooting in a V up into the blameless sky.

Watching the woman in the kimono walk back towards him, her tray now empty, Noah was revisited by an old regret: that he had plied Martin with sherry after Katherine died. Martin, his child-senses frayed by grief, had been unable to sleep, was indeed almost crazy with sleeplessness. Noah began dosing him each evening, watching as the boy became slurry and woozy, his head tilting to the pillow, his eyes drunkenly closing, his breath sounding deep and low, like the suck of the sea. His son had experienced what he now thought of as a juvenile breakdown, but instead of seeking a doctor or psychological help, he had given him booze. In his own defence, had he been asked, Noah would say that he was a mess himself, that he too had trouble sleeping and that alcohol had helped. But it was a disastrous decision, unforgivable. Later, Martin developed chemical and social habits. He resorted to stupefaction when miserable or distressed. For a while he blotted himself with heroin, and then recovered in a clinic. He was a brilliant artist but essentially unstable. It was no wonder his marriage to Angela had failed.

Noah did a calculation: it was 8.54 a.m. in Tokyo, so it was 1.54 a.m. in Rome. It was earlier in Rome, and in his tired body. He had sped through longitudes and retrogrades of motion, he had denied prograde and rotational speed. Air travel: it was outrageous, what people did to their bodies, flinging through space. Noah felt as if he was composed of neon light, a glaring brittle thing, lightly flickering, charged up and gaseous. He might shatter if tapped. He felt manufactured, inhuman. Soon he would enter the tunnel to another long flight, and confuse his body further. Soon he would be airborne and insensible, the bust of

Eleonora resting above him again, his various guilts and shames stored in a compartment while he tried again to sleep. Dora would be far away.

The Japanese woman bearing sake reappeared, her tray replenished. Lady Bountiful. Although she recognised Noah, she approached him again, and offered him another drink. Noah took two. She smiled indulgently, with no hesitation or censure. So Noah sat with a small plastic cup in each hand, like a greedy child, then tipped each into his stinging throat in a single gulp. The gasses inside him fizzed. The woman continued her task, administering to barely awake men in transit. She moved with ceremonial slowness, disguising commerce as ritual.

When she turned away, there was something in the shape of her kimono, seen from behind, that reminded Noah of Katherine in her dressing-gown, pregnant with Evie. It was the strangest connection. He stared at the Japanese woman, grasping the way images slide into and onto each other, the unpredictable metonymies of seeing, the unexpected association. When Katherine had appeared with her new dressing-gown, lapis blue, bought to celebrate her second pregnancy, he had seen her immediately as Piero's pregnant Madonna, the *Madonna del Parto*, in which Mary stands with her gown slightly agape over her swelling belly. One hand rests at the centre, protectively cupping her mystery, the other is on her hip. Noah believed it to be one of the most unusual Madonnas ever painted. Half-sized angels stand either side of her, holding back curtains: *see here, a miraculous pregnancy*, they seem to declare.

Katherine had laughed when he told her. In good humour she derided his arty and sentimental comparisons. But it remained, this vision, this lyrical amazement. He'd stared at her, there, standing in the kitchen, holding a mug of tea in each hand, and was overcome by a feeling he imagined to be both his alone and experienced by men everywhere through countless generations. He dared not describe it to her, this quiver of knowing, or to name it as anything more than a common paternal pride. Still he stared at her, comely, even at breakfast, and ageless in what she meant to him.

The Japanese woman turned and destroyed the shape of the long-dead Katherine. What state was he in, visited by such resemblances, stretched to breaking with desire for Dora Caselli? All that Noah felt was in a ghastly welter. He was demoralised by air travel. Thirsty and lost. If he had seen himself in a mirror, he would have wondered who that old man was, carrying luggage too heavy, bent into the wrong time zone. He stood and fumbled to locate his boarding pass and passport.

At the scanner Noah's bag was hauled aside and placed on a metal trolley. He was asked to unpack his carry-on luggage and display his possessions. Trembling, Noah unwrapped Eleonora Ragusa. It was the first time he had seen her. The sketch was slight by comparison; this face carried especial presence. Noah stared. He was aware that his breath smelled of sake and he must look guilty as hell. His hands flapped like small wings.

The airport official, dapper and stern, rapped at the sculpture, turned it over, and held it up before him, as if it were the severed head of John the Baptist. 'Beautiful,' he said in English. 'She is very beautiful.'

The man was a connoisseur. He asked Noah to repack his bag, and sent him through to his flight. There were no questions, there was no catastrophe, there was no criminal identification. All Noah assumed about to happen had fallen away. 'Yes,' he affirmed. 'Yes, she is very beautiful.'

On the plane, his body shaking, Noah closed his eyes. He must still himself and attempt to regain control. The time at

Narita had been a calling up of phantoms. Katherine in her pregnancy. Martin bereaved, and distressed. He saw again the tousled head of his drunken boy, the way he seemed to drown into sleep. He saw the child-frown on his brow, his small face pinched and suffering. He saw him becoming floaty with alcohol, first quiet, then slowly sinking, his face pacified and finally unreachable.

30

PALERMO WAS ALSO, of course, a city of supermarkets and stadia and multiplexes and chain clothing stores; those places like everywhere else, in the vortex of a blended modernity. Capital. Chrome. A car showroom of new Fiats. The glassy façade of a building committed to the administration of tax. On the outskirts were the high-rises that surrounded most Italian cities, painted pale yellow as if to recall a noble era of architecture. Clunky air conditioners stuck to their sides like ticks. They were of the sixties or seventies, and already crumbling.

It was the other Palermo that Martin inhabited. The old centre of wreckage, of irremissible melancholy. He loved the haywire of the graffiti, the rickety scaffolding, the grimy passages and laneways. He loved 'dilapidation'. The occasional bag of cement, spilt on a building site, did not change Martin's sense that enticing ruin persisted. *Le chiese sconsacrate* still moved his irreligious heart; each time he walked past the 'Church of the Three Kings of the Orient' and saw its concreted windows, he longed for the building to be opened up and filled with people. When a carthorse appeared in the lethal traffic, a beast with bulging eyes, terrified, its neck a clench of swollen veins, he felt it was the past intercepting and becoming visible.

A foreigner was allowed such misconstruals, he told himself. He could never know enough of the history, or what this place really meant. Unlike Evie, who knew so many things, he had only a repertoire of consoling images; he saw only formal compositions and relations of colour and space. He saw the world thinned out, and made more easy. Riding on the bus one night, returning from an excursion to Bagheria, he was sitting in streetlight splash, watching headlights stream in tapers of rain, and saw how Palermo might be a film of surfaces, revealing nothing.

Frank Malone made Martin think in this way. Apart from the food and wine, Frank told him, Palermo was a big disappointment. He had expected something more like Rome, or maybe Bologna. Martin could not resist a private sniff of contempt. They walked together in the drizzle towards the Fontana Pretoria— Martin had agreed to show him the sights—and talk turned to Noah, and what Frank insisted on calling 'the case'.

'Seems Noah left Palermo a day after this woman, this Dora Casetti.'

'Dora Caselli.'

'Her. He followed her to Tokyo. Same flight, actually.'

'My father has never been to Tokyo.'

'Alitalia says different.'

'Ask Antonio Dotti. He can clarify.'

'Antonio Dotti is uncontactable. The university said he's gone on leave. No one knows where.'

'Ask Dora.'

'She refuses to speak to me. I don't have any official power to compel her and the local cops are no help at all. They interviewed her early on. Got nothing at all. I'm fucked. Up shit creek.'

He looked grim again. Martin was zoning out. He was recalling 'pentimento', a word Noah had taught him. He was thinking *abbracci, baci*. His mind stuttered and echoed. He was wondering how Frank Malone managed to swing a trip to Palermo on so flimsy a pretext.

They were skirting Piazza Bologni, walking behind a truck full of concrete and rubble, when Martin looked up and saw an ornate sign carved in marble, set high on a building. He stopped and silently translated.

'What?' asked Malone.

'It says Garibaldi slept in this house for two hours in May, in the year 1860.'

'Garibaldi?'

'Unification.'

'Right.' There was a pause. 'You think I don't know who Garibaldi was?'

Frank Malone sounded hurt. His case was non-existent; there was no crime, no reason for being in Palermo. Martin almost pitied him. He located his camera and took a photograph. Evie would like this one. Only two hours. There was something touching about this verification of weariness, the humble detail of human frailty and time out of time.

'Two hours,' Malone said, addressing nobody. 'So what's the big deal?'

How long could he stand Frank Malone's company? They could have another meal, he thought, a lunch after sightseeing, but then he wanted to draw. He wanted to be alone. His sketchbooks and camera chips were rapidly filling; he had a firm purpose now, unconnected to Noah. He figured two more weeks, three max, and he would head back to Sydney. He was missing Nina. She kept asking by sign when he would return and he wanted to give her a date she could mark on the calendar. Children need this limit, he thought, and perhaps he did too, this limit to stray thinking and dissociated roaming. And he was missing Evie. Now they were in contact again, his life seemed denser somehow; his memories were more accessible, his own sense of self bound with bright threads to her unusual authority. He was just glimpsing her now, as an adult. How many years does it take before siblings know each other? Perhaps—he hardly dared think it—they could not approach each other imaginatively while Noah was alive.

Frank Malone wore a cap, and now, though the air was still damp and overcast, he added sunglasses. A disguise—Frank Malone was adopting a disguise. Frank had donned the look of a tourist and would become another kind of target. He had acquired a sheepish hunch and an anti-policeman manner. At the Fontana Pretoria they were the only tourists. One or two drifting figures crossed the square, but there were no other visitors who came to look at the fenced-off fountain. It was a drenched, sticky monument, grey in the poor light and coated with faded glory. A black dog, which may have been asleep or dead, lay still on the wet flagstones, curled at the foot of the fountain.

Frank looked confused. Faced with fifty nude sculptures, all posing and disporting in a marble circle, he didn't know where to look. 'Bit over the top, isn't it?' he whispered.

'They call this the fountain of shame,' Martin replied. 'Too many *ignudi*, too many naked bodies. High renaissance, mid sixteenth-century. Don't ask me how I know.'

Noah again: Noah had taught him and Evie the art-historical markers. He could recognise Carrara marble at fifty paces. There were fantastical figures, monsters, nymphs, a brawny Dionysus, both too masculine and too fat, and one or two attractive women, demurely looking away. Frank, though embarrassed, wanted a photograph of himself standing in front of the fountain.

'This one,' he said.

From the circus of virile monstrosities he had singled out the sculpture of a woman who appeared reserved in this flagrant company. Martin had not noticed her before: she touched her own naked breast and turned her small head as if blushing and seeking her privacy. He guessed Frank was secretly aroused, like a teenager. The policeman removed his dark glasses and cap, stood near the woman and smiled at the camera.

In the viewfinder Martin saw Tommaso Salvo. He was lingering in the corner of the square, standing near the side of the Church of St Catherine. He was looking in their direction, but not approaching. Martin waved. Tommaso gave an anxious, guilty look and slid away. The moment left him with the strong impression that Tommaso had been following them. Martin thought of mentioning this matter to Frank, but instead took another photograph, and dismissed the idea. Frank seemed less adult and more a gawky adolescent, tragic with insecurity and wishing to impress, but pleased, if only briefly, to be in Italy and now to have a snapshot to prove it.

They walked twice around the fountain. As the rain began again, Martin suggested they have an early lunch, claiming he had 'matters to attend to' in the afternoon. It had been a dull excursion. The black dog, a pool of shadow, rose up when the rain began and moved with arthritic stiffness towards a more sheltered spot. Martin felt such relief: this was what had distracted him. He did not want a dead dog in the photograph or at the periphery of his vision. The dog moved as if puzzled, wavering, to stop beneath an awning, and rested by tipping over as his legs collapsed beneath him.

At lunch the talk was desultory and mostly of Sydney. Football. Rugby. Real estate. They both ate too much. The antipasti, the *primi*, the *secondi*, then the *dolci*: both were eating as if food was filling something missing. Frank tilted the wine bottle towards him to try to decipher the label. He sighed, none the wiser. Martin felt he would die of boredom. Maybe it was the wine: he suddenly laughed for no reason. Martin laughed for no reason and thought of Noah.

31

THERE WAS A timelessness to Skype that Evie found compelling. She heard Martin's ring and was home to receive his call. At once, forward motion ceased and they were both in their screens, in the lucid waft of a satellite drift. She imagined beams diving through space, connecting them in the shape of a colossal A. Martin sat back, so that his face was undistorted; Evie was loose-limbed and relaxed after her zesty swim.

'Evie, I'd like you to meet my good friend Veeramani,' Martin said.

She saw another face enter the screen as Martin tilted backwards. The lustre of warm eyes, and a discreet smile.

'Pleased to meet you, Veeramani.'

'Miss Evie. Your brother, he is an outstanding artist. Truly topnotch.'

'I did a portrait,' Martin explained, 'of his delightful children.'

Veeramani wagged his head. 'And what a portrait. Topnotch. It is an honour to meet you, Miss Evie.'

And then he disappeared. Martin tipped forward. Evie saw that he was jammed in a small, dim booth. There might be dangling wires and sizzling electricity. She would suggest again that he move to a hotel with wi-fi.

'You okay?'

'I've booked the flight home. It's made a difference, I think. Now I can settle better into work. And Nina will be pleased. The seventeenth, two weeks.'

'I saw Nina today. We ate sultanas and played with her doll's house.'

'Yeah, the Barbie house.' Martin was inscrutable. She waited. 'I saw the detective again yesterday,' he announced.

This was why he had called her. He had sent an email a few days ago about Malone turning up in Palermo. Evie assumed the detective had found something and Martin was stalling before a disclosure. It would be something intolerable, she feared, a discovery that would make her want to bury her face in her hands.

'So?'

'So: there's nothing to report. The guy's a wanker. He's discovered nothing at all. It's a relief, Evie. We can stop thinking about this stuff.'

This stuff. Evie couldn't bear it when he talked in this way, flip, unconcerned, reducing the world and its moral conundrums to a kind of cheeky vocabulary. It was heartless, immature. She'd felt from the beginning there might be a subtler story somewhere, not in the protocols of detection, not in a *giallo* or a ripping yarn, but in some more intricate version of her father's time in Italy, and this woman, Dora Caselli, and the missing sculpture. Evie wondered what they would talk about, now that 'stuff' was unimportant, now that he had annoyed her. She felt for the first time that she should have followed her brother to Italy, stood by his side and gripped his hand.

'I've just emailed you an intriguing photo of a plaque,' Martin said. 'It marks a house where Garibaldi slept for two hours in 1860.'

This sober pronouncement was oddly endearing. Martin wanted to hear her voice, to assert their connection in the context of this quest she now considered capricious.

'Two hours,' he prompted.

Evie sensed that her brother wanted to listen, but not to talk. She couldn't understand why he was interested in the Garibaldi plaque; he may have been thinking about timescales, or documenting signs in the city, or recording the nationalist whimsy of such a dedication, minor but for the name.

'Is sleep in or out of time?' Martin asked, prompting her again. He might have been imploring.

Evie was surprised by his question. It was a thoughtful question. Her brother was becoming a philosopher. She looked at him, his head backlit, his face in shadow, as though inside a monk's cowl. She considered his independent artistry and his adoration of his daughter, and his mad-crazy wish to follow his father, and conceded that she must learn to take him more seriously. There was a space opening here, in the streamer between time zones, in which they could meet.

'Let me think about this. It's an excellent question. My first response would be that there is no time without consciousness.'

Martin waited for more. 'Another thing.'

'Yes?'

'Do you remember *abbracci, baci*?'

It was like a wind rushing at her, almost knocking her over.

237

'Of course. Our song. Whatever made you think of that?'

'I saw it printed on a girl's hoodie, as a kind of glittery decoration. I'd forgotten, Evie. I'd completely forgotten about our song until I saw it walking towards me.'

It was not nostalgia or sentimentality, but a mystified recognition that what she'd thought of as ephemeral culture, children's culture, was deeply implanted. Evie considered the plaything phrase, and the hold it had over them. She remembered sprawling on the back seat with Martin as Noah drove through cypress-shaded lanes between small Umbrian towns—his grey head steady, his hands fixed on the wheel, the passenger space beside him poignantly vacant. She remembered Noah turning in exasperation to demand peace and quiet. They would go silent for a while, then start their irritant song once again. It was the power of children, to annoy, and to have more stamina for repetition. When at last they tired of their chanting, they would squabble until bored, then one or the other would climb into the seat beside their father. He would test their Italian by reciting improbable details from the life of one of the saints.

Evie said, 'Recently I thought again about those Piero portraits, the Duke and Duchess of Urbino. Do you remember how obsessed you were by the duke's sword damage, the missing eye you couldn't see, and the bit carved from the bridge of his nose? Noah told you their story. You wanted the portrait painted from the other side, the blinded side.'

Martin didn't respond. Now Evie waited. She realised she'd indirectly spoken to her brother of Benjamin, including him in their circle of seeing.

'Macabre little bugger, wasn't I?'

He remembered; she was sure. They'd been in the Uffizi with Noah, triangulated with the Duke and Duchess portraits before them. This capacity to make images live was the circuit their father had created. Now they were the effects and after-effects of his death.

Evie was startled by a splash sound from the pool, then the muted watery rhythm of regular strokes. Not a kid this time, smashing at the surface, but someone simply taking an evening swim. The sound of moving water ended their conversation. It washed their words away; it was like the breaking of a spell.

32

DILATION, THAT WAS it; Martin felt the dilation of time. Evie would be settling down for the night in Sydney: across the planet he pictured her in their father's apartment, rising from a chair, moving towards the bedroom on bare feet with an air of self-possession. She would have a book with her; she would switch on a lamp; she would lean against the veneer headboard of Noah's bed and open the book to her saved place. A list: she was possibly constructing a list. Martin still envied her canny poise, the way she made her own knowledge, sagely and systematically, always locating a hidden order. Their disorderly lives had needed this incongruity—her lists and his images, her calm, withholding quiet and his noisier rebellion. He saw it now, her aisles of mysterious space, mapped alphabetically step by step, while his gestures were rooms, broad openings on either side. Still, they fitted together; still, they were complements.

Abstract thinking fell away; her location remained. Night. Elizabeth Bay. The everlasting harbour of Sydney. Beyond the window lay tangled undergrowth and a flaunting of tropical flowers, colourless in the night. Martin envisioned the swimming pool, which lately had appeared in his dreams—undulating as if ocean, scrolled with small waves, blue with impossible depth.

He recoiled from seeking a further connection. In Palermo, at daytime, in an earlier phase of the extended day, Veeramani had placed a cup of tea by his side. Martin nodded his thanks and pretended to concern himself with his emails. Although he'd managed to tell Evie about *abbracci, baci*—he heard her surprise and knew he'd recovered something precious—he was still overcome by a feeling of failed communication. This had been his opportunity to speak of the accident, of the man in the three-wheeler van who went under the truck. This, in truth, was why he had Skyped, but then, like a fool, he couldn't say anything. Some day in the future, in Sydney, he would tell Evie of the moment a man's history shut down before him, and of the honking cars and the savage rent they made in the wet air, and of how, though anonymous, it had terribly affected him. It was a magnification of the grief he felt for Noah; it summoned a sense of panic and subjection to fate. Though remote, the man in the accident was a bond to overwhelming feeling, a resumption or culmination of the sight of his father's body.

Martin distrusted exaggerated responses. He was unwilling to concede the drama of the world, and how full it was of unwarranted tragedy. He still needed to believe that one chose what one saw.

Garibaldi asleep. Noah would have liked that one. The Duke of Urbino, with his funny red hat. Evie reminded him that the duke's face had been slashed with a sword, that Piero had hidden the hurt and disfigurement. Martin remembered Noah there, at the Uffizi, lecturing them on the twin paintings. Dates, context, the fact that the wife's face was so pale because her portrait was posthumous. Noah's painterly topic that day was concealment. He was telling his children that concealment was also a function of art.

33

IT WAS TIME, Evie thought, to turn on the lights. She closed her laptop and illuminated Noah's flat. The room might still have contained him, she was so little in evidence. Apart from her beach towel flung across an armchair, her bag and sunglasses resting on the hallstand, the place was still his, with his relics and his various leavings intact. Martin had promised her that if she found it too hard they would clear the place together when he returned; but now it looked like an apartment frozen in time, as if nothing would budge what Noah had placed there.

Other than his library and his icons, he had few valuable possessions. He had a weakness for Indian cushions, covered in fraying embroidery and small cracked mirrors, and, in her reckoning with the discomfort of material inheritance, Evie thought that she might claim these for herself. They were modest and homely. They all seemed to be of some shade of oriental scarlet—cinnabar, perhaps—as was an ornately patterned rug, which he'd bought in Turkey. These were concessions to the hippie days Noah had shared with her mother, the time during which, family lore had it, they were happy and harmonious.

Evie knew that she resembled her mother. Noah had always said it, and so did her grandparents in Adelaide. She remembered them staring at her with a wistful sorrow, insisting she was a copy of someone she didn't know. Here, in her father's house, she was thinking again of her mother, Katherine.

There was something in the sound coming from the swimming pool that troubled her, so that, standing at the window, she shivered in the warm night. Having just lit the apartment, Evie now turned off the light. Darkness fell around her shoulders and into the room. She listened to the swimmer and stood in vague meditation. Reflections played on the wall opposite, streaming in like phosphorescence. Light sparked and swung. There were odd astral spots and a trail of fluctuating ripples.

In the place of her father, Evie slept deep and long. She relinquished time. All that the day had brought with it, even her afternoon swim in the mighty Pacific Ocean, fell away into a private floating darkness. No dreams, or none that she would remember. No disturbance. If there was someone still in the swimming pool, she did not hear him or her. If there was a tragedy in the harbour or a celebration next door, she was unaware. And when the day dawned, Evie knew it would be dark in Palermo, and rose in the morning wishing her distant brother a silent, loyal goodnight.

As she stood in her nightie at the gas ring, making coffee with her father's pot, pouring it into his cup, stirring it with his spoon, sitting down in his favourite comfortable chair, she was mysteriously calm. She noted the diagonal light of the new day. There was the sound of a cat mewing at the door. Evie put her coffee aside and admitted Strozzi. His fur was warm from sun, and he brought with him a benign animal silence. Evie stroked his cheek, rubbed under his chin, and fed him a can of tuna. His body rolled at her touch. No sign of Yours Truly.

'This is the first day,' Evie said to Benjamin, 'that I have felt lighter, and less burdened. I think it was the conversation last night, with my brother, Martin. Memories we shared, small things recalled. It began badly, with me annoyed and upset—no real communication—but in the end there was an ease I cannot really understand.' She was already thinking: this ease cannot last. This was some kind of fake relief, like a childhood song. *Abbracci, baci.*

They were sitting together in a park under the white radiance of a flawless day. Rocky was frolicking before them, mad with his liberty. He ran back and forth, as labradors do, greeting them, then hurling himself away, returning and leaving, returning and leaving. Evie knew that in speaking this way, so personally and so far from her habitual reticence, she was also exhibiting her feelings for Benjamin. But he could not see how she stared at him; she told herself, protectively, that he could not know what she truly felt.

Rocky launched in a friendly welcome towards an approaching jogger and caused him to lose the rhythm of his stride. The jogger swivelled and half-stumbled and shouted angrily at them to leash their dog.

'Sorry, mate,' Benjamin said, and called to Rocky, who obediently gave up his freedom. So they set off for home, Evie's arm linked in Benjamin's, the dog straining before them and sniffing at the earth as they went. Dog-spirit conferred a certain light-heartedness. How she and Martin had longed for a pet when they were children, a Strozzi, suave and silent, or a barely controllable chaos, like Rocky.

As they passed under the ultramarine shade of Moreton Bay figs, Benjamin said he knew they had left the sunlight. The loss of sun on his skin, and a shift in the quality of darkness: both told him so. He was host to an other world, Evie thought. The dimensions of things must be inconstant; objects might strike out at him, or retreat, or exist as points of intensity in a field of reaching and touching. Everything was an invisible betokening, the foundation of apprehensions possible, not given. She realised she was idealising a deprivation. But it was admiration she felt, and her admiration was close to love.

When they walked up the hill towards his home, their bodies moved in step. Linking his arm had allowed her to place her body near his so that their hips rubbed together, and they felt each other's warmth. The confident swing of his stride, the new intimacy of a walk. The triangle in which his arm contained hers was both cordial and suggestive. And during the short climb they seemed to come to an agreement. When they reached the front door, Benjamin asked, 'So, will you stay?' Evie, her mouth papery, her skin alive, replied yes; yes, of course she would stay. They shut the dog in the back courtyard with a huge feed, so that they could have their peace.

Evie undressed Benjamin first. He stood still as she kissed at his throat just inside his collar, then unbuttoned his shirt. There was a formal, slowing ease, pulling the shirt away, resting her hot face against his exposed neck, tasting its salt. She felt without looking for his belt and zip and undid his trousers; then she bent and he helped her by kicking them away. He removed his own underpants, without haste, almost coyly. To her shame, she was reminded of another man. Then he said, 'Close your eyes,' but she did not, and she could not; she continued looking.

Evie was concentrated as Benjamin reached to locate and open her zip. She felt her dress gape behind her and the slide of fabric as he pulled it down over her breasts and hips. She stepped out of her dress and undid her own bra while he knelt to remove her panties, pushing his face there as he did, hungry for her and ready, his hand coming to rest between her legs. They fell together onto the bed with an immense feeling of relief. He breathed into her mouth. She breathed into his mouth. He put his thumb to her lips: *no words.* It was the leaving of a print; now he was entirely specific. This was the first time Benjamin had touched her face. But she saw him strain, remote, his own face far away. He closed his blind eyes as he felt his way into her.

Afterwards, placid, neither said very much. Evie rose and moved securely naked around his house, poured them both a cold drink, then returned to the bed. They sat propped there in silence, feeling the bedroom become still, after they had filled it with waves and agitation. So much beyond the room now seemed unconnected. Evie leaned to kiss him and he took her hand and sucked at her knuckles. Yes, she had to go. Yes, she would ring.

A storm was moving in. When she left the house, softly closing the door behind her, she peered at the sky and saw above her the change in the weather. Thunderheads were sweeping from the east, across the ocean. The sky was flaring with antique heraldic colours, gules and purpure, a touch of azure, increasing the impression of emotional drama. Evie left him before dinner, needing to recover her careless senses, needing to distinguish herself from this couple they had suddenly become. She was exhilarated, but also a little afraid; composed and still ardently discomposed. Habitually diffident, she was acting like a man, she reflected, leaving like this, when she should have stayed longer to talk.

And now there would be a storm and she decided she would walk in the rain. Now she would think of him, but try not to need him. There was some property of rain, all dispersal and inclusion, that it seemed proper to enter, to show her immersion in him. She wrapped herself in the rainfall and stepped forward, looking at everything.

34

THE PLAN WAS that they would catch the bus together to Monte Pellegrino late-morning, so that Maria would be in time for midday mass at the Santa Rosalia church. They would catch bus 812 from Piazza Sturzo. It was decided Maria would return on the bus after mass, but that Martin would look around and walk down the mountain back into the city. He packed his sketchpad and camera in his small backpack, and slid the silver ears, still wrapped in their white tissue paper, into a pocket at the side. He had begun the morning feeling doom-laden, thinking that he would tell Evie about the man in the accident, but after their formless talk he felt an unexpected sense of release. It was the joint recollection of *abbracci, baci*: singing in the back seat, flicking cherry stones at each other, speaking in kiddie Italian, looking goggle-eyed in the same direction.

It was a sunny day. Maria decided this was the day she would talk to Martin. She commented that the fine weather was a sign, that Santa Rosalia would welcome his plea on behalf of his daughter. She was dressed as usual in widow's black, but had donned an almost girlish scarf of peach-coloured flowers, and carried a handbag of red patent leather he'd not seen before. He was moved when she took his arm, so that they stepped out together, looking like mother and son, to walk to the bus stop.

Maria stopped first at the door opposite, knocked, and handed the madam of the establishment a jar of preserved cumquats from her bag. They exchanged friendly talk and Martin guessed they were old friends. He heard giggles from inside, saw a low- wattage bulb and the strands of a multicoloured plastic curtain. A collapsible card table, covered in olive-green baize, stood by the doorway. He had been curious about the brothel interior, but the glimpse was distinctly un-erotic and plain. This too, this glimpse, was a kind of release, the sudden disintegration of a vexatious desire.

They sat on the jolting bus and wound together up the mountain. Shafts of sunlight through the trees striped and decorated the road. So many fuses upwards to the shine falling down on them. No rain, Martin thought, ah, no rain. They passed rocky outcrops, fir trees and giant thorny cactus. A gravel walking path crossed and recrossed the road as they ascended. Behind them Palermo shrunk to a staid panorama, distant and quiet.

Maria was in an expansive mood after her weeks of silence. She spoke of how she had placed a silver image of her womb before the shrine of Santa Rosalia, and been given Tommaso. She had tried again and again after that, but a son was such a blessing, and the saint had so many prayers to answer that she did not see fit to give Maria another child. She had left six silver wombs, she said, and then her husband had died, and she knew she must give all her love to one child. Tommaso's existence had ensured her faith; the five failures were forgotten.

For weeks, Maria had fed Martin and left fresh sheets and towels, she had cleaned his room when he was out, taken away rubbish and bottles, and left behind a sprig of flowers in a small jar, but had not thought him worth talking to. Now, without hesitation, she spoke of her womb. Now her scrupulous silence fell away and she spoke as though he were another older woman, an Italian and a peer, to whom she was summing up her life.

They didn't look at each other. Both fixed on the road ahead, but in the flash of lights and the rocking ascent, in the midst of the noise and the chatter of a bus full of people, they were perfect companions.

The bus stopped near an ugly car park flanked by souvenir stalls. Most sold rosaries, postcards and plastic statues of Rosalia. There were also lurid T-shirts fashioned on the *Godfather* theme, with Marlon Brando silk-screened into a surly death's head, all eye-pit and shadow and distinctive skull. There were few tourists about—still a little early in the season—and everyone from the bus headed up the stone steps towards the church. Maria again linked arms with Martin. He supported her as she struggled uphill, feeling the weight of her physical bulk and presence. Whether from devotion to duty, or a sudden trust, Maria allowed this foreigner to bolster her staggering self. He loved her motherly presumption, and the display of her faith in him.

At the top they halted. The church façade was built into the craggy mountain; it appeared as a mistake in space itself, the building entering the mountain, the form retracted and inserted where there should have been rock. It was the sort of mistake, Martin thought, that one sees in dreams, where exteriors and interiors never seem to match. It was anti-perspectival, as if folded backwards. He wondered for a moment if his father had seen it, had stood here, as he did, bemused by the angles.

Maria became fatigued by the climb up the steps. She leaned on Martin, rested a little, and grumbled in dialect about her aching knees. 'O Gesù biniditto!'

Then they walked across flagstones to the entrance and into the church. She said, 'Inside the grotto the water is holy. If it drips upon you, you are blessed.'

Martin smiled at her. He knew this was her version of a benediction; he could not now reveal himself as a godless non-believer, empty, modern, post-industrially free. He saw how happy she was being brought to this place. He saw that she was grateful for his help up the steps and his company on the bus. She squeezed his hand and murmured to herself.

When they moved inside, Maria became silent. She seemed to forget him. She crossed herself, gave a pert curtsy, and walked slowly through the bright antechamber towards the strange light within the grotto. The antechamber was unusually well lit, and the welcoming saint unusually robust. Accustomed to pale Madonnas of powdery substance, dressed in a flaking and fluted blue, Martin was surprised at the statue of Santa Rosalia, more like a store mannequin or a thirties film star. She was varnished and made up, her marcelled hair smooth beneath a garland of roses and a circlet of stars. She wore a long black robe with a rope at the waist, like that of a friar, and stood with her right arm upraised, holding a cross. Her left hand held a large ivory skull, resting on a Bible.

On a side wall hung rows of silver tokens, the votive offerings of body parts. There were hundreds on display, ordered in categories—rows of breasts, eyes, legs, kidneys, innards uncovered, hearts aflame, lungs rendered in a bloom, like floral arrangements. And yes, there were the wombs, lined like small urns sprouting twin fallopian tulips. They all glinted with the promissory hope they contained. It was easy to be entranced by their aesthetic appeal: stylisation, replication, miniaturisation; the solemn artifice of flesh and its wished-for redemption.

Martin looked around to see where he should place the votive for Nina's ears, and saw a small pile of offerings stacked in a corner before a smaller statue of Rosalia. It was a jumble of notes, baby clothes, money and bunches of flowers. He extracted the ears from his backpack, unwrapped them and placed them on the pile. He felt nothing. No mystic quiver, no visitation. If anything, there was a sense that he had mislaid something. He told himself there was no hypocrisy in his act, only an artful gesture for his beloved daughter. For Maria, in fact; it was also for Maria.

Martin looked around him. People were entering the grotto church for mass. No one saw him lean forward and read the notes, one requesting aid for a palsied child, another asking, in almost sacrilegious terms, for the speedy return of an unfaithful lover. Martin wished them well. There were so few places these days, apart from Skype or talkback radio, where one could make such an appeal, where one could spill the heart and teleport words in desperate communication.

Above the pile of supplicant objects he noticed a marble sign, not unlike the one that proclaimed Garibaldi's sleep. This one said that Volfango Goethe had visited this church, in 1787. *Volfango*—a German remade as an Italian. *Martino*: his own Romantic possibility.

Martin walked under the ironwork archway, from one shaded space to another. The church itself was a dank hollow rock. Water dripped from its ceiling into a system of zinc gutters, so that no holy fluid, but for an occasional drop, would be lost. There was another Rosalia at the back of the church, bathed in a blue light Martin associated with swimming pools, a liquid aquamarine shot through with fluorescence. Overhead it was mostly dark, with small spotlights set high in rocky nooks here and there, lighting a figurine or a wooden crucifix.

The congregation was small but filled the church. Martin could see Maria's head towards the middle, and he heard the priest intoning the service in Latin. His voice swung in the bell of the cave, more impressive in containment. He was visible only as a far silhouette. Martin waited in the shadows until the service was over, so that he could bid farewell to Maria before she boarded the bus back to the city.

When the believers streamed out, he had to tap her on the arm to draw her attention. She was distracted, as if united with spirits in a private delirium. She started at his touch. 'The ears,' she said. 'Did you leave them? Did you pray?'

'Yes, of course. Thank you, Maria, *cara Maria*.' One truth and one lie.

She looked pleased with herself, as if the accomplishment was hers. Martin took her by the elbow for the laborious walk back down the steps to the bus stop. Again she leaned on him; again he was moved to be at her service. At their farewell she reached up, and held his face. She pulled his head towards her and with a popping sound kissed him on both cheeks.

The air was cold on the mountain but the sun was now dazzling. There were no clouds and there was no hint of rain. Martin looked for a sign to the walking path down to the city and when he found it felt a kind of elation. He avoided the tourist stalls and plunged straight into the forest, passing through its unusual mixture of firs and cactuses, feeling the variegated shifts of light and shade, glad of his joggers and their deep clinging tread.

It was a steep path. For the feast of Santa Rosalia pilgrims climbed this path on their knees, testing their faith with their bodies in a gruelling display. From time to time the distant city came into view; Martin wondered how high he was, to see Palermo flattened like this. No peaks and troughs, no brainwaved jerkiness. He thought to himself: no panorama is melancholy.

Martin was perhaps only a fifth of the way down Monte Pellegrino when he realised that he was being followed. He stood his ground and turned around. Two men stopped, saw that he saw them, then continued on.

'*Australiano?*' one asked. He sounded friendly; it was a greeting. He threw a cigarette at his feet, and crushed it.

'*Sì, australiano.*' How could they know?

There was some brusque Sicilian speech; they were demanding something. Martin heard the word 'Ragusa' and knew at once that he was imperilled. 'Where?' he heard. Something in their confidence alarmed him: there was a snarling now, and a mocking, and a taut assumption of power. That they were standing above him seemed to assure them, and to require Martin to cringe.

There was a moment when they all simply looked at each other, estimating in tense silence what might happen next. They had the look of farmers, hard men, workers of the land. They were his age, he thought, but with more difficult lives. Both wore caps. Their clothes were cheap.

One of them flung himself forwards so that he almost slipped on the rocky path. Martin saw his boots skid, raising dust, before he felt the attack. It was impossible to deflect what instantly followed. The smaller of the two men lunged and swung fast with a blow to Martin's throat. He felt a shatter there, a terrible hurt, as if his windpipe had exploded. He reeled back, gasping, imagining this was some kind of mistake, that even as he fell, and saw the trees tip backwards, the men might move away and let him be. But the second man was upon him, kicking at his ribs. Martin tried uselessly to grab at the boot as it came at him; he felt the leather, thought he had it, but as it slipped from his grasp he realised that his right hand had been broken. The burn was awful, more violating than the blow to his throat. He knew only then that he could not defend himself; he was maddened by pain and could not move at all.

A blow came lower down, in the gut, and Martin stiffened, fearing for his genitals. Frantic now, afraid of death, he curled tighter to become smaller, and less a target. He clenched his jaw as if this might help him hold himself together. His whole consciousness was fixed on surviving the assault, screwed into himself, keeping alive. Still they did not cease.

The boots of the heavier man. A rib cracked somewhere near his spine; he was throbbing; he was coming apart; and he shouted something in Italian, to make himself a man again, and stop being their object. The last thing he remembered was a kick to the side of his head, a splatter of light in his skull, his head jerked back. Mouth filling with blood, saliva in the fold of his neck, his busted ear a hot, disastrous thing, as the sky slid into darkness.

And then Veeramani bending above him. Veeramani repeating, 'Oh dear, oh dear.' Veeramani lifting him with great tenderness into the cradle of his lap.

35

ON THE FLIGHT to Italy, Evie could not sleep, or settle, or read, or make sense. Only sixteen hours earlier she'd come home from making love to Benjamin, drenched in the downpour that arrived, as the forecasters said it would, in the early evening, just as she was walking through the colourful twilight to Elizabeth Bay. Like some fool in love she had let the rain wash over her, thinking still of their slow friction, their faces pressed together, the sweet restoration of confidence in her own body. This was the profane and democratic rapture; how essentially good to know and recover it.

Evie had dried herself off, eaten toast and a banana, and fallen happily with a book into her father's bed. The window-panes vibrated and rattled with the storm and she felt the air pressure pump, like exhalation, between the rooms. Outside, black rain fell in noisy torrents. Light flashed through the blinds. And the swimming pool was audible, even loud, a giant drum, plashing.

She'd been dreaming of travel on an ocean liner when the computer sounded its Skype ring. At first the sound chimed in the cabins of her dream. She was calling out against the wet sound of wake and waves, 'Answer that, someone,' but woke to find it actual and rolled like a sailor out of bed. As she stumbled to the light switch, she cursed Martin for forgetting the time difference; he'd clearly miscalculated. The imperative ring continued into the night, with the gravity of a demand.

On the computer screen Evie saw the alarmed face of the man called Veeramani. He looked upset and intense, sweat beading his forehead. In her half-awake state it took a moment before she realised that this was the man she had seen the day before, the man who said 'topnotch' with a vivid smile. He told her that Martin had been attacked and was in the hospital. That Martin had asked that she be informed, and had given over the password details—freely, Veeramani said, wanting to reassure her.

Evie was dumbfounded, afraid. It was the fear of losing someone again, the fear of a harm that is inexplicable, inherent in the knowledge of how swiftly the charmed life of the body might cease. Everything became simple: she wanted to know where and when and why.

In the sunny afternoon in Palermo Veeramani was explaining that, although he was a Hindu, he visited Christian churches, sacred places too, for God is everywhere, after all, God is many, very many, and everywhere about; and that his favourite church in Palermo was the shrine of Santa Rosalia, because he loved the hard walk up and down the mountain, and because it reminded him of a Shiva cave he'd visited as a child with his mother, long ago, long, long ago, though of course he didn't always walk up the mountain, but almost always he walked down, after visiting the shrine.

Evie was perplexed. Why was he telling her all this?

Veeramani had not seen Martin in the church, he continued, nor known he was around, not at all, but when he was walking down the mountain path with a compatriot from the internet café, he came upon two villains attacking his friend. He'd called out, and to his astonishment the attackers had fled. He was a pacifist, he said solemnly, and would never have fought them. He realised that Martin was seriously hurt—'oh, Miss Evie, so seriously hurt'—and he and his friend had carried Martin's body back up the mountain. When the ambulance was called, they wouldn't let Veeramani travel with Martin—'a black man, you see, and no relation at all'—and he had hired a seat in a three-wheeler and followed the ambulance to the hospital, so that he knew where his friend would be kept, so that he could visit, and help him out.

Evie looked at his gleaming face and felt her tears swell.

She remembered the votive ears. Martin had gone to Santa Rosalia to deposit the silver ears, and by happenstance, by ludicrous coincidence, his friend Veeramani had come upon the scene of his attack. Veeramani could not say who had set upon Martin or why.

'It is one of the mysteries, Miss Evie, why one man assaults another.'

The formality of his speech was almost heartbreaking. Evie thanked him for the news, and for his kind assistance. She was decisive. She would come to Palermo, she told him, she would come to her brother's side.

'It will be a comfort,' said Veeramani, and then his flatscreen face said goodbye, and he was gone.

~

Evie sat before her computer, composing herself, staring at the wall. There was some recurring tragedy that pursued their family, a condition of error or a central unhappiness. It was more than the tragedy of their mother, more than their stammered history of uncompleted relationships. It was akin to the fear she had as a child, when a wave, unexpected, pulls too strongly underneath, and there is breath-struggle and sinking-feeling and an aching reach for the light.

Veeramani had been crucially imprecise. Evie realised she did not know the extent of Martin's injuries, or if his life was in danger. She had the name of the hospital, so she located its number and rang. Someone confirmed that a man with her brother's name had been admitted. They would not give details over the phone. She was his sister, she said, ringing all the way from Australia. There was a relenting sigh and a brief blank response. 'Stable,' the voice said curtly. 'His condition is listed as stable.'

She needed to make bookings. She needed to organise herself. Clothes, passport, frame of mind. Veeramani had appeared like the angel Gabriel, the bearer of stunning information, then he'd puffed into darkness and disappeared. No glad tidings, only a fearful interception. But there was insanity in this thinking. She was almost breathless with worry. She felt unprepared for a second tragedy after the still-present death of her father.

Evie booked a flight, returned to bed and lay awake thinking of Martin. The rainstorm had passed. What time was it now? The air had become tranquil, gauzy and quiet. All over Sydney, people were sleeping. In the western suburbs, on the North Shore, over the plains and towards the mountains. East, where the ocean smashed onto high sandstone cliffs. It was some hours before dawn and there were dreamers and sleepwalkers and the slow turn of heavy bodies. There were children twitching with energy and couples with their legs entwined. A lover's arm might rest on the breastbone of another. Evie imagined the entire city at rest, as if under a spell. Outside, for all the torn bushes and floating leaves, for all that had been detonating and disturbing the water, the swimming pool was now still and a copy of the sky.

Then it was ten a.m.; she would leave at noon. It was only when she arrived at the airport that Evie rang Benjamin. He said all the correct things: that she must take her time, her brother needed her. That he hoped all would be well, and that Martin would soon recover. The telephone was a black tunnel stretching between them. She wanted him to lower his voice and say something more personal, to recall what each had known, only yesterday, keenly undressing. But she heard in his tone a practised self-protection. Benjamin said, 'Take care,' and she hated the triviality of it, the dismissal of their complicated day-before. Scrupulous, neutral, he was trying to sound like a patient man, but she knew he was already impatient for her return.

The discontinuity of her experience was almost unbearable. Evie heard a sound that might have come from within clanging overhead in the spacious airport, where feelings went wheeling upwards, hitting the metal ceilings, refracting over signage and escalators and lines of people trailing luggage. The acoustics of airports always seemed to snatch things aloft. Evie thought again alphabetically; it soothed her, thinking thus. The alphabet was her ideal order. Categories of things could be apprehended. The chaos of unlucky accidents, threatened environments and global inequity, of lost mothers and dead fathers and injured brothers. All might succumb to methodical lists.

Airborne, Evie's mind was agile with anxiety. In the sleep-deprived afternoon, she had submitted to be strapped in, lifted up and projected above the earth at 885 kilometres an hour. She flicked through *Scientific American*. She made more lists. She accepted a miniature meal of glutinous substances and a miniature plastic bottle of red wine. After that, she closed her eyes, and must have dozed, because she woke with a start as the man next to her shook her shoulder and asked if he could step out into the aisle. The plane had become dark, she saw, full of sleeping passengers, all resting in vulnerable attitudes of wearied abandon. Some looked like children, curled up, or open-mouthed, or clutching at a blanket as though it were a precious thing. A screen showed their flight path, now over northern India. The calculated alignment, the inexorable route to a destination.

There was a news story, once, of a plane that left Perth—at 6.09 p.m. on the fourth of September in the year 2000 (how pedantic her mind was)—to fly to the mining town of Leonora, in the Western Desert. But it continued flying in a long arc, right across the continent. All the passengers, including the pilot, had suffered hypoxia, loss of oxygen, and had been borne automatically in the plane, unconsciously missing their own deaths, floating at a consistent speed and height until the plane ran out of fuel. Eight people fell from the sky and were killed. Nothing could be done. None could be saved. The hopeless flight was tracked till it crashed near the Gulf of Carpentaria.

Evie remembered the story unfolding on the radio news; how it had haunted her, this canister of drifting souls, this machine-age allegory of insistent engines and the negation of human function. Next day the newspapers showed a map of Australia with the 'ghost flight' arc transecting it. She hated remembering this story now, after years of forgetting. She rose from her seat and walked up and down the dark aisle of the plane. She needed to move. She needed to stop assuming the triumph of tragedy, or the mean omnipresence of fateful symbols. Martin would recover; they would return to Australia together. They would resume their lives. She would stay in Sydney. With Benjamin, perhaps. With Nina. But when she sat down again and strapped herself into her seat, she was still thinking of the ghost plane, silver as tinfoil, arcing out of schedule into the flight path of eight unpredestined deaths. The arc took the form of a perforated trail, such as a child, imagining footsteps, might meticulously draw.

36

FROM THE TALL windows of the hospital she could see the lay of the city, the main avenues, the ruined areas, the harbour and ocean to the right. And in the far distance stood Monte Pellegrino, a block of massive stone rising in dark profile to the north. Evie noted these landmarks with little interest; she had no wish to explore the city or to roam its streets. Her concerns were contracted to this room, and to the horizontal body of her brother, lying disfigured and discoloured before her. He had a fractured skull and four broken ribs, and his spleen had been removed, they said. His shattered hand had required microsurgery.

Martin's face was swollen and split. He was unrecognisable. The pulp of him, all the stuff inside hitherto miraculously in place, had shifted and distorted. Evie did not weep or make a scene. She was brisk and practical, and signed forms and spoke to doctors. Her Italian was rusty, but she learned medical terms, and used them, and impressed the staff with her knowledge. They began in good humour to call her *dottoressa*, and soon, without her assenting or encouraging it, staff were speaking to her as if she were a medical doctor. But she was simply the sister from Australia, visiting her brother.

At first she imagined she was a figment to him, a long shape moving in front of the light. She knew he was trying to make sure she was there. Sometimes his eyes opened and he squinted, then closed them again. When he did see her, surfacing from an immense dark stillness, he worked his rubbery lips and said softly, '*Ciao, bella.*'

Evie put her face on the pillow near his and whispered that she was here, that he would be alright, that she would stay as long as needed, and then she would take him back to Australia. His eyes closed again. Staff in crisp uniforms came and went; Frank Malone visited, bringing a bag of mandarins, and was visibly shaken by what he saw. The local cops, he told her, said an Australian had been attacked, and when Martin didn't turn up he put two and two together. Now this assault was part of his investigation. Veeramani came, sat quietly, and left a small icon of Santa Rosalia hanging on the end of the bed. Both men shook hands with Evie, abashed, it seemed, to be upright in the company of so wounded a man.

Evie read, and waited. She watched the light in the hospital room shift and fade and understood that time was dilated here, and ruthlessly slow. Hospital time. She saw blueness open, spread across the sky like a shawl, then fall away, and darken. In one of the paradoxes of grief, she found herself telling strangers about their father's death, and of Martin's wish to follow his tracks in Italy. No mention of a possible crime, simply of filial piety, and a journey devoutly undertaken. This too endeared the brother and sister. There was a reservoir of kindness in hospitals, Evie thought, a great and good surplus, which went largely unacknowledged. It must be the handling of bodies that created such decency: the wiping of human muck, the cleaning of wounds, the bending over a drained face, transitioning to night-time, as the thready pulse slackened and breath subsided in a rasp or a sigh.

At her hotel near the Quattro Canti, Evie slept like a nun, on her back, hoping not to dream. In the early mornings she wrote emails to Benjamin and Angela, only to them. She knew that Benjamin's computer would translate her emails into an American-accented female voice, so that her news and affection would seem robotically strange. She washed her hair, standing under the shower for too long, and dried it with the roaring machine attached to the wall near the bathroom mirror, so that she could not avoid seeing how a death and a half-death had affected her. There was silver in her hair and twin crescents of purple beneath her eyes; she looked older, she thought, than thirty-nine.

Evie ate each evening at a nearby trattoria, cosily dreary, arousing interest because she was a foreigner, and a woman conspicuously alone. Asked if she was a tourist, she casually mentioned her situation to the waiter—the brother in hospital, she mostly at his side—and found this too meant that she was surrounded by expressions of goodwill. Staff offered up their names; she began to learn small details of their lives, and knew they were whispering about her, giving her a story. She knew they pitied her, an unmarried woman who had recently lost a father and with no child to comfort her. This must have happened to Martin, the foreigner slotted into gossipy knowledge that would make him explicable.

One night the cook, Vittorio, came in from the kitchen and showed Evie a photograph of his dead sister. It was black-and-white and rather worn from constant handling, and showed a woman of about seventeen wearing a cloche, her broad face mottled with shadow. Vittorio placed a bottle of homemade digestif on the table, sat down with Evie and began to talk. They drank from tiny glasses, and this man, who might have been seventy-five, fat as a wine barrel and covered in mess from cooking, spoke in a soft voice about his sister and the past they had shared. They were from the land, a village near Corleone. His sister had a lovely singing voice, and had taught him the old songs of the region. She made the best olive oil. All the boys were in love with her. *Guarda! Che bella!*

Evie reached out and touched the back of his hand, and he ignored what might have indicated a weakness. It was a tender moment. She had entered the world of sorrowful revelations that exist between stranded people, of night-time confessions and the low-tone disclosures that happen in a stripe of hospital light or the fuzzy hours after too much drink. Martin had mentioned several times the melancholy of the city, but perhaps this was no different from anywhere else, or perhaps hospital waiting gave access to the world of ignored feeling. When at last Vittorio bade Evie goodnight, she was almost falling over from her own weary sadness. She stumbled back to the hotel, changed by listening to the story of a man she didn't know, by his assumption that his conversation would somehow support her.

In the morning the nurse who attended Martin was scandalised to learn that Evie had sat up drinking with a cook, and that she went out at night on her own. The nurse warned of gangs in the inner city, bad men with knives. No sensible woman would go out alone in Palermo at night. There were Indians and Nigerians, she said. There were evil Turks. All men want only one thing, she added, her sallow face growing cloudy, her tone baleful and fore-boding. Evie politely thanked her for the advice.

When Martin woke fully for the first time, he began to cry. He'd thought he would die. Then he found he was lying in Veeramani's arms, in terrible pain and barely alive, but rescued. He felt himself lifted up, carried at an angle, and delivered into the pouch of a waiting ambulance. Then there was nothing—the induced coma while they relieved pressure on his brain—until her face, leaning close and incredibly present.

Evie watched her brother weep without ceasing. She knew this was a kind of aggregated weeping: the desolation of all that was spoiled or vanishing, the sense of his own corruptible flesh, the memory of plunging towards death, and the prospect of an arduous recovery. The darkness gone, there was now this elongated twilight, and this dazed, bored waiting, while his body repaired.

He said he hated the tubes around him and the hospital tastes and smells. He despaired to see that his drawing hand was a bulky clump of bandages that rested on the bedcover like a foreign object, pallid and ugly, crude as a boxing glove. The metal bed was a kind of cage. All was din, interruption and unrestful inspections. When a nurse appeared, Evie waved her away, so that only she would see her brother weeping.

Walking that evening back to the hotel, Evie took a new route. She found herself confronted by the high-lit spectacle of the city's famous cathedral. Polished stone and shiny foliage glinted through the darkness. She stopped for a moment, knowing that her father would have visited here, that he would have brought a notebook and a camera and recorded the artworks inside, pernickety about all the dates and details. How often she'd seen him at his task, crested in churchy light, bent over a notebook. This was the first occasion on which Evie had really envisioned Noah in Palermo, and she was disturbed to think how recently he may have stood on exactly this spot.

In the yard of the cathedral rested a wooden boat, and on the bow stood a statue of Santa Rosalia. He may have photographed her too, and filed her away in his catalogue of Italian saints' lives. If she'd seen her father's ghost, it was now, under a narrow rim of curved light, crowned in a halo of scholarly concentration. A nimbus of white seemed to envelop the scene: dust in the air, she reasoned, or moisture becoming visible.

Slightly spooked, Evie hurriedly crossed the street. She did not wish to enter the cathedral, ablaze and apparently open, even at this hour. The shops opposite sold ecclesiastical paraphernalia: embroidered capes, cassocks, monstrances and crucifixes. A little further along, a shop window featured life-sized figures, arranged in a tableau of deposition. The plaster Christ was mauve-coloured and bloody. His cerements were grey. He lay temporarily dead in the arms of his mother, a sweet-faced Mary who appeared, as convention allowed, more or less the same age as her son, more sister than mother.

Evie was flushed and unsteady. She hastened from this scene, appalled by her own disgust. But she couldn't bear it; there it was, in a store window, the tortured body of a man. This was a graphic faith and a rough rendition. And even here, in reverential show, the body was dreadful in its wounding.

For some unaccountable reason she thought of the boy in Sydney, the boy on his bicycle. He visited her as she fled, speeding alongside in a whorl of mist. It was an actual boy perhaps, a Sicilian boy on a bicycle. She peered at a hazy receding form and had a conviction of his reality, as if he was a vision, a gift to a believer patiently waiting in prostration or penance. But then the

269

form was covered over by the black of the night. The cycling boy, unverified, was swept away.

37

WHEN NOAH DISEMBARKED at six a.m. at Sydney airport, he carried his case and hand luggage through customs with barely a glance. He'd not told Martin or Evie the date of his return, so moved through the clattering arrivals hall unnoticed and unremarkable. Other passengers dispersed into the waiting arms of relatives; he lingered in the anaemic light like a man abandoned. A compulsion made him wish to confess his secret load, but when this feeling passed, there was only fatigue in its wake. He needed a shower and a shave. He felt despicable. Ahead was the sunburst signage of a hire-car company and Noah recalled he'd booked a car to drive himself home. He had always loved driving. He would be in control again, and self-directing. Speed would revive his slackened senses.

A tall woman, unadorned but for her Thatcherite perm, wore an orange button that read *Ask me about hire cars.*

'I booked online,' Noah said meekly.

Already, he was unravelling with jetlag. The hall around him seemed to pivot and spin.

'Name, credit card, licence.'

The woman gave him a deadpan, no-nonsense assessment. Noah could see she was unfazed by his dishevelment; people must stumble from flights all the time looking unfit to drive. He hoped she hadn't noticed the rash at his throat.

He fumbled for his wallet and produced his cards. On the licence his stamp-sized face shone up at him, a mugshot, a picture that might appear with a red caption on the evening news. Viewers would look up from their TV dinners and think: *jeez, what a phoney.*

The woman hardly considered him. No corporate welcome here. She inserted his credit card into a machine and asked him to sign electronically. She handed him a paper receipt and a bundle of keys. That simple. No questions.

'The red Corolla, bay H10. It can be returned to any of our thirty-three depots across the state.'

'Thank you.'

Stay polite. Don't be memorable. Be subdued in this home-coming.

Noah felt something rush inside him like radioactive medicine. The chill of a body overtaken by the green rivulets of depression glass. He saw himself as a system of interior channels and canals, of pipes to and from the heart, of cords and strings and little branches opening into cavities. It might have been this woman who summoned his mother and the memory of depression glass; but her presence could not account for his body imagined in this way, anfractuous, as if in an MRI

272

vision, awash with his liquid fear.

Wasted, that was the word. He felt he was wasted. Martin once used it in the clinic, disposing of his whole life in a druggie cliché, and Noah had argued against him. He'd hugged his son and told him that there is no waste, never, that all we are remains perpetual and potentially art.

Even then he didn't quite believe it, seeing Martin's evacuated condition, his muddy stare and slack, incommunicative mouth, and the way he lolled back on the bed, zonked to the eyeballs. But Noah needed to say so. Parental guilt assailed him. He needed to assert pop psychology against his son's suicidal bullshit. He invented advice and pleas for the meaning of life. He referred to the great traditions of visual art, the seeping down of images that bring with them a tide of wonder. But nothing he said made any difference. Martin turned away. Only when Nina arrived with her plastic dinosaur, which she silently grrrr-ed up and down her father's arm, did he register any change in attention.

Noah hoisted Eleonora Ragusa, heavier than ever, and dragged his case along concrete paths to the red Corolla. In Australia, now, and almost at home. Nerve-racked, he was at least on the earth and out of the sky. He started the engine and looked around. Signposts in various fonts instructed the way to central Sydney, but in a spontaneously foolish decision he decided he would spend the day and night in the Blue Mountains. He would not go home immediately, but rest hidden and cosy, up high, with a spectacular view.

He turned away from the city, onto the highway. He steered automatically. The bisected road flowed steadily beneath him and the nifty little hire car hummed soporific. Noah was not driving, but in a haze of driving. Only when he swerved like a crazy man, and jerked awake, did he realise he must stop.

Noah pulled over and discovered he'd driven further than

he thought: he was near a place called Blackheath. Taking a small track off the highway, turning this way, then that, he found himself in a modest lane of bush. There were houses just visible, roofs at some distance, and mostly high eucalypts and a scraggle of ferns and undergrowth. There was abrupt quiet, the country-style quiet of audible wind, things arustle and the low, proximate squawk of invisible birds. And now, Noah was help-less against almighty sleep. He tilted his chair back and fell in daytime into a velvet night, a sleep so deep and so concentrated that the sense was of whooshing collapse, like being the object vanished in a magic trick.

A passer-by was tapping on the window. Noah woke with a start. A face ruddy as raw meat was leaning close to the glass. It was twilight. He must have slept for eight hours or so, only to wake in the next night of another land. Noah wound down the window.

'Just checking, mate. I drove past you this morning, taking a kip, but now, on my way back, thought there might be something wrong.'

It was the most straightforward expression of concern.

Noah was touched. 'I was on a long haul flight,' he explained. 'I was in the sky for hours.'

He guessed the man was wondering what the hell he was doing here and why he had mentioned a flight when he was sitting in a car. Noah was also wondering what the hell he was doing here. He felt like an idiot, ending up in the moun-tains, on an impulse that now seemed to have little logic and purpose.

'You right for the night?' the man asked.

Noah realised he must work a little harder to sound plausible. 'Just heading for Katoomba, a motel. Thanks for asking.'

'Other way, mate. You're completely bushed. Back in the

other direction, about eleven kays.'

Noah thanked the stranger, who was already heading back to his battered truck, and gave a vigorous, jolly wave as he drove off. There would be a loving wife waiting somewhere, with steak and potatoes, and a row of skinny kids, ranged downwards in several sizes. Without looking, he felt for his secret, wedged in the passenger seat.

He started the ignition, turned a loop and headed towards Katoomba. On the outskirts of the town, now a thin pool of light in the growing dark, he took the turn-off too fast, in a tipping skid. He drove down the steep hill of the main street, but was indecisive, wanting no motel now, but simply to keep on driving. He was hungry, actual and wide-awake. Storefronts, billboards, the regular space-signatures of power poles—all flowed past in a systematic flicker. He could drive forever, he reflected; he could turn again and drive over the mountains, towards the centre.

At a service station Noah bought an overheated meat pie, doused it in sauce and devoured it in a few bites. Then, clear-headed, he knew at once of his folly. Home. Of course, he needed to be home. What had he been thinking? So, in his third night of travel, he reversed his plan and set out for Sydney.

On the winding mountain road he was conscious of increasing cold. Somewhere peaceful he stopped and, stepping out for a piss, found himself looking up at the kite of the Southern Cross. His own bright heaven. There were few houses along this stretch of road, so the darkness was darker, the constellations observable, the pace of his own thoughts slower and expanded. He could smell eucalyptus and his unwashed body. He felt a slight beat in the air as cold hit the side of the mountains and slid in a vapour into clefts and gullies.

After he had reached into the back of the car and retrieved

his jacket, he stood a little longer, for no reason at all. Now he knew truly that he was almost at home, and surrounded by what, in the texture of things, felt like real life. He sensed his age, his infirmities and the enduring web of his desires. But he was not yet enfeebled: no. He was not yet pierced by dementia or shuffling in pyjamas along a hospital corridor. He felt the integrity still there, fitting him together as a man. In this huge night, on a mountain, he might have been standing naked before Dora's gaze.

A few cars sped past, Doppler in their effect and disturbing his peace. They inspired the sensation of time itself retreating. Another wave of cold wind. He pulled his jacket closer, slid back into the driver's seat and continued his journey.

He'd made love to Katherine in a Ford Prefect not long after they became a couple, surprised she would submit to such an uncomfortable proposition. She smelled of cigarette smoke and lavender, and he had clutched at her shoulders and devised flowery phrases, desperate to make a good impression. He was fumbling, inept, but still she had gasped. Afterwards, she stepped out into the freezing night, and leaned back onto the car, smoking a cigarette between her still gloved fingers. She seemed ironic and distant when he'd hoped for gentleness and to hear her light laugh. He wiped the misty glass with his palm and saw her facing away from him. She seemed unreachable in a world aglitter with frost, lit by the yellowish headlamps.

He remembered staying in the car, unsure what to do. It had seemed forever, waiting for her to finish her cigarette, wondering if she would consent to remain, worrying what she was thinking, and finding her still a stranger.

He thought now of Dora, and missed her. In the hum of the hire car she was a promise and a newly present spirit. He wanted her to materialise and sit beside him as he drove in the darkness.

PART FIVE

38

AFTER SO MUCH waiting in the hospital, it was good to walk in the streets, to recover mobile life and the rhythm of ordinary time. Before she saw Martin bruised and motionless, prone in a jumble of tubes, hooked to a machine that droned and clicked with registrations of his body, he was like a wilful, younger brother, always in need of counsel. But now he seemed naturally older, and closer to death. They'd been rackety kids, a riddle to their parents, but she'd often considered herself the older one. When she went off the rails in her teenage years, refusing the decorous model of a clever girl from Adelaide, she'd wanted, in a sense, to become immature, to be Martin for a while, sniggering and sulky. And when Martin had taken to heroin, she'd half-wanted that too, to be released into negligence. In the clinic he'd looked like a scolded child. He was gruff, stingy with feeling, and fearless in his self-destruction.

The sun was out but it was not yet warm. A cold snap in Central Europe was to blame for the chill and the unseasonable rain. Like her father, Evie had always been intolerant of cold. She wore a bulky overcoat and a woollen scarf and noticed that locals also disliked the lower temperatures. She thought of the refugees she'd seen on television the night before, how frozen they were, huddled in shiny orange blankets, their eyes enlarged both with fear and with rescue. Syrians, Eritreans, Nigerians, Sudanese. There was a child being lifted upwards, away from surging water, and a man's stiff arms reaching out to claim her. There was the bucking of a rowboat, hands groping in appeal, and glistening wet faces. There was a woman from Syracuse saying, 'They are our brothers, they are our sisters.' Evie had burst into tears.

The city didn't have the seedy decrepitude Martin had described, but there was a breath of pathos to its ruined spaces. She saw the closed-up churches and palmless trees, and the way everything existed beneath a thin coat of pale dust. She saw slouched beggars and street kids and a man dragging a rubbishy foam mattress. She saw a lingering population who must have come on the boats. They lived in the shadows, regarded as a social nuisance. These were not the suffering outcasts of every city, but the newly dispossessed, incautious in their desperation as their hopes burned to nothing. She hugged her elbows and was tempted to look away.

And there was more—there was something elegiac in the air. Something that contested the sunshine and the tapering clouds and the round loaves of bread she had seen a man selling from the boot of his car. She felt it too, disquieting and close. Could one feel history? Might there be seances of the past, or intimations of antique places? She was more susceptible these days to anti-rationalist suppositions. She was regressing, she thought, to the credulity of a child.

A line of graffiti read: *Aprire tutte le gabbie!* Open all the cages.

Evie pushed at the heavy wooden door and entered the court-yard to Dora's apartment, unsure what to expect. Dora had been cordial on the phone, but asked little about Martin. Told of the beating, she simply moved to another subject. Evie thought her attitude aloof, and cold.

She looked around. There was a lemon tree in the centre of the courtyard, hung with the last knobbly fruit of the season, and large ceramic pots of crimson geranium, surely unseasonal, arranged on the perimeter.

Dora waved from her first-floor balcony and called out to come up. From a distance her face looked amiable and familiar. When she opened the door, Evie was struck again by a sense of familiarity, some revenant detail or feature, some mannerism that struck a small flame to see her by. Dora held a black open-weave shawl around her chest, and leaned forward, a sheathed figure, to kiss Evie on both cheeks. 'I have wanted to meet you,' she said. 'Noah spoke often of you and Martin.'

She took Evie's coat and scarf and led her into the elegant sitting room of old furniture and crammed high bookcases. Papers were on the floor, her reading glasses rested on an over-turned book. There was a plate of biscotti on a low table set with two small cups, and Evie could smell fresh coffee.

'One moment.' Dora left and returned with a large silver pot.

They sat facing, in that pause of formal interregnum before conversation begins. Dora poured Evie an espresso and proffered the biscotti.

'So now,' she said. 'Now we shall have our little talk. Your father, Noah.'

They were assessing each other. It had only been minutes and Evie knew already that this woman had been her father's lover. It was nothing she could name, but a conviction came over her, the hands and their openness, the glance, solicitous, the way she smoothed down her dress and squared her shoulders. Martin had not guessed. Caravaggio, he said. She was an expert on Caravaggio. But Evie saw in this short time what Noah had seen, and knew that she was dear to him. Despite Dora's posture of withdrawal, something in the way her head moved, a slight nod when she said his name, showed intimate contact. The body confides, Evie thought, even when one might sit in silence attending to the Italian ceremony of coffee. She looked down: fine porcelain cups, old silver spoons with a Florentine design on the handles, biscuits newly released from their cellophane and arranged in a fan, just so.

'Forgive me, I should have asked first about your brother.'

'Martin is slowly improving. Soon he will be able to travel, and we will return to Australia. But the doctors think he will need a second operation on his hand.'

Dora said nothing. Evie was expecting her to say: how terrible, I was stunned to hear of the attack. Instead she was looking down, preoccupied, pressing a fingertip onto fallen crumbs. Evie realised at once that Dora wanted only to speak of her father, and to hear her speak of him, as a figure of love.

'Is that it?' Evie asked. Above a sideboard hung the face of Eleonora Ragusa. The detective had shown them a photograph of the sculpture; this must be the initial sketch. It was more erotic than Evie had remembered, the face receptive to a kiss, the garment falling away, a breast exposed.

'Apparently the sculpture has been stolen from the museum,'

Dora volunteered, 'but no one knows by whom. I know what Antonio Dotti has been saying, but the man is delusional and not to be believed.'

Dora spoke as if concluding an argument, with nothing more to say on the subject. She spoke as if dissembling. With a single tilt of the head, she drank her espresso. So it would be like this— the stiffening of conversation into tough declarations. Evasion, façade, the smothering of feeling.

'You will forgive me, Dora, but my father is dead, and accused, and my brother was attacked. Left for dead.' She was conscious of her own theatrical plea, wishing to insist on her right to an explanation.

A strain of concern or denial swept over Dora's face. Her free hand seemed to dangle; her other grasped tighter at her shawl. 'And my Uncle Vito is also dead,' she said. 'I want no more of this matter; I want no more people hurt.'

She rose, moved to the window and lit a cigarette. Evie waited in polite silence while Dora composed herself. Her thoughts were spinning. She was in a rage that she had been banished from truth, and that she would perhaps never know what her father had done in Sicily, or the whole story of what might have involved and killed him. The logic of things was retreating before her, in this art historian's room, full, like her father's, of trinkets and souvenirs, foxed prints, reproductions, heavy art books on old masters. Who was this Vito? What role did he play?

'Forgive me,' Dora said.

It was an incomprehensible echo. Evie expected a confession or revelation, but nothing followed. In a startling flash she imagined her father sitting where she sat now, looking at this woman standing posed before a square of cold sunlight, the sash a shadowed cross, the apartment opposite just visible, a tiny band of clear sky in the far-right corner. Her mind dithered at the substitution, and at the return of her father's eyes.

'We were meant to talk, Noah and I, to arrange our future,' Dora said. 'But I had to leave, you understand. I had to find Uncle Vito.'

A tight, wrenched sentence. It was some kind of explanation. Evie heard Dora's insistence but could not interpret her meaning.

'Did you love my father?'

'Yes, I loved your father.'

She was still turned away, blowing smoke at the half-open window.

'I was to follow him to Sydney,' she said. 'We had a future planned.'

Evie was thinking: Noah didn't mention you when he returned. Not once. Not once did he mention a woman with whom he might have a future. An Italian woman. But she looked at the black figure, held firm in the shape of her shawl, rigid with the effort not to divulge, and felt overcome by a surge of pity. Dora too was bereaved. She was a woman holding herself in, unable to speak freely, possibly unable to weep.

'Who is Uncle Vito?' Evie asked.

Dora turned and stared at her, stricken.

'Uncle Vito is my father, you might say.'

Again, there was a strict conclusiveness to her tone. The announcement of a special relationship was left in darkness.

'The lemon tree is looking well,' Dora announced. 'So much rain.'

She was unrelaxed and vigilant. She bent and extinguished the cigarette she had just begun. She sat again and leaned forward and poured them both a second coffee, this time with a kind of fidgety agitation, her slender hand ever so slightly atremble. They heard a prolonged howl from a dog somewhere, and a volley of high-pitched yapping.

'It's left alone, locked inside,' Dora explained. 'There's a point every day when that dog becomes distressed. I hear it often when I'm working at home.'

They were both quiet then, listening. The sound was piercing and intrusive, impossible to ignore. Evie thought it unbearable. Dora caught her glance, rose and closed the sash window.

'I hope we will be friends,' Dora said, as if beginning their conversation afresh. 'And I would like to come to Australia, *need* to come to Australia, to see where he lived and breathed, to see his home. It is important to me. Especially now.'

'Can you tell me what happened?'

'No, I cannot tell you what happened. Here, in this city, knowledge is dangerous. We are used to guilty silences. I tried to warn Martin, but for some reason he stayed on.'

Evie gulped her coffee and took a second biscotti. She was consuming in order not to think or feel. Noah was dead, her brother was maimed, and the woman who had loved her father was after all not without feeling, but by temperament or necessity adamant, and withholding her story.

'See how tragic we are?' Dora smiled sadly.

It was a weak attempt at conciliating humour; it was a protest at her failure to be consoled. Evie could have wept then, for all that had not been said. The howls of the distraught dog were still faintly audible. It might have been the soundtrack of a greater disheartening.

'We'll meet again,' continued Dora, implying it was time to leave. No more questions. No answers. 'We'll speak again, in other circumstances. There will be a time when it becomes possible to speak of what matters.'

She looked pale and mysterious, like an elderly film star, Evie thought, who was asking in accented English to be left alone.

'You Australians are so direct,' Dora added.

~

It may have been a compliment. It may have been a rebuke. In any case, Evie took the hint and left. She gathered her coat and scarf, and walked back down the steps, past the flourishing lemon tree, and out through the doorway onto the street. With the dry cold she saw more clearly the floating dust in the air, and the way it coated everything, sprinkling evenly over the shape of the city. Thousands of years of human habitation: the violence, the love-making, the celebrations, the vice. It occurred to Evie there must be human skin floating in this dust, the abrasions and frottage of brutality or of sex. Ambient, there must be forensically physical remains. But this was the thinking of a madwoman, she reflected; it was sordid, and unworthy.

Evie paused for no reason in the shadow of an archway. She felt as if she had visited Noah's widow. This was unanticipated, to feel for Dora as she might have felt for her own mother, had she known her, had they been adults together, had time and death cracked open in a different pattern. Again, it was unworthy to think in this way, to see tenderness ramify so that everyone was included in her grief, so that everyone she met was among the forsaken.

39

WHEN HE'D FIRST opened his eyes to see Evie, Martin thought
that he was back in Sydney.

Evie, Sydney.

Then he felt how swollen and wounded he was, his hand a
weighty lump, his body encased and invaded, his very breathing
a sear across his broken ribs. In the amendment of his understanding, which formed its own kind of anguish, he saw that he
was in hospital and a figure in pentimento: redrawn, misshapen,
a mistake of a man. He discovered he was out of danger and, in
a torrent of relief, began to tell Evie his story. Then something
occurred that his old clinic would have described as an 'episode';
he found himself weeping and could not stop. Martin hadn't cried
in this way since the death of his mother, and in truth he was not

sure what impelled this copious weeping. It might have been for Noah, or for himself; it might have been for some kind of shame, or regret. All were muddled in the hospital and infected by its sickly light. Delayed shock, finding himself delivered, *rescued*, seemed to have swung back at him like a pendulum, with stunning gravitational force. Evie sat by the bed, quietly waiting. She leaned over him and touched his forehead. He thought he heard seagulls wheeling outside the window, but it could have been pigeons, or doves. In that time close to the wounding, so benighted, all presences were indeterminate.

Now, sitting up, on the mend, Martin found it hard to believe he'd lost control of his feelings in this way. He trusted Evie not to mention it, his lack of dignity. She'd always seemed the discreet one, the older, in a sense. Frank Malone was asking him questions and Martin knew he must keep his grip. An Italian police officer, Giordano, stood alongside, surreptitiously flirting with a nurse.

'Two more things,' said Malone. 'You say only this bloke Salvo'—he looked at his notepad—'Tommaso Salvo, knew you were heading to the mountain. So he must be involved.'

'No,' said Martin. 'Tommaso is a friend. He would not be involved.'

Evie was sitting opposite Frank. Martin gave her a warning look. He knew she suspected Tommaso of something, but could not say what. She'd gone to the Salvos' to collect some of his things and there met Maria, red-eyed with lamentation over 'her two lost boys': Martin, in hospital; Tommaso, disappeared. She'd embraced Evie like a daughter and, undone by distress, spoken rapidly in dialect. *Disappeared* was the word Evie was sure she'd heard. Maria had hit at her chest with her fist, speaking of her love for her only son; she'd swallowed dust from the bones of Santa Rita, protector of widows; she'd prayed to Santa Rosalia on her knees, all through the night. Martin had listened to Evie's account of her visit with a sensation of mounting dread. He imagined Maria immobile, her bulky form on the floor, pleading for intercession. What in another context might have seemed an almost farcical detail—consuming the pulverised bones of Santa Rita—oddly moved him. He felt both admiration at Maria's fervency, and a nagging guilt. But he could not imagine Tommaso, where he might be hiding, whether he too had been hurt. Tommaso was gone, disappeared. He'd retreated like a shadow into shadows.

'He's disappeared,' said Frank, as if he had heard Martin's thoughts. 'My Carabinieri mates checked him out and found that he's pissed off somewhere. Petty crook, it seems. All-round dodgy character.'

Here the Italian policeman nodded, to show that he understood.

'Giordano here will interview his mother,' Frank added.

'Disappearance proves nothing,' Evie said. 'He may have succumbed to some kind of pressure. He may be afraid.'

'Nevertheless.'

Frank had nothing to go on. He was a detective without a case. And what had all this to do with the missing Ragusa?

'And this bloke Veeramani,' he insisted, 'who just happened to be passing by.'

And then Veeramani was there, standing in the doorway.

'So, it is me you are seeking?' he asked, hearing his own name. Veeramani looked indignant. Evie looked indignant. Martin wanted Frank to shut the fuck up. The detective with no case was trying to justify his time in Palermo by nailing the poor immigrant.

Veeramani hovered at the doorway. Giordano demanded to see his papers and there was a tight interval during which all waited for the procedure to conclude. Martin was scratching at the cannula in his good hand with the exposed fingertips of his damaged one. He felt the infant imprecision of his impeded movements.

'Come in. Please.' It was Evie, making things right.

'For your information, I often visit Santa Rosalia on Monday, my free day, and always walk down the mountain. But often'—he paused—'I take the bus up. Such a hard, hard climb.'

Veeramani offered Martin a small plastic bag of pumpkin seeds. 'For your good self.'

'Thanks, mate. Frank here didn't mean anything. He's just a fuckwit with no answers, aren't you, Frank?'

It was an unnecessary insult. The detective looked gloomier than usual, more crosshatched, Martin thought.

Frank folded away his notepad. 'I think we're about done for now.' He was avoiding eye contact and holding himself erect. The room was tense and unhappy. A second nurse peered in at the door, then retreated. 'I have to ask these questions, Martin.'

And now Martin knew that he had been cruel. Frank was the man who had eaten a meal with him, and sat next to him at the movies, and wanted Palermo to be Rome, and asked for his photo to be taken in front of a marble nymph at the Fontana Pretoria. Not a cartoon cop, but a damaged man, like himself. A man whose marriage was failing, whose job was dull, who confessed he was missing his kids. He would leave for home in two days.

'Right. No hard feelings,' Martin said. 'We'll catch up in Sydney for a drink, righto?'

Frank rose, looming over him, the notebook stowed away. He hesitated for a moment, and then leaned across the bed to shake hands with both Evie and Veeramani. It was the gesture of a man who was trying to make amends, and to signal that the official questioning was over, and inconsequential, after all.

Veeramani was gracious. 'You have to ask your questions. Of course.'

Frank nodded, policeman-like, and slipped away, banished. When the three were together, they talked for a while in a stilted manner, unsure how to recover the ease of conversation. Martin saw that Veeramani was made awkward by Evie's presence and would not look at her. Within minutes he made an excuse and left brother and sister together.

'None of this makes any sense, Evie.'

'No, none of it.'

'It's not like I found any information, or made any discoveries.' *A hole in the water.*

'None of that matters now,' said Evie. 'Rest, recuperate.'

He wanted to say that none of his life made sense, that the misalignment he felt was not physical, but metaphysical, that he and Frank shared the profound loneliness many men share, linked back into life only by their children. He thought of Nina climbing over his chest as he lay on the grass at the park. He thought of her strange high laugh, which she herself could not hear, and the squeals of her anger, and her frustration at not being understood. He liked the way she brought her face enormously close to his.

'I saw Dora,' Evie began. 'She was in love with Noah.'

'Are you sure? He never mentioned her. And she seemed fairly distant.'

'Yes, I'm sure.'

'So what does this mean? Did she commit a crime and involve him?'

'Who knows? She's protecting someone—she will not speak of it. She may even be protecting us, or think that she is.'

'Jesus.'

They were quiet, then. A wave of drowsiness flowed over

them. The day nurse came and went, and a large woman in a pale pink uniform deposited a mug of weak coffee. They shared the cup, Evie lifting it carefully to Martin's mouth, tipping slowly, catching the drips, wiping his chin with her fingers.

'Get me out of here, Evie. This stuff will kill me.'

And so they began to relax and trade stories. Evie told Martin about the cook and his tale of his sister, the photograph marked by his greasy hands. Then shyly she told him a little about Benjamin. She said it had been unexpected, the embrace of a blind man, that her heartsick self fell away at his touch. Martin was conscious of her making a sort of proclamation, and pleased she had taken him into her confidence.

'You'll like him,' she added. But she seemed reluctant to say more.

Martin was recalling, from nowhere, the attractive woman at his father's funeral. A postgraduate, perhaps. How might he find her?

Listless with analgesics, content just to be in her tender company, Martin asked Evie to tell him about Noah's theories of painting and time. Noah had tried once, he said, years ago, on the beach at Glenelg.

Through the fug of hospital potions, he heard Evie speak of pleated matter and folds in the soul. He heard 'multiplicity, not unity'; he heard 'co-presence of the finite and the infinite'; he heard her say something about serial time giving way to curves and bending motions. He could understand nothing. Was it the medication? When she began speaking of the fresco sequence called *The Legend of the True Cross*, he had at least a few images to pin to her words. A piece of wood appearing and disappearing throughout history, and its afterlife in millions of icons around the world, substance remade as an image, continuing in time.

Still, he felt stupid. His old paranoia about early dementia seized him. Evie's words seemed to fall into cavities in his mind. Was he losing it, density of substance and presence? And since they were both atheist barbarians—as Noah once called them—this account of his sister's seemed in any case beside the point. They did not believe. They had never believed.

'Enough folded time,' he said, weakly.

Evie smiled. 'Yes, enough already. I'll see you tomorrow.'

She kissed him on the cheek, pulled up his sheets as if she was tucking him in, and then left.

Martin lay alone in his hospital room. He thought of Frank and Evie. He thought of Noah and Nina. He thought of Tommaso and Antonio, both disappeared, and of the men who had bashed him. And then he thought of Veeramani. Dear Veeramani.

Afraid for Nina, and wishing to offer advice, Veeramani had told him a terrible story. The Mughal emperor Akbar the Great conducted an experiment in the sixteenth century to discover if language was innate or learned. He'd imprisoned twenty babies in a room, tended only by mute nurses, never hearing a word of human speech. Of course, none of the children learned to speak, and later, as adults, they still could not learn.

Martin had been appalled by this story. He was worried his friend might think him a harsh experimenter, or a neglectful father. He ought to tell him of the tin ears, left with Santa Rosalia. More than anything, he wanted Veeramani to think well of him; he wanted his respect and esteem. He wanted to show this man of rare quality that he had been worthy of being saved.

40

IT WAS PERHAPS only ten p.m. when Noah arrived in Sydney, though it felt much later. He was lucid and wide-awake. His vision seemed to have sharpened. It occurred to him that his jetlag might be a complete reversal, so that his series of nights would continue, and he would sleep throughout each day, losing them forever in the fitful nothing his sleep now resembled. His world was counterfactual now; he had bent the laws of physics, he had travelled back and forth, he had entered a zone of alteration.

In Elizabeth Bay he steered the hire car between the shell-shaped lights, up the flowery driveway into the communal car park, intending to slide into his usual spot. There he discovered his own car, left about three months ago, before his life in Sicily commenced. He'd forgotten its existence; he'd simply forgotten his own car. There it was, a black beetle, blocking his way. So Noah had to reverse down the driveway and find a park nearby, difficult at this time of night, when most residents were at home. He drove around in the patchy darkness until he found a spot. Then he had almost two blocks to walk with his luggage back to the apartment.

The sculpture in the duffle bag was heavier now, and his case seemed a dead weight, even on its efficient wheels. The last stretch, up the steep driveway, almost did him in. Noah felt his heart banging at the strenuous movement after so many hours of inertia; he felt unfit, an old man, a kind of carcass. Ahead lay the glittering swimming pool, which he had never used. It looked dark and glassy, a window facing upwards, with a full moon floating like a face in its centre. He'd paused to register confusion, but was moved by what he saw, the symmetry, the illusion, the ordinary remade. It was a whole other world, a true apparition. Only the far sound of an ambulance siren, rising in the whine of interruption, broke the seal of this graceful, almost Japanese scene.

As he approached his apartment, a black cat tiptoed forwards to greet him.

Strozzi.

He adored Strozzi and almost considered him his own. Noah bent to stroke the small head, finding the bowl of his ears, and then scratching the rumbling spot beneath his chin. Strozzi's warm, curving body twisted to his touch, recognised him and sounded a welcoming purr.

Noah left his luggage by the door and did not unpack. Instead, he took a long shower, feeling his body revive, feeling with immodest pleasure the endowments of his hands, and his arms and his sinewy legs, patting at his chest, rubbing the back of his neck, cupping his soft genitals, poking between his toes, holding up his face, eyes closed, to the benign cascade of water-fall. When he inspected himself in the mirror, with a towel at the waist, the image he saw did not match what he had just experi-enced, that something, after all, was restored and vital. He was a grandfather now, but sensuous life still coiled in him. He still had this compact body that made love, and drank wine, and swam in the ocean. If only for the time of a shower, he'd cast off all the fear of the last few days. It took a moment to name it: gratitude. It was old-fashioned gratitude.

Noah dressed in a T-shirt and familiar trackpants. He made himself a cup of coffee, found some dry biscuits to snack on, and felt at once rested and recomposed. Sleep was impossible. He wrote a long love letter to Dora, even though she had told him not to write for at least two weeks after he arrived. He did not mention the journey or the Ragusa. He described the Australian night and the swimming pool holding the ghost face of the moon; he described Strozzi's greeting, coming towards him out of the darkness. Then he wrote about their time together, and his deepest emotions. In the solemnity of insomnia, he was a truth-teller and a man of feeling. He was pulling her back, bringing her into the vicinity of his lamplight, into the warm embrace of Sydney air.

The apartment was unchanged. Here was his favourite reading chair, his books and the two icons he had bought not long after he was married. Katherine and he had argued over the cost, but he could not resist the dubious offer from a man who claimed to be Russian, but did not know the language, or under-stand the concept of provenance. He was offered a special deal, if he took them both. Even then, reflected Noah, he was in the shady world of art dealing that moved images and objects into private hands, when they should have been communal and left at home. The Madonna and Child was conventional—he would admit, if pressed, that it was nothing unusual—but the St Jerome, the scholar saint, the renowned lonely saint of biblical translation, was another matter entirely. The face of the old man might have been his own: slightly drawn, long, with heavy-lidded eyes. It was as if in purchasing it he'd recognised his own face in the future, and wanted to buy himself back. He cherished this image with a passion he could not explain to anyone.

Noah lifted the icon, inspected it, then put it down again. With his T-shirt he wiped away a thin coating of dust. It was the only thing among his possessions he truly cared about.

In the next week Noah readjusted a little to his old world. He met with Martin for an Italian dinner in his favourite restaurant in Potts Point; he later visited his son's studio and gave his opinion on a series of sketches. He rang Evie in Melbourne and talked about his new interest in Caravaggio; then she rang back, excited, to continue their conversation. One morning, he visited Nina, presenting her with the gift of an Italian puppet, one of those obsolescent wooden toys children like to avoid, and a copy of Collodi's *The Adventures of Pinocchio*. Nina loved both gifts. She'd climbed onto his lap and half-strangled him with her happy hello and wordless thankyou. She'd clung to his neck and covered his cheek with kisses. And each night, lovesick and longing, Noah thought about Dora. He waited restlessly for the moment he might again hear her voice.

Noah could not remember the last time he'd felt so bereft of a lover. It was like a condition from the past that he ought to have outgrown. The sort of thing a schoolboy would experience, or wish to mock. One was meant to discard such romantic intensities. One was meant to *mellow*—that was the word. But he was unmellowed and fierce in his wish to touch her. His feelings were stretched across the planet, leaning in her direction.

An *ellipse*: Piero, master geometer, for whom everything fell in a pattern, would have called his condition an ellipse.

In that week, for all the semblance of everyday busyness, Noah's sleep did not become regular. He felt nocturnal and worn down. He imagined his face was flattening out to the disc of an owl. One night he heard the hoot of an owl, or thought he did, and smiled. It was a lunatic response, he told himself later, fantasising affinity and identification. The patter everywhere of night wings—he noticed it now. Sydney was full of birds.

He adjusted his mealtimes; he listened to music late into the night: Albinoni, Fauré; he watched movies; he cleaned the belly of the stove, rearranged his records and books, brewed coffee at all hours. Reading was hopeless; his mind would not organise the words. In his tidying up, he came across keepsakes from his children's lives: photographs, letters, a little tin-plated trophy with scrolled handles that Evie had won. There was a chalk drawing Martin must have done when he was about fourteen— such effortless skill—of Evie, sleeping. Her face appeared now as an ashen smudge, but above her head, in biro, was a scalloped dream cloud, and in the dream cloud Martin had rendered her sleeping alphabetical: *zzzz*. This drawing lay in Noah's trembling hands like a living thing. He looked away, dashed by powerful feelings. He could hardly bear to contemplate what this image summoned. The face a spectre, disappearing. He stared at the zigzags of this mystery, then tucked the drawing back where he'd found it, in an old cardboard box beneath his bed, next to his tartan slippers. He'd forgotten that he slept above his children's things.

Slowly, for all his activity, the night was overtaking him. In the distortions of his mind, in its incapable troubled sea, he could not find enough distractions to hold back the tides. He felt aggravated, serious, alert, embarrassed. Maddened, bitter, mild, rebellious. The blur of his attention beleaguered him, but there were also moments, alone at night, in which his sense of useless waiting fell away and he recovered a kind of peace. There was even sublimity, when he went outside and looked upwards. The vault of night-time was as daunting and spacious as a cathedral. A name returned to him: *Santa Maria dello Spasimo*, Mary of the Swoon, a roofless cathedral in Palermo. Without the irony Martin and Evie practised, he felt a helpless awe, like an ancient man deciphering the drama of weather.

At some point Noah understood one source of his sleeplessness. He could not stand having the Ragusa in his apartment any longer. It was an incriminating object, and a reminder of Dora's absence. Its proximity made him feel vulnerable and afraid. On the internet he located secure lockers in the city, in a backstreet not far from Central Station. This was action, not waiting. This was an assertion of control. He devised a code of numbers for the lock based on the name *Ragusa*. If anything happened to him, the statue could not be reclaimed. Only Evie would understand the code, since it employed her alphabetical mania.

On a humid Saturday morning, Noah took the train to Central, walked with his load to the nondescript storefront that advertised itself as a storage facility, and deposited Eleonora Ragusa in a large locker, using his arcane numbers. It was a huge relief. He could hardly believe how unburdened he felt to leave her there, locked away. He returned home with his empty bag and slipped the word *Ragusa* and the address of storage into the back of his St Jerome icon, in the fissure between its cardboard backing and the splintery wood of the artwork itself. If anything happened to him, Evie would inspect his St Jerome and discover what he had stored there. And she would know instantly that numbers might decipher the name. She would consider *Ragusa*, and look him up, and this would lead to Eleonora Ragusa, resting in her locker—but also to Dora, as if to a long-lost mother. His reasoning may have been fevered and devious from lack of sleep, but he knew his daughter and her unusual processes of thinking. He knew he must protect himself if anyone came looking. He felt a small sense of achievement. If all went well, Dora would arrive in Sydney, and they would plan a future together.

His weary reasoning stopped there. *A future together* was a culmination he could not imagine. Though she permeated his longing, he could not bend time towards them. His failure to imagine Dora in the future, to pull her from tenuous unreality, pained and tormented him.

41

AFTER THE AGREED two weeks, exactly, and at the prearranged time, Noah rang Dora. He was desperate to communicate, imagining her lips close to the telephone, parting and closing, her face pale with their separation and all she had been through, her words wary but intimate. Noah needed to find out what had happened, to hear of Dora and Uncle Vito, and to learn if he could organise her visit or the return of the sculpture. There was no answer.

Noah rang again, and again, then emailed, several times, and after that rang Dora at hourly intervals throughout the night. The next day he rang again. It would be her night-time, now, and he rang into it as one casts a lifebuoy onto the heaving swell of the ocean, wanting a sign in the darkness against engulfing odds. It was as if their secret life together had sunk into a void.

He could not ring Antonio—Dora had warned him against it—and he knew no one else in Palermo well enough to contact, or to trust. He'd agreed not to tell his children or solicit support until after he heard from her. He'd conceived many terrifying scenarios, all more or less derived from movies—guns, hold-ups, stealthy intruders in the night—but he had not conceived this, a telephone ringing out in a dark room. How difficult love was, when it had no reply. How impossible and deadening this turmoil of not-knowing. He continued shaving and washing and feeding the cat, he continued being a father; but the response that would have subdued him did not come.

It was late November, summertime. Above him, Noah heard rain wash in from the harbour, then pass. The air pressure swayed and brought with it an impression of unsettlement. In the long hours of waiting he heard the susurration of the jacaranda tree, the high calls of night-birds—but no owls—and what might have been the beat of batwings heading away from the Botanical Gardens. He let his mind drift outside, through the flimsy moon-light, down the shell-lit driveway, out towards the waters of the harbour, and then beyond, so that he saw in his mind's eye the Pacific Ocean, thunderous and vast. He saw wave on wave, turning like the pages of a book. He stayed there, and may have dozed, resting on the water, feeling its pull beneath him and its ripples heading back to the shore. There were birds swerving and veering in circles, but the wrong birds, not seagulls or seabirds, but creatures lost, disorientated, flung by wind from their homes.

He slept long enough to dream he was in the position of St Peter, hauled upside down, unconsenting to death. Noah was tilted and pulled in Caravaggian blackness, an object of bitter mockery and scorn. His guts tipped over, he was strung and hopeless. When he woke in the dark, he was neither relieved nor rested. And as if no elapse had occurred, no elapse at all, he was thinking still of the telephone in the empty room. Noah had no explanation of why Dora had disappeared. His throat was inflamed and he knew that his childhood rash had returned, bringing with it a feeling of self-contempt. His jaw had become stiff. He felt constriction in his chest, and in the waiting that now defined him.

He was an idiot to have agreed to this ridiculous theft. He was an idiot to have left her at Narita airport. They should have taken Uncle Vito together, at the beginning, and simply fled. How could he have surrendered to her plan, surely doomed from the beginning?

Her room in Palermo, the sashed window, the lemon tree in the courtyard. Those little flowers on the tree, sparks of radiant white.

It was late at night. Noah tried to ring again, and still there was no answer. He thought once more of the hazy drive on the road heading away from the Blue Mountains, with the stretch of telephone wires alongside, wave-like, in a trivial repetition. There was no connection, only the wires, rising and falling.

And now he was rising and falling and drifting towards her. There was a vast, disastrous ocean between them; there was peril and fear and useless striving. He tried to bob as birds do, his head prim and perky, but he was all sag, and exhaustion, and a netted tangle of feeling.

Noah drank malt whisky slowly, a man waiting without hope. His fingers were tingling and his arms felt tremendously heavy. He could barely open his jaw to sip at his drink. He wanted to think of his family and Dora in the hotel room in

Syracuse. He wanted to consider his life's blessings and all that had quickened him. But there was no control in his thoughts. His mind was fraught, and ungovernable.

What returned to him first was Francis, the boy he'd loved, the boy he'd turned into a pariah in the tale of his own heroism. He'd made Francis a cover for his own unspeakable cowardice. With a kind of desolation he knew then that shame lasts a life-time. And still he could not recall the name of Francis's uncle, the man holding a felt hat at the funeral of his father. He seemed almost present, as if standing in the periphery of his vision. Who was this man? The man in the jeep, the custodian of memory, who drove away in a cloud of orange dust. Noah tried. He tried again. In his spent state and sheer tiredness the name would not return. He could think of no extenuation for this vaguest of shames, or why it returned at this time, and with such commanding force. And now a flux of images: Joshua's large hands, Katherine as the Madonna, a black swan, a flying shadow, angled in uplifting.

And a baby—not Martin, his darling Martin, in that early ecstasy of adoration, but Evie, blue-coloured and almost drowned, barely breathing in Martin's arms. How it had caught his heart in a net, how it had pulled him towards them.

My son, my daughter.

He had lurched to save her, and both his children had screamed, wet and confused and made afraid by his fear. Martin stood apart from him, melodramatic, struggling to hold on to Evie. Noah remembered wrapping them both in the towel, making them by instinct one beloved package. He could not disguise the pure fear of losing them. His arms trembled and he knew his face was distorted and scary. But he thought: *saved, now they are saved.*

~

He may have nodded off. There was a period of dark nothing. When he felt his chest cramp again, it came with some other, softer notion. What returned was a sensation he could not at first comprehend. His hands lifting something, patting something, feeling a fine material, submitting to his touch. The gesture was a smooth one, but there was swift clicking, too, and his hands working together over the dome of a head. There was delicacy, exactitude. He was recalling the act of cutting his son's hair, and the truth of this sensation was a revelation, as if it was the most important act of his life. Brushing at his neck. The neat shape of his son's skull. His own breath blowing away minuscule lengths of cut hair. It was almost blissful, recalling this, the strands resting weightless between his fingers, the curve of bone that shaped his hand into an upside-down cradle.

Noah thought he heard Strozzi at the back door, mewing to be admitted. He struggled to his feet, feeling heavy, as if he carried another body hung like a cloak over his own. He opened the door and saw only the still glossy night. The rain had passed now and there was a dripping, languorous calm. Noah peered out, seeing the world made nebulous by shadow, and in a trance of precision he saw the fall of raindrops from the jacaranda, each a crystal, and singular. There was the tiniest splash, then another. If he shook a low-hanging branch, he could make his own rainfall.

Then he heard mewing once again and thought it was at the front, so he turned, stumbling back, passing through scrambled aeons and a swirl of breathy smoke. Noah opened the front door. Ahead of him lay the swimming pool, and it was the loveliest thing he'd ever seen. The moon stretched there, and all the stars. It was a pool of Prussian blue. It was how one might imagine the end of time.

Noah advanced, in pain now, his chest crushing in on itself.

And when at last he fell forward, he fell into the stars, and his arms were so heavy they could not move to save him, and his senses were so tired he could not struggle to rise, and the shape of that extra body weighed him down, and down.

42

LIGHTLY, THE WINDOW shudders in a gust.

Nina rests her palms on its surface, feeling the vibrations as if blind. The whole world is shuddery now, as she fights the thunder of surround sound and the raucous jumble of spoken words.

She's screamed in frustration and hit her mother's face with her fists. She's banged her head against the bedstead and thrown her toys at the wall. It helps, sending things flying, showing the chaos of white noise. This is the world now, this monster-roar, and Granddad gone, his itchy chin, and his gifts, and the way he drew messages with her crayons, and hid his thumbs as if they disappeared, but she knew, and he knew, and he knew that she knew, and his ten fingers would reappear—pop!—but he will not return—pop!—because this is what dead is. They don't come back, Mum said; it's sad, but never-ever.

The boom of sound, it assaults her, and here is her own heavy tongue, fat as a slimy slug. A lady comes in the morning to help her practise words, she opens her mouth to show where the tongue should lie, and places Nina's fingers on her wrinkly throat to feel what happens. How close that lady comes, like Evie, like Daddy, eyes shiny with little Ninas and her skin like a mesh. When Nina tries to echo, she is all grunts and something unclean. Her slug-tongue sticks fast, she feels it blocking, not saying. She has swallowed dirt and is driven to baby tears. Words are harder than anything, she's a weeny baby, and stupid. She's a baby boiling and bubbling with unexpressed meanings. Spoken words, she hates them. They have somehow undone her.

Nina stands at the window waiting for the boy on the bicycle to appear. It is a Saturday morning, and he will come. She waits and waits. And when he slides into view—there! not even touching the handlebars—she leaps up and waves. Nina waves and calls out, but the boy does not see or hear her. He rides on, beyond the glass. He grows smaller, and is gone. A sob starts inside her chest. She taps at the window with her fingernails, and peers as if into the otherworld of a vast aquarium.

So Nina is alone. She is alone, thinking of Granddad. She remembers him slowly buttoning her pale blue cardigan. He had such enormous hands. There he was, kneeling before her, buttoning with his pincer fingers, his pointers pushing each circle through each tight hole—and what pretty buttons they were, glinting in hard plastic, flower-shaped and faceted—and she will remember his enormous hands, joining button and buttonhole, patient, lovingly slow, until her own end of days.

IN THE LONG now of grieving, Dora is refashioned widow-like.

There is no one left for her to love; she is steeped in calamity. Those who know her see immediately the alteration: how her speaking feathers at the edges and drifts away, how she loses her trains of thought, how she lacks energy for anything. An old nonna, dressed all in black, says, 'Bless you,' on the street, recognising instinctively her companion sorrow. Dora avoids the black-clad women of her city; she wears beige and coloured scarves; she makes herself look youthful. But these women know, they're a secret tribe, they move in their own sheltering darkness and speak in low, silky whispers. Self-effacing, they are also a superstitious force. She is almost afraid of them, how they assign her a membership.

When she was a child, Vito took her to see the annual *presepi*. She loved the semicircles of figures looking down at the infant Christ, the Madonna, the useless Joseph, the three foreign kings. She loved the shepherds' fat hands and familiar faces, and the way all stood with their animals in postures of wonder. She loved knowing who was who, and their role in the story. Vito would squat at her height to point out details; the clay figurines were a folk art he had cherished as a boy. They trailed from church to church to make comparisons, she reaching to clasp him, and allowing herself to be led. Why does this memory return now, in the time of bereavement?

'Unblinking,' Vito teased her. Now she wants to close her eyes.

Dora stands at her window, seeing nothing. She inhales, she exhales. It's come to this, mere continuance. She finds herself brushing at her skirt, as demented women do, or turning in a piazza, thinking she hears Noah's voice, or Vito's. She is tired. She feels old. Now there is dog-whine and cigarette stench and her own heart heavy as lead. She has endured years of lead.

How long has it been? She's lost all sense of time. Vito, Noah.

The lumpen shape of Australia drifts like a cloud in her mind. It won't go away, this other island, and there is a worrisome beckoning. Noah placed the idea of Australia before her. She would meet his children and granddaughter, he said; she would have a family and a safe place. But it is Vito's death that complicates; it is Vito, beloved Vito, more truly father than uncle.

When she heard herself announce this, it was an act of truth-telling after so much deception. It named that grief precisely. So she knows, with conviction, that she will never leave Palermo. She needs her sepia ghosts because they keep her company. She needs her old city and its aura of secrecy and cunning.

Dora thinks of the Ragusa and imagines it hidden somewhere in darkness. She no longer wants it. Once, it meant all to her, it was worshipful, rare. From hope, or premonition, it was her idea of art crafted by love. Noah had understood it too. But she killed them both, Noah and Vito. She should have fled immediately, and not risked her soul.

The telephone rings and Dora ignores it. She has the irrational thought that it is Noah, calling her from his death. Still, she ignores it.

Ah, but his voice. How she'd loved his voice.

IN BED, BESIDE Benjamin, Evie hears the word 'abide'. Before she opens her eyes, the old hymn is playing in her head, and when the lines fade, there it is. *Abide*: it summons him. She half-expects to see Noah, resurrected in light. An 'a' word, abide. A and B together. If she were inclined to religious feeling, she would think it existed here, kept alive with gentle purpose in an ancient word.

Inside the ampoule of the long window, there is the rosy glow of a new dawn. Benjamin looks older in the early morning light. Still asleep, his features are sunken and relaxed, his blindness now a true state, and not a deficiency or loss. His face says he is dreaming: his eyelids flicker, his brow is furrowed, he is engrossed in a world of images that is private and elsewhere. There is a weak sound, like a child's moan, that he offers up to those images. It is a plea, or a complaint. It is a sound without alphabet, she thinks, that arrives only with images. She does not yet know Benjamin well, but they are learning to be together. They are learning together to contest the decay of time.

His skin has a dark tone she finds arousing. She's still surprised how easy it was, after their confiding pleasure, after the sharing of movies and grief had eroded their reticence, to meet him as her lover. In Palermo she'd thought it more a casual affair, but since her return realised that she was coming not to Sydney, but to him. He was there at the airport, his chin raised, listening for her call. When they embraced, he held her tight, and she smelled the musk of his body as a home. Martin stood beside her, waiting to be introduced. With his good hand her brother shook and blurted a clumsy greeting. They are still awkward with each other and remain mutually suspicious.

Now Evie rises from the bed in the modest flat she has rented. She's not sure of her future, but this intermission will help her decide. She does not want to live with Benjamin; she wants independently to know him. Her few possessions here are enough to sustain her: clothes, books, objects that belonged to her father. She pads on bare feet, half-awake, moving to the kitchen to brew coffee. But some instinct directs her instead to the St Jerome icon, leaning on the windowsill.

She lifts and examines it. The face is Noah's. She had noticed the likeness before but now it strikes her with especial force. She almost cries out in surprise. She sheds a tear, then smiles. There is a new delicacy to her observance, that pays a tribute to the dead. Evie turns over the icon. There, tucked between the wooden image and its cardboard backing, is a triangle of paper she'd not seen before. Evie pries Noah's message from its hiding place. She reads the code carefully. She knows its meaning almost at once. There is incredulity and solace—and there is his belief that she would understand.

MARTIN IS STRUGGLING. He finds unendurable his father's mystery, and his own abject failure to discover answers. He does not know why he was bashed, or who commissioned the deed. He does not know if his father stole a sculpture, or if it was Tommaso who betrayed him, or Antonio, or perhaps Maria. He wasted his time, and now he is wasted. He feels unmanned, and hopeless. There might be a recovery in the future, but he thinks the damage is permanent, and more than just a hand. Nightly, in hideous dreams, he falls through a hole in the water.

The telephone rings. It is Nina, caught in her own lonely struggle. Part of her therapy is an obligation to ring her father each day, to practise words without the clue of a visible face. He can hear her valiantly trying.

'Daddy.'

She sounds alien, her mouth misshapen around the word.

'Nina. Sweetie.'

There is a long pause at the other end.

'The boy. I saw him.'

A complete sentence.

'The boy?'

She tries the word 'bicycle', but cannot quite manage. Still, he understands.

'Bicycle,' he helps her.

Their breathing hangs in the telephonic darkness between them. She tries again, with no improvement. He hears her snorts of impatience and frustration.

'Bi'cle,' she says, still missing a syllable.

'Well done!'

But she has hung up, or thrown the phone, or walked away from her own disappointment.

Martin holds the handset for a minute, then realises that Nina will not resume their conversation. In the hush, he understands that she now knows her own imperfection, that spoken words have driven her to awe and fury, that her suffering is something he cannot hope to alleviate.

Evie, darling Evie; he might tell her his secret. That when they packed their father's apartment he found a letter Noah had written to Dora. That he destroyed it, without reading it. In a glare of pain and annoyance, urged by despair, he had acted in spite. He regrets his foolishness. He burned the letter in the kitchen sink, pleased to see it flare and disintegrate. The smoke alarm had sounded a screeching witness.

Martin is already thinking about his father in artful terms: *The Death of Noah Glass*. This is how he will cope. He will convert his father to art and place him in the world of images. He will forget Piero and Barbie and his wavelength fantasies, and start again, tomorrow, with something new. Something new for Nina.

'I DON'T KNOW,' says Evie, in response to his question. '*Non lo so*.'

She is examining her brother's hand, newly unbandaged. The scars are raised in silver threads across the skin; there are pink indentations where tiny screws have been removed. It is a heavy hand; they are all heavier now. Martin allows his hand to be lifted and turned. He watches his sister stretch the fingers, as the physiotherapist advised, and examine how the tendons extend in a slow uncurling. There is a slight twang of pain, but he doesn't mention it.

Winter has arrived in Sydney yet it is a bright, clear day, the sky high, full of yellow light, and with no sign of rain. They sit together beneath a grapevine that has recently borne purple fruit. Now it is bare, leafless, but the shape and twist of the vine wood is beautiful to behold.

'I don't know,' she repeats.

ACKNOWLEDGEMENTS

The leprosarium in this book is based on Bungarun, which existed near Derby, Western Australia, from 1936 to 1986, established by the Sisters of St John of God for Indigenous patients. I've taken many liberties here, but wish to honour this sad history. I thank Dr Charmaine Robson for her scholarship, and pay my respects to those communities and families affected by Hansen's disease.

Simonetta Agnello Hornby piqued my interest in Sicily, and Dr Valentina Castagna offered a small symbolic tale and the gift of conversation and encouragement. Valentina's students at the University of Palermo reminded me of the youthful vitality of the city. Professor Giuseppa Tamburello and Dr Brigid Maher both read this book with generous attention. Special thanks to Meredith Curnow and Catherine Hill, whose early support means more to me than I can express here.

Students and colleagues at the Writing and Society Research Centre (Western Sydney University) have provided intellectual community. I'm deeply grateful to the Australia Council for the Arts for the use of a working space in Rome, and to Jane Novak for her wise service. Close friends have offered consistent support, for which I am indebted in ways only they can know. Above all, my daughter, Kyra Giorgi, has been an extraordinary inspiration.

Michael Heyward was a feisty, intelligent and patient editor. Thanks to Chong Weng Ho for his sympathetic artistry, and to everyone in the hardworking team at Text.

The recalled line of poetry on page 72 is from Francis Webb's 'Five Days Old', in his *Collected Poems* (UWAP 2011).

This novel is dedicated to the memory of my father, Arthur Jones.